Missi

Producer & International Distributor
eBookPro Publishing
www.ebook-pro.com

Mission Senator
Charlie Wolfe

Contact: Charlie.Wolfe.Author@gmail.com
ISBN

MISSION SENATOR

CHARLIE WOLFE

MISSION SENATOR

Washington, DC

The four black quadcopters were flying in loose formation along Delaware Avenue, which led to the US Capitol. They were launched moments earlier from the roof of a building near Union Station, and once they cleared the building, they dropped down to an altitude of twenty-five meters. It was dark, and at the height they were flying, they were above the area illuminated by the streetlights. Their electric motors were quiet enough so they couldn't be heard above the din of traffic in the early evening hour. Just to ensure that a stray pedestrian couldn't hear them, a noisy motorbike traveled in the right lane of the avenue just below them. They kept low to avoid being detected by the extra security measures put in place after 9/11. As they got closer to their target, several fireworks were launched from an open space in the Washington Mall to distract the guards and confuse security devices. The four young operators were concentrating on the images sent by the lightweight miniature cameras that were installed on the quadcopters. An older man was overseeing their work, closely watching the same images, and instructing the biker to control his speed to stay directly below the quadcopters.

A window had been left open in one of the restrooms on the second floor of the Capitol building. The two most highly skilled operators guided their quadcopters to enter the room, which was unoccupied at that time. They crash-landed, and a small charge of explosives broke the thin glass capsule that was fixed between the two parts of the landing gear. The pressurized radioactive radon gas was released from the broken capsules. Some of it started seeping through the crack at the bottom of the restroom's door into the hallway that led to several offices. However, the more serious hazard was from the fraction of gas that was sucked up by the air-conditioning system and spread throughout the building. For anyone inhaling the radioactive atoms, there was a chance that some of the material would settle in the lungs and continue to decay there by emission of deadly alpha particles.

The other two quadcopters flew to the west side of the building that looked over the reflecting pool and hovered there. One of the security guards, Jefferson King, caught sight of the two small flying machines quietly hovering above his head. All the other security guards were still watching the display of fireworks and were startled when Jefferson shouted a warning and drew out his pistol. The quadcopters went into a crazy dance, and Jefferson had trouble aiming his weapon. Seconds later he was joined by the three other guards, and the four men opened fire without thinking of the consequences. Ricochets were whining off the walls and the ceiling but miraculously no one was hurt. A direct shot hit one of the quadcopters, and it exploded in a burst of flames. Moments later the second one followed suit. The capsules carried by the quadcopters were shattered, and fine particles of radioactive cesium chloride were dispersed all over the west side entrance of the building. Invisible deadly gamma radiation was emitted from these innocent-looking particles. The guard who was the first to reach the downed flying machines received a dose of radiation that would kill him within minutes. He was the lucky one because the other three guards were sure to die painfully within hours.

The older man on the roof congratulated the four young men for accomplishing their mission successfully and then drew out a silenced automatic pistol and shot the one closest to him in the head, execution-style. The other three were paralyzed by the sight of blood and brain matter that spurted out of the poor guy's shattered head, so the man had no trouble shooting them all. He quickly checked their pockets to make sure that the only documents left on their still-warm bodies were those that he had planted. Two had French passports that were stamped by the US Immigration and Naturalization Service, the INS, which was now part of the Department of Homeland Security. They had legally entered the US and like all French citizens, they didn't require visas. One of the others carried a Syrian passport without any entry permit—indicating that he had entered the country illicitly. The fourth youth was an African American who had a District of Columbia driver's license. A quick investigation would show that he belonged to a Muslim cultural center and regularly attended a mosque just a few blocks from the Capitol. He knew that these fake identities wouldn't hold water for long, but all he wanted was the preliminary report that would show that Muslims had attacked the core of American democracy.

CHAPTER 1

The reactions to the attack on the most prominent representation of democracy in the United States swept across the globe, were quick to come, and held few surprises.

The president of the United States, known by his acronym as POTUS, responded in a typically short statement, "The United States of America will not tolerate heinous attacks on its soil. This attack with radioactive materials crossed a lot of red lines for me. My attitude toward the radical Islamic perpetrators and Muslims in general has been reinforced, and a forceful American response will be delivered." POTUS refrained from specifying how the US would respond but hastened to add, "The enemies of the United States will soon learn that there is a new sheriff in town." These sixty-seven words practically exhausted his vocabulary, so he signed off by saying, "Sad. So sad."

Political analysts viewed this statement with a lot of skepticism. The commentator at the international desk of CNN said, "POTUS has not understood that the attack on the Capitol was carried out by anonymous terrorists. There is no 'return address' for a retaliatory strike by cruise missiles, like the one he launched on Syria after it was caught red-handed using chemical weapons on its own citizens in 2017. There is no viable, verifiable target for the US forces. POTUS can huff and puff and blow hot air and superheated steam, but unless the perpetrators can be identified, there is nothing he can do. Or in his own words, 'Sad. So sad.'"

The king of Jordan, who was on an official visit to the US capital when the attack took place, said in his perfect British accent, "The Hashemite Kingdom of Jordan stands behind its American ally and will give the US authorities full support in investigating this dastardly crime and bringing the perpetrators to justice." The cynics commented that the US would have been happier if the brave king would have stood in front of its American ally rather than behind it.

The prime ministers of Britain, Germany, and Italy and the newly elected president of the French Republic issued similar statements, promising to cooperate with the US intelligence agencies. However, Marine Le Pen, the head of the National Front, the right-wing French opposition party, could barely conceal her joy, "The American public can now get a taste of the horrors instigated by Muslim terrorists in France and on the continent." She ignored the fact that the deadliest terror attack in the twenty-first century occurred on American soil on September 11, 2001.

The BBC, with its usual facetious attitude that it was purportedly giving its dwindling audience a "balanced picture," gave its regular "on the one hand and on the other hand" show. The talking heads in the studio condemned "acts of terror wherever they hurt innocent civilians" but quickly added that they understood the frustration of the Muslim people who had been humiliated and deeply offended by the American military presence on Arab soil and by the multinational industrial companies that exploited their natural resources. They handily ignored the fact that the British companies were there before the Americans set foot in the Middle East. A professorial type on the panel of experts didn't bother to remove his unlit pipe from his mouth when he said through clenched teeth that most of the Muslims were peace-loving people and terror was carried out by a small minority of misguided people. Conveniently, none of the honorable academicians in the studio referred to the recent wave of home-grown Islamic terrorism in London, Manchester, and other places in Europe. Typically, nobody mentioned the massacres, genocide, and terrorist acts against fellow Muslims that "peace-loving" Muslims carried out in Syria, Libya, Iraq, Tunisia, Turkey, and other Islamic countries.

The president of the Russian Federation was ambiguous at the small press-conference that he held, "The Russian Federation condemns all terrorist attacks against innocent citizens. Such shameful attacks have been launched in Moscow and Saint Petersburg, as well as in other cities in Europe, Asia, Oceania, and Africa. Muslim extremists are behind most of them, but let's not forget that the United States has made many enemies in all these countries. My grandmother taught me, 'friends come and go, but enemies accumulate,' so I am not surprised that one of them decided to act against capitalist oppression and aggression." He saw the astonished expressions of the faces of the reporters, so he quickly backpedaled, "I only wish to say that the world should not rush to conclusions and should wait until irrefutable evidence is gathered. The Russian Federation will assist in finding those responsible."

No official statements were issued by North Korea and Iran, but off the record, the supreme religious leader of Iran commented, "Allah punishes the infidels in many ways. Although radioactive materials were invented by the Big Satan," alluding to the American World War II Manhattan Project, "they, too, are part of Allah's arsenal in times of need."

The most interesting reaction came from China. "No comment," said the Chinese prime minister, standing in front of a map of the South China Sea in which the Spratly Islands and Paracel Islands were marked with red circles. He could barely control the smug expression on his face when he delivered his short statement.

Sheikh Ibrahim Salah, the imam of the Islamic Center of Washington and one of the national leaders of the Muslims in the US, issued a statement. "The acts of a few extremists do not represent Islam and the loyal Muslim citizens of the United States. The members of the Islamic cultural center unanimously condemn these acts of violence and consider them as sacrilegious. Islam is a religion of peace and love and tolerance." One of the cynics watching the imam commented that Islamic tolerance lead to the burning of a newspaper in Denmark, to the murderous attack on a journal in Paris that published cartoons of Mohammad, and to the 1977 siege on the Islamic center in Washington with the demand to destroy a movie that described the life of Mohammad, without even showing his image or the sound of his voice. Sheikh Ibrahim was, of course, unaware of this cynical remark, and he continued, "I am proud to remind the American people that President George W. Bush and many dignitaries visited our cultural center just a few days after the heinous events of 9/11, quoted from the Quran, and assured Americans that most Muslims were peaceful." He paused, took a sip of water, and continued, "Unfortunately, there are distinguished members of Congress and the Senate who will try to exploit this act of terror for their own political purposes. I hope that the American public will not place the blame for the crimes committed by a handful of radicalized people who claim to represent Allah or all Muslims." The same cynic who had been listening to the sheikh whispered that he was glad the sheikh was not connected to a polygraph because the apparatus would certainly blow a fuse with so many lies delivered so quickly.

The editorial of the New York Times would have infuriated the president had he bothered to read it. In a nutshell, it read, "Once again, we see that 'America first' and isolationism will not spare the United States from attacks on our soil by our enemies. They will continue to avenge real or imaginary injustices caused by this administration and its predecessors. The policy of shouting in a loud voice and carrying a small stick will not work any longer. Only an open and candid discussion with our enemies and willingness to acknowledge previous wrongdoings and take corrective actions will bring us peace. Mutual respect will bring shared prosperity."

The prime minister of Israel made the most elaborate statement in an American accent, with traces of Boston from his days at Massachusetts Institute of Technology. He tried to avoid using words that he thought may not be part of the vocabulary of POTUS, "My government had predicted that such an attack on American soil was imminent and repeatedly warned the previous US administration that its lenient policy toward radical Islam would backfire. As the prophet Hosea warned, 'For they have sown the wind, and they shall reap the whirlwind,' quoting the phrase in King James's Bible, translated from my ancient Hebrew. Now this has come to be. Israel will take an active role in helping the law enforcement agencies of its greatest friend and supporter, the United States of America, in finding the perpetrators." He didn't add that Mossad would also be happy to help punish the perpetrators.

The network of the National Public Radio (NPR) radio stations interviewed one of the leading scientific experts on radioactive and nuclear issues. Dr. Eugene Powers, a senior scientist in the National Nuclear Security Administration (NNSA), said, "The ease of obtaining highly radioactive materials, such as the cesium chloride used in this terrorist attack, is troublesome. This material is widely deployed in medical devices for the treatment of cancer patients, but in the wrong hands, it can be extremely dangerous. The regulations regarding the handling, storage, and disposal of radioactive substances must be strongly enforced. Radioactive materials removed from medical devices have been used by different terror organizations in the past in radioactive dispersion devices, commonly known as 'dirty bombs,' like the one detonated in Zurich. They have also been used to produce other nuclear materials," he was referring to incidents in Europe. He added, hoping to prevent mass panic, "The attack on the

Capitol building has a psychological effect as a weapon of mass disruption, but the actual physical and health effects are quite negligible to the public. So, the American public should put things in proportion and not lose focus of the big picture—how do we prevent such attacks in the future."

The narrator of the radio show thanked Dr. Powers and then heard the show's producer on his earphone. He added that there was a last-minute item and pleaded with the listeners to stay tuned. One of the followers of the NPR program was a scholarly professor (emeritus) of American history. He called the station and said that he had a comment that would interest the listeners. After hearing what he had to say, the producer of the radio-show put him online and asked for his comment. The professor said, "Few people know about the bomb that was planted in the Capitol on July 2, 1915, during World War I. The explosion occurred close to midnight under the Senate's telephone switchboard when there was no one around. The perpetrator was a professor of German from Harvard University, Erich Muenter. After the blast, in a letter he sent under an assumed name, he explained that he wanted to appeal for peace and protest America's involvement in financing Britain and the Allies. A few days later, the professor showed up at J. P. Morgan's private home and shot him with a pistol. Morgan, who had been Britain's principal financier, was only wounded and recovered quickly. Professor Muenter was caught, tried, and sentenced to jail. There he took his own life." The narrator asked him what his story was based on, and the professor replied that is available in the records of the US Senate. He added, "It is a pity that the people of the US know so little about their own history. I can only quote words of wisdom, 'History appears twice, the first time as a tragedy, the second time as a farce.' I don't think this latest attack on the Capitol with radioactive substances is a farce, but unless we understand the motivation of the perpetrators, we may see it repeated." The narrator didn't want to be bothered by any more obscure facts and wise mottos, so he thanked the scholarly professor and signed off.

David Avivi, at Mossad headquarters in Tel Aviv, closely followed the news reports from Washington and the reactions by the world leaders and the media. Thus, he was not surprised when he was summoned by his boss, Haim Shimony, the Mossad chief, and told to be in contact with his friend Dr. Eugene Powers and to get up-to-date information on the incident, the suspects, the preventive actions, and counterterrorist operations that the US authorities were carrying out. Shimony added that this was a direct order from the prime minister.

***

Senator Jim McCorey, the junior senator from New Mexico, famously recognized by the media as MBJ, or Muslim-Bashing Jimbo, made a fiery appearance on Fox News. The good-looking, flaxen-haired reporter asked, "Senator McCorey, what do you make of the attack on the Capitol?"

To MBJ, the trite question sounded like the starter pistol fired at the final of the one hundred-meter dash at the Olympic Games. He was like the fastest sprinter in the world, flying out of the starter block, "As long as there is a single Muslim in this country, such monstrous acts will continue! This strike in the heart of our capital, against the seat of the representatives of the American people, the most revered symbol of our country's democracy, is something we cannot, and will not, tolerate. The perpetrators are obviously Muslims. We saw the documents that the four dead terrorists were carrying. Two of them were allowed into our country—legally, I regret to say—as they were French citizens. Nobody at the Department of Homeland Security considered the fact that they were religious zealots whose loyalty was to a fake God. For the DHS, the fact they carried French passports was enough to allow these rabid foxes into our chicken coop! One of the other terrorists was a Syrian who entered our country right under the noses of the DHS people who are supposed to protect us and secure our borders. The worst of the dishonorable lot is the homebred African American who converted to Islam and turned against the country that provided him with health care, social security, and a chance of a better life. The blame for this disregard to the public's safety rests with the former administration and its left-wing, liberal supporters who betrayed our country. Until we lock up all these bleeding-heart liberals, we will not be able to live here in peace. So immediately after we deport, or incarcerate, all the Muslims in this country, we'll have to deal with these traitors. I call on all like-minded, red-blooded, honest, and patriotic Americans to show their support for our ideas. Send us 'likes,' put up signs in your windows and on your lawns, and proudly fly the Star-Spangled Banner above your houses. I call on you to boycott stores that are run by Muslims, stay away from any activity that is sponsored by left-wing communists, socialists, and liberals. Let us, true Americans, regain control of our country."

The blond narrator looked at the senator and thought that she saw his mouth foaming. She surreptitiously wiped a little dribble from her face and eventually found her speech, "Thank you, Senator McCorey, for your candid opinion so eloquently expressed. We have to go to a commercial break." The senator stood up and, before walking out of the studio, mumbled something about her having a drink together at his hotel suite afterward. She ignored the comment and did her utmost not to stare at the front of his pants and to ignore the bulge that formed there. She picked up a glass of water and looked helplessly at the producer of the news show.

He whispered in her earpiece, "Great job. This will boost our rating."

She sheepishly answered, "I only gave him the microphone. It is all his doing."

***

Le Docteur, or Jacque Deleau, the name he had used since his arrival in Canada a few years earlier, watched the interview with Senator Jim McCorey and barely refrained from laughing. They first met a couple of months earlier at a social gathering sponsored by the MAGAFU society, one of the thinly disguised racist societies in Washington whose acronym stood for Make America Great Again For Us. Le

Docteur was there on what he considered a scouting mission to get to know the enemy, while the senator was mingling with his electoral base.

Le Docteur had introduced himself as a French-Canadian professor of political science and European history. This was not far from the truth, or more precisely, a small part of it. These had been his fields of professional expertise while he was a lecturer at the Sorbonne under his real identity as Dr. Albert Pousin. However, when the true role of Dr. Albert Pousin was exposed as the founder and head of the new Islamic terrorist organization, NEMESIS, he had to flee Europe as the notorious persona at the top of the most wanted list of several countries. He changed his appearance so profoundly, while maintaining his handsome presence, that even his mother, had she still been alive, would not have recognized him. He had learned to alter his voice while keeping his slightly French-accented English that appealed to certain people. In any case, he refrained from public appearances and avoided the electronic media so that his speech patterns would not be readily available for voice recognition analysis. He preferred to meet with people privately or in small groups and did not allow recording or filming of the lectures and seminars he gave. Security and his own personal safety were at the top of his mind always, and he evaded meetings with known members of intelligence agencies.

In his identity as a French-Canadian political scientist, he had gained prestige in his new country as a leading expert on European history. More importantly, he was much sought after as a political consultant on the current situation in

Europe, particularly on the treatment of the waves of Islamic immigrants. He spent weeks, sometimes even a whole semester, as a visiting professor and guest lecturer in several universities and think tanks in the United States. He impressed his colleagues on the faculty with his broad knowledge of world affairs and charmed his students, mainly those of the female persuasion, with his handsome looks and his alluring French accent.

He had met Muslim-Bashing Jimbo a few times over the past months and established that they had mutual interests. The senator was losing popularity in his home state of New Mexico as he was perceived by more and more of his constituents as a self-serving politician who cared little about the people who sent him to represent them in Washington. Even worse for him was the fact that he was practically ignored by the media because other outspoken and more colorful politicians stole the limelight. Jimbo was so predictable that once he began a sentence, every intelligent viewer or listener could complete it in unison with him. Only Breitbart and Fox News still retained some interest in interviewing him after particularly heinous incidents. The recent attack on the Capitol building was just such a case. Unfortunately for the senator, his bigotry and sexism got the better of him toward the end of that interview. He knew that he would be the laughingstock of the liberal media the next day and probably the target of endless barbs of satire shows. He knew that his outburst and rudeness would be the centerpieces of John Oliver's show and that every half-bit stand-up comedian would mock him. This was something that he did not have in mind when he made the agreement with the man he knew as Professor Jacque Deleau.

For his part, Le Docteur wanted to carry out an attack in the heart of his most hated city, Washington, DC, and didn't care if this involved making a contract with the devil himself, or his representative in the US Senate, Senator McCorey. He fully understood the senator's motives, and they coincided with his own plans to bring the fight against the colonialists and Crusaders to the United States of America. True, the US didn't own colonies, but in his mind, their very presence on Arab soil, in military bases, or as oil-drilling companies was a new form of colonialism. He regarded their army bases and armed forces as equivalent to the Crusaders almost a millennium earlier. Cynically, he viewed his cooperation with the Muslim-bashing senator as the components of fire—where one provided the fuel and the other the oxygen, and together the flames would consume everything in the area. Le Docteur believed in Lenin's motto, 'the worse, the better'—the worse it got for Muslims in the United States, the better it would be for them in the world. The Ummah of Islam would awaken, and Muslims would unite and rebel against their oppressors. Inciting hatred would serve his cause well. Naturally, Senator McCorey had no idea that his partner-in-crime was a Muslim and that Le Docteur was using him, just as Jimbo believed that he was using the scholar.

***

After being convinced that the senator would stop at

nothing to increase his popularity, Le Docteur carefully proposed a series of provocations in the United States that would be blamed on Muslims. Both men knew that if these were to become unveiled, they would be charged with everything from conspiracy and murder to treason. Each understood that they were mutually dependent on each other. Thus, the senator's response to Le Docteur's proposition was encouraging. Regarding the attack on the Capitol building with radioactive materials, Senator McCorey unashamedly stated that he wouldn't mourn the murder—or untimely death, as he euphemistically put it—of the four young Muslims that controlled the quadcopters. When Le Docteur mentioned that some of the security people in the Capitol may be exposed to lethal levels of radioactivity, the senator just smiled and mumbled that as far as he was concerned, Black lives didn't matter, knowing full well that most of the guards were African Americans. Le Docteur was a little surprised by McCorey's attitude—he had expected cynicism from the politician, but he didn't think the senator would be so blatant.

Le Docteur wondered if the senator suspected that he was a radicalized Muslim and amused himself by speculating how he would react if he found out who he really was. From his own point of view, the senator tried to understand the real motives of his new friend. Le Docteur had said that he thought that Muslims were plotting to take over the US—something he truly believed, but from the exact opposite reasons—and that Senator McCorey was one of the few patriotic people in the country who realized that. Le Docteur believed that if the US government could be driven to take extreme measures against Muslims in the United States, like those taken against people of Japanese descent during World War II, then the global reaction by Muslims and by liberal governments in Europe would provide the ultimate excuse for the War of Civilizations that he was trying to instigate. He had no doubt that the West was technologically superior to Islam but thought that the people in the Western societies were spoiled by their affluence and were softened by their sheltered way of life so that Muslims who were used to hardship and suffering would prevail in the long run.

***

Le Docteur's terror ring in Europe had not been annihilated when his right-hand man in Paris, Amir, was killed by the French police's elite antiterror unit. Because of the strict security measures that he had imposed on his followers, each member knew only a few other operatives of NEMESIS, and no one, except himself, knew all the operatives. When Le Docteur fled the UK to Ireland and then to Canada, several sleeper cells remained intact, waiting for orders to reactivate. For almost two years, they heard nothing from Le Docteur and assumed, based on the media reports, that the NEMESIS organization had been eliminated. Nevertheless, some of the more fervent members remained dedicated to the cause of fighting the colonialists, communists, and Crusaders. Some new recruits also found their way to the organization, and some of the cells, particularly in France and the UK, were just waiting for their marching orders to resume their activities.

When Le Docteur clandestinely reestablished contact with a few of the cell leaders, he noticed that some refused to take his calls, while others were still loyal members and anticipated his call for action.

Le Docteur decided to recommence the operations of NEMESIS in a place where it would be least expected. Not in Paris but in the quiet and peaceful country of Portugal, where Muslims were not regarded as a problem because very few of them lived there. He decided to call on one of his most trusted operatives, Fatima, who had successfully pulled off the bombing operation at Sainte-Chapelle in Paris and afterward had relocated to the UK, thus evading the French authorities searching for her. She was delighted to receive his call for action and renewed her vows to NEMESIS and to him personally.

CHAPTER 2

Coimbra, Portugal

A long line of people, mainly elderly tourists, stood quietly in front of the stairs that led to the Biblioteca Joanina, the library that was donated by King Joao the Fifth to Velha Universidade, the famous university of Coimbra that was founded in the thirteenth century. Some were keeping themselves busy staring at the large ornamental doors or the vast courtyard that housed the royal palace, the chapel, and the library. All eagerly awaited the opening of the doors and permission for the group that held tickets for the 11:40 a.m. tour to enter. One of the ushers verified that all people in the line had the tickets for the correct time slot. Some of the tourists were engaged in small talk with each other or with the people next to them in the line, others stood quietly, while some of the more energetic tourists were busy snapping photos of the impressive courtyard. The tower with the clock, the trademark of the university, was the subject of many of those photos. A few of the younger people in the line kept taking selfies and making funny faces for the photos. The doors opened to let out members of the previous tour group. These were the people who didn't go down the steps to the library's store and the so-called students' prison that was used to hold the students who broke the laws governing their behavior.

Among the people waiting in line was a young couple who were dressed like typical tourists. In the month of May, with its unpredictable weather, this meant that they were wearing light jackets over a short-sleeved shirts and caps and sunglasses to evade the bright sun, and they were holding an umbrella in case it started to rain again, as it had been doing on-and-off throughout the morning. Ahmed, a thin, dark-skinned teenager, obviously of Yemenite or Saudi descent, was gingerly holding his backpack by its straps and appeared to be troubled by something. Anyone who knew how to read body language would have noticed that he was trying to make himself as small and inconspicuous as possible. His overweight girlfriend, Fatima, stood on the other side of the backpack, and a sheen of perspiration covered her face, despite the cool weather. She looked very uncomfortable with the canvas backpack that was strapped to her back. She took Ahmed's hand and held it firmly, as if trying to instill some courage into him and perhaps gain some from him.

They entered the library and, just like everyone else in the group, couldn't avoid an expression of awe in view of the beautifully arranged leather-bound tomes that were stacked on the wooden bookshelves, the hardwood tables, and the decorative ceiling. In the corners, there were small alcoves covered by velvet curtains in which small tables and a single chair per table were placed for the use of scholars who wanted to quietly study the old books and carry out research. Photography was not allowed, and when one of the Canadian tourists ignored the signs, she was removed, almost with brute force, from the library, and her camera was confiscated. Everyone looked at the commotion caused by the Canadian tourist. Ahmed was quick to take advantage of this unexpected diversion and placed his backpack underneath a table in one of the alcoves. This was observed by other tourists, and a fragile-looking woman tried to explain in French that it was forbidden, but the young man shrugged, said in English that he didn't understand, and slowly stepped into the next section of the library. The woman muttered something to her friends about rude young men, and they all just continued their tour of the library. After fifteen minutes, a bell rang, and everyone was instructed to leave the library and make way for the next group. Most of the tourists, including Fatima and Ahmed, now free of the backpack, took the flight of stairs at the corner of the first room, down through the store, and exited the building through a side door.

The young couple walked up the stairs back to the courtyard and headed toward Capela de Sao Miguel, the chapel that was adjacent to the clock tower. They showed their tickets to the smiling girl at the door and entered the chapel. They were impressed by the colorful decorations on the walls and ceiling and especially by the organ that was coated with gold. While everybody else was looking at the ceiling, Fatima placed her backpack behind a velvet curtain that hid a small alcove on the left side of the chapel. Her boyfriend, Ahmed, was impressed by the speed with which she moved despite her excess weight. He smiled at her, took a long look at the crucifix, and restrained himself from spitting at the wooden idol the Christians worshipped. They left the chapel and walked out of the courtyard holding hands.

They made their way through the winding streets and down the steep hill and returned to their hotel that was on Avenida Fernao de Magalhaes. They were greeted by the balding man at the reception desk and politely avoided him, trying to escape from another lecture about why the Portuguese were not like the Spanish people. When they had checked in the previous evening, the same man gave them a history lesson about Coimbra and Portugal. Ahmed thought it was interesting, but Fatima tugged his sleeve and said she was tired. The receptionist apologized for his lengthy talk, but anyone could see that he was disappointed to lose his audience. Anyway, the couple took the elevator to the fifth floor, where their upgraded "superior room" was located. Both stood on the veranda and watched the hill on which Coimbra stood, noting the distinct top of the university's clock tower. Ahmed looked at his watch and quietly started to count down from ten to one. When he reached three, a column of fire and smoke arose next to the clock tower and seconds later, the sound of an explosion, like thunder, was heard. A moment later, a smaller explosion took place and another column of smoke was visible. From their viewpoint, they couldn't tell whether the bomb in the library was detonated before the one in the chapel or vice versa.

Fatima looked at Ahmed with shining eyes and dragged him to the bed without bothering to close the glass doors that led to the veranda. In the blink of an eye, she undressed herself in a hurry and removed his clothes. Before he could utter a word, she was on top of him. She started to grind her pelvis without bothering to look at him, as her eyes were focused on the two smoke columns on the top of the hill that had started to disperse. Both came simultaneously with the accompanying music of the sirens of ambulances, police cars, and firefighters that to them sounded like the sweetest sound in the world. Ahmed felt that Fatima's weight was strangling him, but when he tried to move from under her, she indicated that she wanted, and desperately needed, another round of lovemaking. Ahmed had no choice but to perform again, getting a second wind from the incessant sound of the sirens. This time, when she came, she made a sound like a siren and smiled at him. Her expression was so ludicrous that he burst out laughing. Fatima was slightly insulted by his reaction but was too well satiated to take offense, so she slapped him gently and placed the full weight of her body on his chest. He just couldn't continue laughing and breathing at the same time with the extra weight, so he just patted her back and gently moved her to his side, continuing to stroke her back.

Despite the sound of the loud sirens in the street below their hotel room, they fell asleep for an afternoon nap. Fatima's sweet dreams were interrupted by Ahmed. He wriggled out of the bed and went to close the large glass door that led to the veranda to shut out the noise of the sirens that didn't cease even an hour after the explosions. He looked out and saw that people in the building across the street were standing at the windows and on the verandas and watching the commotion on the street between the hotel and their building. Regular traffic was still blocked by the police to keep the street open for the emergency first responders and ambulances. To his horror, Ahmed suddenly realized that he was naked, and three old women on the veranda across the street were pointing at him and laughing. He quickly closed the glass door, drew the curtains, and, with an embarrassed smile, made his way to the bathroom. He took a quick shower, wrapped the large towel around his body, and returned to the bedroom.

Fatima was smiling contentedly when she saw him. She stretched, removed the sheet that covered her body, and, in a suggestive fashion, cupped her ample breasts so that Ahmed could see that her dark nipples were erect. Before things got out of hand, he got dressed and said, "I am going to the cafeteria to get a cup of coffee. Would you like something from the bar or cafeteria?"

She shook her head, "Nothing from the bar. Only something from you." She patted the empty space on the bed.

Ahmed didn't want to offend her, "Sure, Fatima. But I must have coffee first, and I need a few moments to recharge my batteries. Why don't you take a shower?"

Fatima said, "Hurry back. I need you." She rolled over on her stomach, closed her eyes, and mumbled, "I'll shower after you come back to me."

***

Ahmed stepped out of the room and walked through the short corridor that led to the bar-cafeteria that was also located on the fifth floor of the hotel. He ordered a double espresso, swallowed it with a single gulp, and then asked for another one. He added two packets of sugar and slowly sipped the syrupy drink. The barman knowingly smiled at him, "A tough day at the office?"

Ahmed didn't understand what he was talking about. He thought that there was a language barrier, but then it dawned on him, and he shyly said, "You know women. Can't live with them and can't live without them." A moment later, he added, "What's the commotion outside? What are all these sirens?"

The barman pointed at the large TV screen. Ahmed looked at the muted picture that showed a female reporter standing in front of the Biblioteca Joanina with an expression of awe and shock on her face. Smoke was still coming out of the old building and seeping through the once-magnificent wooden doors. Ahmed asked the barman to turn the volume up and translate what the reporter was saying. The barman listened for a while and said, "She is saying that a section of the two-hundred-year-old library has been destroyed and thousands of old books have been ruined." He saw Ahmed's face lose its color and added, "I think that this is a barbaric act carried out by vandals. By people who have no respect for culture and history and are willing to destroy our heritage. They should be punished for what can only be considered as an act against civilization and God." The TV camera showed the damaged section of the ancient library and the leather-bound books scattered all over the floor. The wooden bookshelves and hardwood tables were strewn on a pile of smoldering ashes. A crowd had gathered in the courtyard and was held back by police barriers. They were shouting something in Portuguese. The barman looked at Ahmed, noting his dark complexion, and asked, "Are you a Muslim?"

Ahmed didn't like the question, so he tried to evade by asking, "Were any people killed?" The barman just looked at him, without saying a word. Ahmed continued, "Do they know who did this?"

The barman watched the TV for a while before saying, "Must be some psychopaths. Probably the Islamic State or other Muslims. There were more than twenty dead, mostly elderly tourists, and dozens of injured people. There was also an explosion in the chapel of Sao Miguel, but fortunately the beautiful chapel was only moderately damaged. The police say that the bomb failed to detonate completely." As an afterthought, he said, eyeing Ahmed, "If I were a Muslim, I would lay low and get out of this country as soon as possible."

Ahmed finished his second cup of coffee, left a nice tip for the barman, and returned to the room.

***

Fatima had also turned on the TV and was watching the carnage with a smile on her face. When Ahmed entered, she said, "We did a good job today. This will show the colonialists and Crusaders that the Muslim people will rise again. There is no place in the vast lands of the Crusaders in which they will be safe. The long hand of Allah will destroy everything that they have accomplished, starting with what they view as 'civilization.' We know that the riches of Portugal were stolen from the people in the colonies they had in Africa, Asia, and South America. Come to me, Ahmed. Let's celebrate once more the small triumph of Islam over the infidels." Then she noticed the solemn expression on his face and added, "Come, rejoice, be happy. Islam has dealt another blow to the Crusaders."

Ahmed stood by the door and said, "The Portuguese people are so nice and hospitable. What have they ever done to Muslims and Islam? Why have we attacked them? Why have we hurt innocent people? You said that the bombs we planted would only make some noise, a big bang, and produce smoke. You didn't mention that people would be killed and that old cultural treasures will be destroyed. Why, Fatima, why? What have we done?"

Fatima saw that his eyes were moist and that he was about to burst into tears. She admonished him, "Ahmed, behave like a man! Do you know that the Portuguese murdered and expelled all Muslims from their kingdom in 1249, two hundred and fifty years before our people were driven out of Spain? Do you know that the Portuguese had established the first European colony in Africa by attacking and capturing Ceuta in 1415 and thus gaining access to the Mediterranean Sea? Do you know that Portugal had one of the world's largest empires, enslaving and repressing millions of people? Do you realize that they only gave up the last part of their empire by granting sovereignty to East Timor less than twenty years ago? Those easygoing, peace-loving, nice people ruled an empire of sorts for almost six hundred years! Do you still feel sorry for them?" Then she added as an afterthought, "My name, Fatima, is a household word in Portugal. No, not because of me, but it is the name of a small village where three young girls allegedly had an epiphany and saw Maria in 1917. Where do you think the name came from? It must be from the time our ancestors, the Muslim Moors, ruled Portugal."

Ahmed was at a loss for words. Fatima continued, "I hope that the tourist trade, on which Portugal depends, will suffer. I am glad that the dead people in the library are mostly elderly tourists. I am sure that in their long lives they had caused a lot of injustices. Anyway, Ahmed, it is much worse to kill innocent young girls and boys as our friends from ISIS had done at that concert in Manchester. Come here, Ahmed, and I'll make you feel better."

Ahmed just grumbled that he wasn't in the mood and went out to the veranda to watch the town of Coimbra slowly return to its normal life. After Fatima had showered, she joined him on the veranda. He told her about the barman's advice that Muslims should keep out of Portugal. Fatima listened without commenting and let him blow off steam. Finally, she said, "Let's stay in the room until it gets dark outside and then go out for dinner somewhere near the hotel. Tomorrow we'll check out and drive to Porto." She took Ahmed's hand and gently pulled him back into the room, saying, "Let's go up to the roof, have a drink, and watch the sun set over Coimbra." She was thinking that it would be nice if the sun would also set on Portugal and obliterate western civilization.

Ahmed followed her to the short stairway that led from the fifth floor to the open roof of the hotel. They sat at a table that was close to the roof's door and within minutes, the barman came up to take their order. He acknowledged Ahmed's presence and greeted him like an old friend, but they could feel that he appeared to have some reservations about Fatima. Perhaps he could sense that she was too joyful, considering the situation, or perhaps he was simply upset to be serving what he viewed as unconcerned and unsympathetic tourists. Nevertheless, he took their order and returned with two glasses of semisweet ruby port.

After he left them, Fatima raised her glass and said, "Ahmed, my dear, this ends the first part of our mission. I understand that the 'gift' we left for the infidels in the chapel didn't work well, but we have achieved the effect we wanted. Once we reach Porto, we will separate and probably never meet again in this life. I am sad, so sad, that it must turn out this way because I really got to like you. I am sure that if we spent a few more days and nights together, with proper training and some practice, you would become the man to fulfil my dreams. Drink up, and let's return to the room for another close encounter of the ecstatic kind before dinner."

***

Ahmed just nodded and timidly followed her back to the room. He thought that he now understood how sheep on the way to the slaughterhouse must feel. Then another analogy came to mind, and he shivered: a female black widow spider that devoured her male partner after having sex. Well, he thought, this was not exactly sexual cannibalism since Fatima didn't intend to literally eat him to provide nutrition to her eggs and only meant to sap some of his strength to energize herself.

She understood his physical condition and was gentler with him this time. She didn't pounce on him but slowly undressed him, watching his body begin to respond to her articulate maneuvers. She took off her top, unhooked her bra, freed her breasts from all restraints, and then removed the rest of her clothes. She commanded him to face the full-length mirror and peeped from behind his body to watch his reaction to her machinations. Her initial disappointment was soon replaced by a smile as she saw what effect rubbing her breasts against his bare back had. She clung to his back and let her hands wander over his slim body. When he tried to turn around to face her, she pinned his hands to his sides and then slowly caressed his chest, pinching his nipples until he cried out in pain and pleasure. Only then did she bring her hands down his flat belly until they struck an obstacle that stopped their downward motion. She allowed her hands to explore the obstacle and more cries of pleasure escaped his lips. Then, she loosened her grip and spun him around. She watched closely as his eyeballs rolled over until only the white of his eyes was visible and then, in a low, husky voice, said, "Do you think seventy-two virgins can give as much pleasure as one experienced woman?" She didn't wait for his answer.

He panted, "I never knew that my body could feel such a sensation. Fatima, please allow me to stay with you."

***

The next morning, they checked out of the hotel. Fortunately, the woman on duty at the reception desk made no small talk with them. She only instructed the valet to bring their rental car from the parking garage, made sure that they signed the bill, and bid them a good day. Not a word was said about the terror incident that took place the previous day nor about the fact that several Muslim organizations made claims that they were responsible.

Fatima and Ahmed knew that the legendary Le Docteur, and NEMESIS, had sent them on this mission that had been in the planning stages for over two years but was put on hold due to the circumstances. She had not met Ahmed prior to the mission, and when she received a plane ticket from London to Porto on one of the low-cost airlines, she was pleased to see the tall, dark-skinned young man sitting next to her. When he quietly said the coded recognition phrase—"Have you ever flown over the Bay of Biscay?"—she was delighted. She answered, "I prefer flying to sailing," and squeezed his hand. He said that he had almost missed the flight because of confusion about the correct gate, and she squeezed his hand harder and said that she was happy he made it. She told him that she was twenty-five years old (she was closer to thirty but didn't admit it, even to herself), but nothing else about her background and upbringing. She added that she had been on a couple of previous missions, recalling the bombing of Sainte-Chapelle in Paris that she had carried out with Rafiq, but this was the first time that she was in charge. He said that he had just turned twenty, which she thought was a lie as he had practically no facial hair. Nevertheless, she liked what she saw, and she saw what she liked—a lithe, young man who could be molded like silly putty into whatever shape she fancied. His dark complexion indicated that he was from Arabian origin, and his thin body showed that he was not spoiled by the ways of the West. His English was good, and from his accent, she gathered that he had probably attended a good school in the UK.

After the plane landed in Porto, they walked over to the car rental office, and she produced the voucher that she had received with the plane ticket. They picked up the car, checked it for dents or damage, and then they drove to Coimbra and checked in to the hotel that had been reserved for them. Fatima saw that Ahmed was very shy and inexperienced and decided to be his tutor in earthly matters. She encouraged him to make physical advances and guided him. Ahmed had seen naked women only in porn videos and didn't know what a real woman felt like in the flesh. With Fatima's guidance, this changed very quickly, and by the time they went on their mission, three days after arriving in Coimbra, they were already acting like an old couple.

Fatima received a coded e-mail with instructions and was directed to contact a local businessman. In fact, she never saw the businessman and, when she called his number, was told to leave a message and the number of her prepaid phone. She got a text message telling her to go to the old convent of Santa Clara and look for a package in the deserted atrium. Fatima and Ahmed crossed the Mondego River on the bridge closest to their hotel and saw the abandoned convent. They read the sign explaining that in the seventeenth century there was a big flood that buried the convent in a layer of mud and that it had to be moved to a new position on top of the nearby hill.

The site of the old monastery was being cleaned and restored, and therefore there were no visitors or workmen in the early evening hours. It took them a few minutes to find the two backpacks behind one of the columns of the atrium. There was a note pinned to the canvas backpack. They opened it and saw that it was a tourist map of Coimbra with the sites of Biblioteca Joanina and Capela de Sao Miguel marked with a red *X*. There was no text attached nor was any necessary.

***

During the drive back to the Porto airport, there was almost no discussion in the car, as they were thinking of what they had done in Coimbra and the expected consequences. Fatima drove, and Ahmed checked the navigation system and helped find the entrance to the rental car return position. Together, they boarded the flight back to London, and after landing in Stansted, they went their separate ways, in accordance with the instructions they received before the mission. They knew that despite their personal preference, they would never see each other again.

CHAPTER 3

London, United Kingdom

On the same day that the explosions in Coimbra took place, another NEMESIS-inspired attack was carried out to remind the residents of London and the many tourists that perpetually crowded the city that despite the enhanced security measures, they should not feel complacent and safe, even while attending church.

The choir at St Martin-in-the-Fields church had just finished its second part of the Thursday afternoon performance, and the Reverend Doctor Lockwood-Smith rose from his chair and walked up to the podium. He looked at the audience, that almost filled the entire church, saw that they were mostly elderly Britons who wanted to enjoy an hour of free choir music and some tourists trying to escape the light rain. He knew that they wouldn't like to hear what he had to say, so he started by thanking the choir and the audience. Then he got on with his sermon. "The Good Book doesn't tell us anything about democracy. There is a king, or some other ruler, who orders the people around; there are prophets who deliver the word of God, and there are disciples who spread these words. Yet, my friends, there is nothing wrong with the system if the leader cares about his subjects, knows what's good for them, and follows up on providing them with sound guidance. Years later, the idea that all people have an equal right to decide who will rule them spread in Western culture. When democracy began in ancient Athens, the right to vote was reserved for men who were free and had property. Women, slaves, or poor people were denied the vote. These privileged people had to be responsible when they elected their officials, or else they stood to lose their property and privileges." He paused to see whether he was getting across to his audience and was glad to see that only a few of them had their heads down and were snoozing, while the great majority had their eyes, and hopefully their ears, focused on him. He went on to say, "Democracy is the rule of the majority, or at least, most of the people who cast their votes. This is a good system if people act responsibly and make rational decisions after studying all the facts. However, there are times when people vote impulsively, or self-servingly, without considering the consequences. For example, imagine a democratic society in which two wolves and a sheep vote on the dinner menu by a majority decision." He paused a little to allow the message to sink in and was rewarded by some smiles. He continued, "We have recently seen that a majority of the British people voted to leave the European Community. Yes, it was a democratic decision, but look at the supporters of Brexit and, more interestingly, at the opponents. Those who voted for remaining in the EC were typically the more educated, more ambitious, more sophisticated people and the young people. The very same class of people who had made Britain the empire it once was. The people who believe in an open society and feel confident enough that our British way of life can be preserved, even flourish, when we play a leading part in the economy, science, and progress of the European Community." Reverend Doctor Lockwood-Smith could hear the whispering in the audience, and although he couldn't make out the words, he knew that most of the elderly people in the crowd didn't agree with him. They wanted to "make Britain great again" by turning their island into a fortress and to isolate themselves from the problems of Europe. He said, "I would like to conclude my little sermon by referring you to what's happening in our streets. Terror bombing at a rock concert, murdering almost two dozen young girls and boys, murderous drivers nose-diving their cars into crowds on sidewalks and then getting out with a knife in their hand and the name of their God on their lips, beheading of a soldier here in London, not in Mosul or Baghdad, and openly preaching in mosques for destruction of our Western, democratic society."

He stepped away from the podium, and the choir started singing another hymn when a loud explosion was heard. The terrible sound reverberated in the church, amplified by the excellent acoustics for which the church was famous. A flash of light was seen, and smoke started rising from the cafeteria, appropriately named Café in the Crypt, located in the basement of the building. People came rushing up the two flights of stairs that led from the cafeteria to the street level. Some of them ran out of the church, down the stairs that led to Charing Cross Road, and crossed into Trafalgar Square. Panic spread, and the crowd gathered around the street performers and pavement artists began to run away from the church. Small children were trampled by the panic-stricken mob, older people who couldn't get out of the way of the mob fast enough were shoved aside and pushed to the ground. Tourists standing on the veranda of the National Gallery watched the crowd and filmed the whole incident from a safe position. Within minutes, video clips were sent to news agencies, and they in turn were glad to pour more fuel on the flames and further contribute to the fright and terror.

***

The NEMESIS video clip was simultaneously released to all major networks and news agencies. In accordance with the strict media control imposed by the new US president, who vowed to sue and prosecute anyone responsible for the dissemination of "fake news," none of the major news agencies in the West dared to show the footage on network television. However, that cat had long been out of the bag, and the social media that also got copies of the clip were only too glad to post it on their websites. So the plot to deny the public of this juicy news item only served to amplify its effect and repercussions.

In the clip, Le Docteur said, in his slightly accented but perfect English, "The recent act in Portugal against the cultural heritage of the colonialists and the small tour de force in London show that the news of the demise of NEMESIS was premature. This time, as in the past, NEMESIS was not trying to impress the world by causing mindless mayhem and by the number of casualties but by the quality of its acts. We are not like the fundamentalist Muslim barbarians that didn't hesitate to send a suicide bomber to a rock concert in Manchester or to use a car as a murder weapon and run over pedestrians in central London in an act of vehicular homicide. These primitive acts can be carried out by any brainless individual who is willing to die for the cause he believes in. Those lowly terrorists were brainwashed, perhaps even drugged, and sent to die by some armchair mastermind or, more likely, by some mullah in a mosque. NEMESIS believes that dying for the cause is for fools. Wise people should remember the quote attributed to General George S. Patton, 'The object of war is not to die for your country but to make the other bastard die for his.' Patton is also quoted as saying, 'It is foolish and wrong to mourn the men who died. Rather we should thank God that such men lived', which may be construed as encouraging suicide bombers, but most Americans, quite rightfully, remember only the first quote.

"NEMESIS is back and ready to fight its dire enemies—colonialists, communists, and Crusaders—the three Cs. You can now add to the list two subspecies—I would like to say 'subhuman species'—of these people, capitalists and Jews, who are responsible for participating, if not publicly leading, the three Cs. The Jewish entity, referred by some misinformed individuals as the State of Israel, and its intelligence organization were behind the hunt for NEMESIS operators. Israel and its 'big brother,' the United States of America, have been placed at the top of our list of enemies." He paused, adjusted the keffiyeh that covered his face, and continued in his old tone of voice, not the newly adopted French-Canadian manner.

"I am sure that you are familiar with the Beatles' song from five decades ago, 'Listen, Do You Want to Know a Secret?' So, here is one secret I would like to share with you." Le Docteur paused dramatically before continuing, "The attack on the heart of democracy, the Capitol building in Washington, DC, was carried out by the US branch of NEMESIS. Our supporters in the US are not only radicalized Muslim citizens, as those responsible for the recent ISIS attacks in the UK, but people from all walks of life who have suffered from the repression and usurpation by the old establishment." In a theatrical gesture, he waved a small stars-and-stripes banner that he pulled out of his pocket. He was sure that this would gain more attention than the words of wisdom he was about to say.

In a resounding tenor, he said, "Regular folks in the US who feel that their tax money is used to give expensive medical treatment to people who have intentionally impaired their body and mind by abuse of alcohol, tobacco, and drugs. Folks who see their hard-earned tax money being spent on building and maintaining armed forces that are ineffective in defending their country and way of life. People who cannot afford to buy a home or give their children the type of education that will enable them to advance in society. People who have lost hope of getting a better life for themselves and their children. No, my friends, our supporters are not only right-wing extremists, heart-bleeding liberals, or minority members who have been discriminated against all their lives. No, stop deluding yourselves. Unless you rise against the establishment, things will not change. NEMESIS calls on you to fight—not to die fighting, but to live and win fighting."

Le Docteur refrained from mentioning the other objective of NEMESIS, to enforce the rule of Islamic law, the Shariya, on the world. He reckoned that it would deter potential supporters; therefore, he emphasized the rebellion against the establishment. He only mentioned in passing the desire to avenge the acts against Islam and Muslims because Americans, unlike their European ancestors, were not a colonialist power in the past. He ignored his hatred of Americans who instigated a war against Muslims on Islamic soil in Iraq, Afghanistan, Syria, and other countries. He tried to draw a fine line between the establishment and the people. He believed the common man didn't want to go to war in foreign lands, while the establishment, impelled by the military-industrial complex, needed wars to continue its growing sales of weapons.

***

CHAPTER 4

Santa Fe, New Mexico

Jacque Deleau, Le Docteur's new name, looked at Blossom, the young woman sitting across the table, and raised his glass of wine. He looked at the reflection of the liquid in the sunlight, swirled the wine, took a deep sniff of the intoxicating aroma, and said, "New Mexico is now producing some of the best wines in the nation. And if I may add, also some the finest women in the world."

His partner blushed at the compliment, and her skin took on a particularly beautiful hue, which was a composition of her natural color and the excitement she felt. She said, "Dr. Deleau, I am flattered by the attention you are giving me. Since the first time you stepped into class and started speaking, I had hoped for a moment like this. I had tried to get you to notice me and, as you know, followed you to your office after class many times. I thought that you ignored me and therefore was overjoyed when you invited me to dine with you."

Le Docteur contentedly said, "Blossom, please call me Jacque—we are not in class anymore, and I am no longer your teacher. Of course, I noticed you and your interest in me, but I couldn't respond in kind while you were one of my students." He picked up his glass of wine and added, "Here's to our new friendship. Tell me a little about yourself."

Blossom told him that her mother, Nadia, was originally a Palestinian, who nowadays worked as a nuclear physicist at Sandia National Laboratory. Her father, Jonathan Bearskin, was a Native American who was Nadia's boss at Sandia. When Jonathan was eight years old, his unique mathematical talent was identified by his second-grade teacher, Miss Gordon, and he was transferred to a special class, where he received advanced lessons in science and math. When he was twelve, he was sent to boarding school on the West Coast, far away from his family who lived on a reservation close to Roswell, New Mexico. He did exceptionally well at the school and started to take university courses while still in high school. He earned a double doctorate in mathematics and engineering a couple of months before his twentieth birthday. He immediately received several lucrative and prestigious job offers from leading universities on the West Coast, but he wanted to be close to his parents and extended family so turned down those offers. His reputation preceded him, and within two weeks after receiving his degree, he was recruited by Sandia. At first, he was "a scientist at large," meaning that he had no formal responsibilities and was free to roam the lab, ask questions, and offer advice. That way, he got involved with many different ongoing projects and quite frequently managed to solve problems that appeared to be at dead ends. Within a couple of years, he became so well known as a "mister know-it-all" and "doctor problem solver" that he got calls for help from different parts of the lab.

One day he was summoned to the physics department and was presented with a particularly difficult question involving transmutation of radioactive elements. Nadia, a fresh graduate from the University of New Mexico in Albuquerque, had been experimenting with the effects of neutron irradiation on a mixture of heavy elements. She believed that she had produced a new, hitherto unknown element, but nobody else was convinced by the experimental evidence that she had submitted. Jonathan was called to review her experimental results but spent even more time viewing Nadia. Within a short while, he was convinced of two things. First, she had misinterpreted her results and no new element was produced, and secondly, he was in love with Nadia. She was deeply disappointed by his conclusion about her scientific results but greatly buoyed and pleased by his proposal to marry her. The wedding ceremony was carried out in a traditional Native American style, with some influences of Islam interjected by Nadia's parents who flew over from the Palestinian town of Nablus. Whenever Jonathan and Nadia talked about the reaction of the in-laws to the unfamiliar ceremony, they burst out laughing. His Native American parents didn't understand what Nadia's Palestinian parents said, and her parents found the entire ceremony to be bizarre, to soften what they had actually said about it. The only thing they agreed on was that the young couple were deeply in love with each other.

When their only daughter, Blossom, was born, the grandparents from both sides practically worshipped her. The scene of the adoration of the three wise men, or Magi from the East, paying tribute to baby Jesus, came to mind when they were close to the baby. They brought gifts, they looked at the baby girl with loving eyes, they jumped to console her when she cried, and they made funny faces to make her laugh. Only through her strength of character did Blossom avoid becoming a spoiled princess and turned out to be an adventurous young woman. Her mixed heritage didn't make life easy for her in a society that often judged people by the color of their skin, but her natural intelligence and beauty had made her self-confident enough to ignore the racist-based scorn of her peers. She viewed the young men in her class as immature boys and the young women as spoiled girls whose only interests involved parties and shopping. That included shopping for brand-name items at the mall during the day and for a husband at school or at parties held in the evening and night.

She came across Jacque Deleau when he had given a series of seminars as a visiting professor of European History at New Mexico State University, NMSU, in Las Cruces, where she had gone to college. He was spending a semester in New Mexico, dividing his time between NMSU and the larger University of New Mexico in Albuquerque. Blossom instantly fell for the charismatic professor with the charming accent and followed him to his temporary office after class. He could tell from her questions that she was as intelligent as she was good looking and, from the admiring look in her eyes, that she would abide by his every word. When he heard that her mother was Palestinian, his interest in her grew, as he reckoned that she was excellent material for recruitment to NEMESIS. Yet, while the semester lasted, he couldn't make any advances without risking getting in trouble with the university authorities. However, the semester had just ended, and they were no longer in an official teacher-student relationship, so Le Docteur invited her out for dinner and was sitting across the table from her, enjoying the excellent wine and her company. He gave her a heavily edited version of his own life. He said, "I was raised in a French-Canadian family in a small village on the Saguenay River in the Province of Quebec. I couldn't really speak English until I was sent to boarding school in Montreal after my parents died in a car accident. Therefore, I still have some accent."

He looked at her and saw her smiling, "Jacque, I love your accent. It makes you much more approachable and human. But I am sorry that you were orphaned at such a young age. Tell me more about yourself." This was the first time that she used his first name and was thrilled by the shiver of excitement this mere act sent through her body.

Le Docteur continued, "I took a great interest in political science, and then I understood that most of what is happening in the world nowadays has its roots in the actions of the European colonial powers. That is why I decided to focus on European history because of its past and present influence on global politics." He saw her nodding in agreement and added, "Anyone who wishes to understand what is happening in the world—the reason for the waves of terrorism, the deeply instilled resentment of the people in Asia and Africa toward their former colonial oppressors, the hatred of people who suffered a similar fate in the hands of the communist occupiers—must look for the reasons in the history of the last century or two. You said that your father is a Native American and your mother a Muslim from Palestine, so you should be aware of the burden you are carrying."

He looked at her to assess her reaction. He was disappointed when she said, "I feel like an American. I don't deserve any special treatment because of my heritage. I just want to live my life like any other young woman, excel in my career, raise a family, and receive my share of happiness. But, Jacque, what brought you to New Mexico?"

He answered, "I didn't want to settle down in one place. I thought that I needed to see different places in which past colonialism shaped the present. I have taught courses on political science in several places in Europe and in North America, and I was glad to be offered the opportunity to spend a semester here in New Mexico. This is the most northern place that the Spaniards reached from their base in Mexico, as well as the site of some of the battles between the American settlers spreading west and the original residents, your paternal ancestors. In my field, this first-hand experience is important."

She thought about this, "Jacque, I have looked for your scientific publications on different websites but have not found any."

He had expected this, and before she could continue, he laughed, "My dear Blossom, this is because I use a pen name. I try not to brag about my scientific achievements but let me assure you that I have published many highly regarded articles, as well as a few books. For the sake of modesty, please allow me to retain my anonymity. In due time, I promise to tell you all about these publications." He had anticipated her query and had this answer ready. He added, "I have spent time as a visiting professor not only in academic institutions but also in private and government research institutes. In fact, I'll be returning to Washington, DC, in a few weeks to assume a position at one of these institutions."

He knew that he should take his time getting closer to Blossom and didn't want to rush things. So, after dinner, he escorted her to her apartment, refused her transparent offer to "come up for coffee," and arranged to meet her again the following evening.

***

Blossom's mixed parental heritage gave the devious Le Docteur a new idea, which he later came to regard as nothing less than an epiphany. Blossom's father, Jonathan, was a member of one of oldest tribes of Native Americans and proud of his ancestry. Blossom said that he regarded himself as being exceptionally fortunate for receiving the opportunity to succeed in a highly competitive society, as he was fully aware that his fellow tribesmen didn't get the same chance. Le Docteur thought that Native Americans carried a deep loathing and profound bitterness against the White Man for what he had done to their culture and traditional way of life. He reckoned that he could channel these feelings of animosity to support his own cause, especially with the endorsement of one of their most respected members. Blossom could well be the key to progressing with this idea. Once again, Le Docteur smiled to himself when the thought of combining business and pleasure—recruiting the Native Americans in his fight against the hated colonialists and Crusaders while enjoying the delightful company of the most delicate blossoming flower.

***

Office of Senator McCorey, Santa Fe

Le Docteur arrived at Senator McCorey's office in downtown Santa Fe right on time for their scheduled meeting. The senator told his secretary to take a long lunch break and personally stepped out to greet his guest. "Professor Deleau, it is good to see you here in New Mexico. I understand that you spent a semester in Albuquerque and Las Cruces teaching European History. How did you like living here, on the edge of the desert? It must have been quite a change from Canada."

Le Docteur smiled, "Senator, please call me Jacque. After all, we are partners with common goals. Yes, I love the dry heat of the desert. It will make me better appreciate the rain, cold weather, and green trees in Quebec."

The senator opened the ornamental liquor cabinet, took out a bottle of bourbon and a couple of Glencairn whiskey glasses, and poured a generous amount of the amber liquid in both glasses. He raised his glass, "Jacque, our last operation was a resounding success. I got excellent exposure on TV, strengthened my electoral base, and was quoted by the national and international media. Let's drink to many more fruitful operations."

Le Docteur, with his finely-honed French palette, was not particularly fond of bourbon, a drink that he considered as being fit for rednecks and uncouth country bumpkins. He thought Senator McCorey fit the bill, but he smiled and raised his glass, "Jim, I love win-win situations like these. True, there was some collateral damage, but this is unavoidable when you are playing for high stakes."

The senator finished his drink and refilled his own glass. He saw that his friend had not yet drank his bourbon and figured that perhaps as a French-Canadian, more precisely a Quebecois, he preferred cognac. He went to the liquor cabinet, took out a bottle of cognac, and poured a generous amount into a snifter. Le Docteur was favorably surprised that the senator knew that cognac should be served in a snifter. He raised the snifter, "Jim, you certainly know how to treat a friend. Please let me tell you what I have in mind for our next joint venture." He started to explain his plan and watched the expression on the senator's face change from surprise and rejection, to a skeptical look, and finally to apprehension and admiration.

Senator McCorey said, "This is the boldest and most audacious plan I have ever heard. If we can pull it off, I will be my party's leading candidate for the presidential race when the incumbent is impeached or completes his first term. If we are discovered, then I won't have to worry about anything because I'll be dead . . ." his voice trailed off. He knew that it wasn't entirely true—he could use his new dear friend, Jacque Deleau, as a scapegoat.

Le Docteur understood what was going on in the senator's mind. He nodded, "I am sure that it will work, Mr. Future President." He rose from his chair and shook hands with the senator. He thought that some people would stop at nothing to gain power, or money. He didn't stop to wonder if his own motivation, revenge, was morally better justified.

***

Le Docteur was glad to step out from the senator's stuffy air-conditioned office into the busy commercial square where street vendors displayed their goods. He was surprised to see that one of the stores displayed a sign with the name "Mimosa." It reminded him of his mother and her Albanian roots and the tragic circumstances of her untimely death in Paris, when she suffered severe burns while saving kindergarten children from a fire set by an anti-Muslim arsonist. This further strengthened his resolve to avenge the maltreatment of Muslims by Americans and by the hated Crusaders and colonialists. He wondered if the unholy alliance with Senator McCorey would serve his objective of vengeance.

His dark mood lightened when he saw the tourists crowding around the small stalls and rough woolen blankets spread on the sidewalk. The merchandize on display consisted mainly of beautifully woven rugs, quilts, and blankets with motifs from the life of the Native Americans (no one referred to them as "Indians" nowadays), or more correctly, from what Hollywood depicted as their lives. There were also several types of dream catchers, the traditional Native American object that to him looked like a fishing net with feathers, which was meant to protect the sleeping person from negative dreams while allowing positive ones to slip through the holes in the net. Beside these artistic items, there were colorful beads of various sizes, traditional dancing regalia, knives of different sizes and shapes, and other knickknacks that were supposedly originally handmade Native American products, but probably, he thought, mass produced in China. He suppressed a giggle when he thought about the ironies of history: one hundred and fifty years earlier, the White Man gave Native Americans glass baubles in return for land, horses, and other precious goods, and now the descendants of those Native Americans were selling the descendants of the White Man worthless glass beads for good, green dollars.

His mood received another uplift when he arrived at the restaurant where Blossom was already waiting for him with a cool beer in her hand. The beads of condensed water vapor that formed on the chilled thick glass made his mouth water, and he signaled to the waitress to bring him the same, pointing at Blossom's glass and raising two fingers. Such a gesture to a waiter in France would have earned him the everlasting animosity of the waiter, and he would be assured that he would be ignored completely, but here, in the US, prompt service was to be expected, as was the reward of a large tip.

The couple took a minute to study the menu, and both decided to keep things simple by ordering cheeseburgers with home fries and another couple of beers. They took their time eating and appeared outwardly to be relaxed, but the tension between them was high because they were both anticipating the next move. Le Docteur had reserved a room at the Hilton hotel, which was just a short walk from the restaurant. In fact, he had already parked his car at the hotel's parking lot and had checked in, although he was told that the room would be ready only at three o'clock. Blossom drove up to Santa Fe from Albuquerque, and her car was at one of the parking lots that surrounded the old town.

After lunch, they strolled along the streets of the old town, looking at several of the artists' galleries, entering some of the small shops, and reading the signs posted in front of historic sites and some of the older houses. Once again, Le Docteur was amused by what was considered as a "historic site 'in New Mexico—buildings that were constructed one hundred years earlier, while things that were slightly older were titled as "ancient." He thought of France, where medieval castles and fortresses were spread all over the country, and about the roots of Islam in the Middle East, where there were structures more than one thousand years old. When Blossom's foot slipped over a pothole in the road, he instinctively took her arm to steady her, and the electric jolt they both felt made him remove his hand quickly. Blossom's reaction was different—she took his hand in hers and stroked his fingers with an unabashed promise of what was to come. This was to be the first time that they would spend the night together, and she was excited about this and wondering what it would be like.

***

Le Docteur considered the unique ethnic composition of

the population of New Mexico and the opportunity presented by it. While in the entire US the Native Americans (including American Indians and Native Alaskans) constituted a mere 0.8 percent of the population, they were 8.8 percent in New Mexico. The Hispanic population in the state was a whopping 46.4 percent compared with the 16.9 percent in the nation. Asians and Blacks together were 3.5 percent in New Mexico, while in the entire US they were 18.4 percent of the population. He knew that Senator McCorey was also aware of these statistics and that his election strategy was based on receiving almost all the votes of the White people and some votes from the more affluent Hispanics, as well as those of the Asian minority. Le Docteur thought that if he could manipulate the votes of Native Americans to support the senator, it would ensure his reelection. He understood that he could use this to manipulate the unscrupulous senator.

***

The plan Le Docteur had presented to Senator McCorey was bold, daring, and dangerous. He had devised it after considering the matter for a long time. What he had found most interesting as a professor of political science with a keen knowledge of history was that there were two contradictory viewpoints regarding the relationship between Muslims and Native Americans. On the one hand, Le Docteur could adopt the approach that both populations were exploited, oppressed, and denigrated by the White Man, meaning European and American racists and White supremacists. This would place the Native American population on the side of the Muslims and diagonally opposed to Senator McCorey—not the desired outcome for the senator and Le Docteur. On the other hand, if he could turn the Native Americans against Islam and Muslims, they would be inclined to support the senator—"my enemy's enemy is my friend"—although there was no love for him in their community. To do this, an extreme act was required, just the type Le Docteur excelled in pulling off, something so outrageous, so monstrous, so dreadful that it would force the hand of even the moderate leaders of the Native American community and push them to support Muslim-Bashing Jimbo.

Le Docteur didn't share his self-deliberations with McCorey and whispered in his ear only in general terms what he intended to do. This promoted the warm response he had received from the senator.

***

The main problem he faced, though, was how to introduce the senator's well-known hatred of Muslims to Blossom and her parents. Bringing Jonathan's family to the foreground was especially crucial because Jonathan was a true patriot of the United States, despite what he perceived as the systematic mistreatment of Native Americans by representatives of the administration. Obviously, Jonathan couldn't be persuaded that Muslims were enemies of the Native Americans, certainly not when his love and devotion to Nadia were so complete. Nor would Blossom ever believe that, considering the relationship between her own parents and two sets of grandparents. The devious mind of Le Docteur came up with a different approach—he knew that Jonathan was respected by the educated tribesmen and by the more sophisticated Native American leaders, but the common folk envied his success and regarded him as a renegade for marrying a Muslim woman, who was considered as an insult to the proud tradition of the tribe. He also knew that Blossom's independent-minded behavior was anathema to the traditionalists, and he intended to exploit this as well. He thought that the perfect setting for his atrocious plan would be at the biggest annual gathering of Native Americans from all over North America—the powwow at Gallup, New Mexico.

CHAPTER 5

Washington, DC

Senator Thomas J. Buckley, Jr., chairman of the Senate Committee on Foreign Relations, the Honorable Republican from Tennessee, couldn't stand Senator McCorey, who headed the subcommittee on the Near East, South Asia, Central Asia, and counterterrorism. The senator from New Mexico represented everything he despised—he was self-serving, he used his influence to promote policies that were sure to sink America deeper into the quagmire of the Near East, and worse of all, he did this so blatantly that even the conservative press frequently refrained from supporting him. A case in point was the embarrassing TV interview he gave Fox News after the drone attack on the Capitol building. Senator Buckley knew that the resentment was mutual and tried to avoid being in the same room with McCorey, a feat that was not always possible because of the biweekly meetings that they held. Buckley knew that McCorey wanted nothing more than to take his job as chairman, but even he didn't think to what lengths the manipulative senator would be willing to go to in order to achieve his goal.

The two senators were sitting across from each other at

both ends of the long table, while the members of the subcommittee were seated along the sides of the table. Coffee, tea, and soft drinks were placed on the sideboard, and sweet and salty pastries were laid next to the beverages. The discussion on the policy toward the rising threat of Islamic terrorism on US soil, as exemplified by the drone attack, became heated. Muslim-Bashing Jimbo had the floor and was obviously out of control as he raised his voice to a disagreeable volume, "You must understand that Muslims, like rabid dogs, comprehend only one language—that of brute force. Attempts to reason with them, to negotiate a deal with them, and to reach an understanding are doomed to fail and will only encourage them to toughen their position and demand more. Give them an inch, and they'll demand a mile and raise their middle finger to show you what they think of you. Forget about them showing gratitude for helping them eliminate starvation of refugees in Syria or Iraq. Don't expect them to curb violence among themselves and to carry out a democratic election. There is no such thing as democracy in the Arab world, and there never will be. We have to carry a big stick and use it to bash their heads." He saw that the members of the subcommittee were unable to suppress their sniggering at his use of the verb that was part of his nickname, and his voice rose by another octave, "To demonstrate that we are serious, I propose that we take out the city that hosts the leadership of the Islamic State terrorist organization."

Before he could further advance his proposal, Senator Buckley, the chairman of the committee, intervened, "Senator McCorey, you are out of line and, I don't hesitate to say, also out of your mind. Do you seriously propose that we drop an atom bomb on a city with hundreds of thousands of innocent civilians who are held as hostages by ISIS against their will?"

McCorey's face turned crimson, and he almost choked on his own spittle before he retorted, "Mr. Chairman, with all due respect, you are not only soft-hearted but also soft-minded. You don't know these people, these subhuman camel drivers. I assure you that all it takes for our beloved United States to reestablish its dominance and the fact that we make the rules for everyone else is one lousy little A-bomb. Who cares if a quarter of a million of those hateful people die in an instant? In Syria alone, double that number perished during the first six years of their so-called civil war, and who knows how many more will die before it ends. Almost half the population of Syria was forced to leave their homes and live as refugees in their own country or elsewhere. If we do what I propose, what our destiny as the mightiest power in the world has called upon us to do, then we'll end this sordid affair with a single sharp blow. No more refugees, no more casualties, no more terrorists flooding Europe and the US. One blow and finished." He emphasized his words by opening his fist and spreading out his fingers, like a puff of air, and then sat down and looked around the table. The expressions of deep resentment he saw on the faces of his colleagues conveyed a clear message that they didn't agree with him.

Chairman Buckley looked as if he was about to have a heart attack. All blood drained from his already pallid face. In a weak voice, he managed to say, "I think that Senator McCorey is way out of line. If a transcription of this meeting ever reaches the press, then we are all doomed unless we strongly oppose his proposal. For the public record, I call for a vote on the senator's proposal." Every single member of the subcommittee raised their hands to vote against the proposal, except, of course, McCorey. The chairman said, "The meeting is adjourned," and left the room in hurry, probably to report to POTUS that McCorey is dangerous and should be removed, preferably in a straitjacket, from the Senate.

After everyone left the conference room, Senator McCorey walked calmly to the sideboard and took a bottle of sparkling water out of the ice bucket. He didn't bother with a glass and took a long sip directly from the bottle. He smiled to himself and mumbled inaudibly, "The seed was planted. Now all I need is to nourish it and let it grow." He took the miniature tape recorder out of his pocket and switched it off. He returned to his office in the Senate and called his press secretary, who also served as his lover, "Dolly, please take the recording and leak it, anonymously, of course, to your contacts at Fox News and Breitbart. Make sure that it receives favorable commentary by some of the more respectful political analysts. Meet me at my hotel at nine p.m., and we'll discuss some innovative strategies that haven't been tried before." Dolly nodded and rushed off to carry out his task.

***

Fox News ran a banner that promised "News at nine. Revelation of the secret transcription from a closed meeting of the subcommittee on counterterrorism," not bothering to mention the full name of the subcommittee that would take up most of the banner. Breitbart didn't wait until the evening and had repeatedly played the recording and showed a transcript, with commentary that left no doubt that it was in favor of the proposal to nuke the "A-rabs." In fact, the resident "expert on terrorism" said that taking out the cities of Mosul in Iraq and Al Raqqah in Syria should have been carried out years earlier and suggested using an H-bomb on Tehran, just for good measure. No one contradicted the "expert" or bothered to think what the implications of such an act would be.

Compared with Breitbart, Fox News was the epitome of sanity and impartiality. A serious discussion took place, and pros and cons of the proposal were debated. The narrator mentioned that Senator McCorey was not available and his press secretary only said that she couldn't comment on transcriptions of closed subcommittee meetings. The discussion in the studio was interrupted by a call from Senator Buckley's legal adviser, who said that disclosure of confidential proceedings from closed sessions of the Senate Committee on Foreign Relations and its subcommittees was illegal and could be considered as high treason. When he was asked if the recording was accurate, he quickly said that he couldn't deny or confirm its originality. He added that there have many cases in which recordings were fabricated.

Senator McCorey and his press secretary were seated on the couch in the senator's hotel suite, sipping bourbon and laughing. Dolly looked at the senator with admiring eyes and refilled their glasses. The senator said, "Let's celebrate," and asked the press secretary to show him how much she appreciated the little publicity feat. He was not disappointed when Dolly did a small victory dance, followed by some quite incredible gymnastics.

***

The National Museum of Nuclear Science and History, Albuquerque, New Mexico

The staff member who was the first to arrive at the museum, a part-time student by the name of Greta, couldn't believe her eyes. As usual, she entered from the employees' side door that served the staff, not the main doors through which the visitors entered. After she placed her backpack on her desk and went to the ladies' room to freshen up, something that she saw from the corner of her eye caught her attention. One of the museum's centerpieces, "The Critical Assembly," which included some of the original equipment that was used by the scientists who developed the first atom bomb, as well as a model of the core of that bomb and other components was strewn on the floor. The large racks that held the electronic equipment were lying face down on the floor, and the thick cables that interconnected were sliced to small bits. The wall was covered with graffiti that depicted a cartoon of Uncle Sam holding a nuclear mushroom in his hand, and scribbled in red letters, a sentence read, "I have my nuclear umbrella and don't give a damn about anyone else."

Greta rushed back to her desk and called the museum's director, Dr. Steve Montal, a retired physicist from Los

Alamos, and described what she saw. He told her to keep everybody out, including the staff, and not open the museum to visitors. He instructed her to call the police immediately and ask for a forensics team, while he got into his car and headed to the museum. Dr. Montal and the police arrived at the same time. He guided the police officer to the employees' entrance and called for Greta to open the door. The other staff members who had arrived and found the door locked peeped over his shoulders and tried to see what was going on inside. When the door finally opened, the director ordered them to remain outside until the police finished their investigation. The police officer said that the forensics team was on their way and took a quick look at the scene of the crime. He had visited the museum with his kids several times and viewed it as one of the major attractions of Albuquerque, so he was upset by the sight of the ruined scientific display. He said, "Dr. Montal, who would do such a barbaric thing?"

The director shrugged, "I hope you catch them and punish them severely. This exhibit is a piece of history and is irreplaceable. I gather from the caricature that it is someone who hates the United States. This is not a blind act of vandalism—this was done by someone who wanted to convey a message. We have the entire museum covered by surveillance cameras, so it should be easy to see who did this. Let's go to the room in which the feed from the video cameras is stored." He led the way to a small room that served as an office for the security staff and contained the computer that recorded the output from the surveillance cameras. The police officer and the director saw an open gap where the hard drive had been, looked at each other, and shook their heads in dismay.

The officer said, "Our forensics team has just arrived. Let them do their job and collect whatever evidence they can. We'll have to do without the security camera videos." The team's photographer started taking photos of everything, while another member of the team tried to collect fingerprints. He complained that there were so many that it would be impossible to process them all. Dr. Montal muttered that the perpetrators were probably careful to avoid leaving fingerprints and that he thought the forensics guys were wasting their time, but they pretended they didn't hear him and continued to methodically do their job.

Greta approached the director and said, "Dr. Montal, I have checked the museum's social schedule and saw that the place was used for a small party, given in honor of a professor from the University of New Mexico who is retiring after fifty years at the chemistry department. Although the museum can seat two hundred guests, there were only about fifty at the party last night. Our regular cleaning staff tidied up after the guests left and everything was in order when the head of the staff locked up. Perhaps one of the guests hid somewhere and then destroyed the exhibit and let himself out."

The director looked at her, "Good work, Greta. Please find out what you can on the party, the guests, the caterers, cleaning staff, and everything you can about the event. Then tell me what you have found, and we'll update the police. Meanwhile, once the police finish their work, please close off the area where the Critical Assembly was placed but open the rest of the museum for visitors. We'll try to act as if nothing happened, business as usual. Tell the rest of the staff to gather near the entrance and wait for me to address them."

An hour later, Greta entered the director's office. "The police have left, and the entire staff is waiting for you."

Dr. Montal got up from his chair, straightened his suit, and walked to the main entrance where the staff was assembled, anxiously waiting for him. "A barbaric act was committed here last night. One of our main exhibits, one that represents an important event in American history and a symbol of the greatness of our science, has been maliciously destroyed. This is not a simple act of vandalism; it is nothing less than a blatant hate crime. The chief of police has assured me that it will be treated as a hate crime and receive top priority. The FBI and Department of Homeland Security are also involved, although this may be out of their jurisdiction, unless proven different. I ask all of you not to talk about this with anyone and to help the authorities seize the perpetrators." He stopped talking when he saw many employees lift their cellphones and show him the major news stations were already showing photos of the ruined exhibit and the graffiti. He shook his head, "As a veteran of Los Alamos, I can only be thankful that such devices didn't exist in my time. It is impossible to keep anything secret anymore. Still, I implore you to avoid the media. Thanks for your attention. Please get back to work."

***

Le Docteur watched the local TV station, KOAT Channel 7, and was pleased to see the announcer's fixed smile fade away. He solemnly said, "A hate crime against the United States has been committed, here in Albuquerque. Some perpetrator has destroyed one of the most important exhibits at our city's very own National Museum of Nuclear Science and History. Our reporter, Marjorie Star, is at the scene."

The comely brunette held the microphone in one hand, and her other hand pointed at the main door of the museum, "This is the site where a mindless crime of vandalism took place last night. With me is Dr. Steve Montal, the director of the museum. Dr. Montal, can you tell our viewers what happened here?"

The director would have preferred to be on TV for other reasons but responded, "An exhibit of historical and scientific importance was damaged beyond repair. This heinous crime took place between eleven p.m. last night when the museum was closed after a social event and seven thirty this morning, when the first staff member arrived to prepare the museum for visitors. The police forensics team has gathered physical evidence from the scene of the crime and will study it. Unfortunately, the surveillance video is missing—the perpetrator removed the hard drive from the security computer."

The reported said, "Can you tell us about the exhibit?"

Dr. Montal was now more in his element, "This is, sorry, this was the most complete, and perhaps the only, exhibit that displayed a model of the innards of the very first atomic bomb, the "Gadget," detonated on July 16, 1945, at the Trinity site, not far from here. This was the first time that the powerful force of nuclear fission was demonstrated and the harbinger of the atomic age. This is the quintessential symbol of what made America the greatest country in the world. We will do our best to reconstruct the exhibit, but the damage is extensive." He choked and almost burst out in tears but managed to continue, "The graffiti on the wall proves that this was not a random act but was meant to humiliate our grand country and to convey a message. I am not sure what exactly this message means, but I am sure that we'll hear from the perpetrator or perpetrators."

A still photo of the graffiti was shown. The reporter signed off, "From the ugly scene at the National Museum of Nuclear Science and History, this is Marjorie Star."

Le Docteur turned off his TV set, got up from his chair, and poured himself a large glass of red wine. He raised his glass to his image in the mirror and silently congratulated himself. He had been invited to the event in honor of the retiring chemistry professor, who was one of the few acquaintances he had made on the university campus. After the event started to wind down, Le Docteur hid himself in the staff's restroom and waited for everyone else to leave. After the place was empty, he entered the museum's storeroom, in which he found a sledgehammer, a sturdy wire cutter, and a spray can with red paint. Nonchalantly, he walked to the security office and removed the hard drive from the computer. He then went to the most revered exhibit, the Critical Assembly, and methodically trashed it with blows from the sledgehammer. Then he toppled all the cabinets with the historical electronic equipment and sliced the wires that connected them to each other and to the centerpiece. Finally, he used the spray can to draw the graffiti and write the sentence that he knew would be quoted by the media.

After drinking half the bottle of wine, Le Docteur called Blossom and invited her to dinner. She was glad to hear his voice and said, "Jacque, did you see the news? Someone broke into the Nuclear Science Museum and destroyed some exhibits. Terrible."

Le Docteur pretended that he knew nothing about this, "Blossom, what happened? Can you tell me about it when we meet? I need to complete some writing before dinner."

***

After some self-deliberation, Le Docteur decided that NEMESIS would not claim responsibility for the successful attack on the centerpiece of the National Museum of Nuclear Science and History. He thought that the risk of drawing attention to himself was too great, but he reserved it for future use, to show how far the tentacles of NEMESIS could reach. However, he wanted to make sure that Senator McCorey would give him credit for the new opportunity to grab some prime time in the limelight, so he called him and told him to turn on his TV to KOAT Channel 7.

Marjorie Star looked at the cameraman as he was beginning to pack his equipment and head back to the Channel 7 van. She waved to him to attract his attention and pointed at her cellphone. He understood that she wanted to continue to broadcast live, so he focused his camera and pointed at the microphone she was holding in her hand. She said, "I have Senator McCorey on the phone, and he wishes to state his opinion on the senseless act of vandalism that was committed here, at the National Museum of Nuclear Science and History. Senator, please share your thoughts about this dreadful act with the audience."

Senator McCorey cleared his throat, "Marjorie, this heinous attack on another landmark of our cultural heritage and a symbol of American technological superiority is an indication of the far-reaching tentacles of the Islamic terrorism."

Marjorie didn't like the senator and his bigotry, so she interrupted, "Senator McCorey, how do you know that the perpetrators were Muslims? There is no evidence in the cartoon or graffiti of Islamic involvement. The graffiti 'I have my nuclear umbrella and don't give a damn about anyone else' denounces the United States."

The senator, who was experienced in handling difficult questions from the media, turned to the safe ground that always worked, "Marjorie, you know I cannot divulge my sources of information because of national security considerations. Take my word that sooner or later the whole world will know that Islamic terrorists are behind this. I have said time and again that Muslims are not welcome in our country, and most certainly we don't want them in New Mexico, the land of enchantment. They penetrated the museum dedicated to commemorating one of the greatest achievements of our nation, a place frequented by schoolchildren, one of the symbols of national pride. I shudder to think what could happen if they attacked the museum when hundreds of young schoolchildren were visiting. These Godless people would stop at nothing. I call for investigating every suspected Muslim in New Mexico and taking corrective measures to remove them, temporarily or permanently, from the company of God-fearing, red-blooded, patriotic Americans."

Although only his voice was heard, one could easily imagine his face distorted with rage and hatred. Marjorie was grateful that she didn't have to see him. She signed off, "Thank you, Senator McCorey for your candid opinion. I am sure that many of our viewers would agree with you. This is Marjorie Star at the National Museum of Nuclear Science and History in Albuquerque." She signaled to the cameraman by crossing her throat with her right hand in a gesture that could be interpreted simply as "stop filming" or perhaps as an expression of her opinion of the senator.

Senator McCorey was not very happy with the way the interview developed. Firstly, he wanted to be seen, not only heard, on live TV. Secondly, he really detested the still photo that the station showed when he talked. It showed him with a five o'clock shadow of unshaven stubble and black circles around his eyes. Thirdly, he thought that the young reporter was being disrespectful when she asked for his source of information regarding the Islamic involvement. Finally, he felt that his rhetoric was not as inflammatory as it should have been. After all, such an act in his home state was a good excuse to be on national TV and not just on a local station.

CHAPTER 6

Albuquerque, New Mexico

Le Docteur told Blossom that he would soon have to return to Washington, DC, to resume his position as an expert on international affairs and European history at one of the prestigious institutions. He didn't specify which one because he had made up the whole thing on the spur of the moment at one of their first meetings. He thought that after being so close together, he needed time to consider his next move. He had not told her about the part he played in creating NEMESIS and conducting its operations in Europe and certainly nothing about his plans for causing havoc in the USA. Whenever he raised the issue of her Muslim maternal heritage, she stated that she felt more like a Native American and regarded herself as a patriotic American who was fortunate to be born and grow up in this great country. She had expressed her dislike of politics and politicians and frowned upon his close ties with Senator McCorey. Le Docteur wasn't quite sure what to do about these differences, so he felt that being away from her would help clarify his mind. He said, "Blossom, I need to fly to Washington after the weekend. I don't know when I'll be back, so let's enjoy the weekend.

Your father has told me that there is a nationwide powwow of Native Americans in Gallup and said that it would be interesting for me to see." Le Docteur planted the seed in Blossom's mind, and he now hoped she would take the bait.

Blossom had been feeling for quite a while that Jacque, as she called Le Docteur, was troubled by something, and she knew that it affected their relationship. They had practically been inseparable for the last three weeks. She had introduced him to her parents, who were a bit concerned about the age difference between their daughter and Jacque, as well as by the way he swept her off her feet. She was so young and impressionable, they thought, and they feared that she was too naïve and gullible. They liked Jacque and his intellect and were impressed by his charisma but would have preferred him to be a friend of the family rather than Blossom's boyfriend. Blossom responded to Le Docteur's offer, "That is a good idea. My father took me to a small powwow in Las Cruces when I was nine years old. I was a bit afraid then of the big, burly, solemn-faced men with their colorful clothes and headdresses, while all the women looked to me as if they were all overweight. However, when they started chanting their monotonous songs, accompanied by the rhythmic beating on the drums, I was enchanted. I could feel the rhythm in my bones, my breathing and heartbeat fell in time with the drumbeats, and it seemed as if my blood flowed differently. I would love to go to the powwow in Gallup, as I heard it would be one of the largest social gatherings of Native Americans from the Southwest with representatives from tribes from across the nation, and even from Canada."

He said, "I have never been west of Albuquerque, so I checked the map. It's one hundred and sixty miles from here to Gallup, and the drive should take just under three hours. So, I suggest that we should leave in the early afternoon to get there by early evening. Your father said that the social gathering begins at seven p.m., but he joked and said that seven p.m. 'Indian Time' is closer to nine p.m. I have made reservations at a hotel in Gallup, and we can rest there before going to the gathering."

Blossom said, "Many people do not understand the profound meaning of these powwows and regard them as a Halloween party for grown-ups. For the Native Americans, this gathering is the place for an intertribal meeting that has two main aspects. On the one hand, this is a cultural event, in which artists and traders meet with filmmakers and writers, where traditional dances and songs are performed, where toddlers and young kids learn about their proud heritage, and where people come to party. On the other hand, the leaders of the different communities of Native Americans discuss their common problems and seek solutions. They try to assess their political power, particularly in states in which they constitute a sizable part of the population and where they can wield their electoral influence to better the lives of members of their community. Tourists can only see the first part of what I just said, but the real work is carried out far from the public's eye. That is what my father has told me. He used to participate in those meetings, but after being insulted time and again for marrying outside the tribe, he was offended because whatever he said was considered as the words of an

Indian Uncle Tom, so he stopped going to these powwows. It is a pity because he is one of a handful of Native Americans who has earned the respect of the White Man, in addition to being one of the cleverest people in the country." She had tears in her eyes when she said that, and Le Docteur gently took out a tissue and wiped her eyes and hugged her.

He said, "Blossom, if this is too emotional for you, perhaps we should just go up to Taos and spend a quiet weekend in one of the cabins." He was sure that she wouldn't accept the alternative, so he pretended that he wasn't keen on going to the powwow.

Blossom looked at him for a long moment before saying, "Jacque, if you want to get to really know me and to understand me and the burden I am carrying, we must go to the powwow. I only ask that you come there with an open mind and do not be judgmental." She didn't realize that Le Docteur drew many parallel lines between the treatment of Muslims and of Native Americans by the White Man but that he intended to do something that would create a deep rift between the two communities.

***

The drive from Albuquerque to Gallup was quite boring. Soon after leaving the city of Albuquerque behind them and heading west on Highway I-40, they passed a couple of RV parks, and then there were almost no signs of civilization for miles. When they passed a sign "Route 66 Casino Hotel" Blossom told Le Docteur that this highway was also part of the famous Route 66. When he asked why it was famous, she told him that this was one of the first US highways. It had originally connected Chicago with California but became known because of a popular song called "Get Your Kicks on Route 66" and an old TV series. Le Docteur was once again impressed by what was considered as "historical" in this part of the world. The only village on that part of the highway was called Grants, and they stopped there for coffee and the restrooms. Posters on the walls of the café displayed impressive photos of the two main attractions in the area: El Malpais National Monument, with its caves and rock formations, and the Bandera Volcano and Ice Cave. Blossom said that she had been to those places as a child but, much to Le Docteur's relief, didn't express any interest in taking a diversion to see them again.

The rest of the trip was uneventful, and they reached the Best Western hotel in Gallup in the late afternoon. Blossom didn't notice the green trolley bag that Le Docteur had left in the car's trunk when he brought the rest of their luggage up to the hotel room. The small, innocent-looking trolley contained eight kilograms of an explosive substance known by its acronym, TATP. As its full chemical name—triacetone triperoxide—implied, it could be formed from two household items—acetone and hydrogen peroxide. Indeed, it was favored by terrorist organizations because it could be readily produced in dozens of kilogram quantities in a bathtub. However, amateur chemists must take care to avoid a premature explosion if the components are not treated properly. Such accidents have cut short the career of many terrorists and budding engineers of death, as Le Docteur was well aware when he synthesized the improvised explosive device—the IED—he now had inside the small suitcase. The IED would be set off by dialing the number of the cellphone that was connected to a broken light bulb. Le Docteur had also used a primitive booby trap to make disarming the device more difficult. If someone opened the trolley before neutralizing the trigger mechanism, the IED would explode, killing everyone standing too close to it and maiming or injuring people at a radius of two dozen meters. He intended to set the booby trap only when he planted the trolley at the target.

***

They were glad to take a shower and a short nap in the king-size bed, and after that they made love patiently and gently. They showered again and went out for dinner at a nearby restaurant. Because of the powwow, the place was crowded. Blossom commented with distaste, "Most of the patrons here look like tourists on an anthropological mission, coming to ogle the primitive Indians."

Le Docteur, somewhat cynically, said, "I am also a tourist."

She took no offense and just patted his hand across the table, "No, you are my very own guest of honor, not an ogling tourist."

They left the restaurant and headed to Red Rock Park, the site of the powwow. Le Docteur was impressed by the poster claiming that in 2017 the ninety-sixth powwow would be celebrated. He had thought it was a much more recent occasion, created for the tourists. Blossom noted that the event was organized along purely commercial lines and was more of a showpiece than she remembered from more than a decade earlier when her father brought her to a powwow as a kid. She added that she felt that it was now less authentic.

They wandered through the exhibition of Native American arts and crafts, and Blossom tried to explain the differences between the tribes and pointed out the importance of the geographical location and its influence on the motifs represented in the artifacts. Le Docteur thought that the differences were minor compared to the many common themes. They watched part of the dancing competition, stayed for a while to see the Gourd Dances at the powwow arena, and even watched a couple of short movies from the Native Film Series at the cinema.

Le Docteur said that he needed to fetch some antacid medication from the car. He suggested that Blossom watch another movie, excused himself, and rushed to the parking lot where he had left the car. On the way, he purchased three bags of glass beads. He removed the green trolley and nonchalantly wheeled it to the cinema. He showed his ticket to the usher and headed directly to the restroom. He entered the larger stall reserved for the handicapped and relieved himself. Then he opened the trolley, placed the bags of glass beads around the neatly packed explosives, and set the booby trap. He left the trolley in the stall's corner and exited. From outside the stall, he used a small screwdriver and set the lock to indicate the stall was occupied. He then returned to his seat and watched the end of the movie with Blossom.

It was quite late when they returned to their hotel, but they had quite a long discussion on the fate of the Native Americans under the rule of the White Man. Le Docteur tried to prove to Blossom that there were great similarities between all the native people who were under the rule of colonial powers, regardless of the identity of the colonialists. He claimed that in all cases, the colonialists thought that they were inherently superior to the natives and treated them as servants, and certainly not as equals. He kept on with this theme, emphasizing that modern colonialism was not much different than the old type. He said that for the sake of appearances the "natives" were given a form of self-rule, but the colonialists still called the shots. As a case in point, he mentioned Saudi Arabia that was supposedly ruled by its own king and royal family, but the true power lay in the hands of the American oil companies and US government agencies. He added that the situation was not much different in Syria because Russia controlled the president or in Lebanon, which obeyed the dictates of Hezbollah, who were in turn directed by the Iranian Islamic Revolutionary Guards.

Blossom listened attentively and said, "Jacque, I think that there are more differences than similarities between the examples you have quoted and the condition of Native Americans in this country. True, we are discriminated against by politicians and by many bigots, but we have opportunities to advance. Just look at my father and the position he had attained or at the privileges I have enjoyed growing up."

Before she could continue, he said, "You must see that you and your father are the exceptions to the rule. How many other Native Americans have reached what you have? No, Blossom, there is a long way to go before equality is achieved."

She didn't like his outburst and was intimidated by the fervent look in his eyes. She meekly said, "So, what can we do?"

This was the opening he had hoped for. "Being passive and 'behaving yourselves' will not get you anywhere. Only decisive action can gain the attention of the White Man. Look at the struggle of African Americans, the politically correct name for Blacks in this country. Just over fifty years ago, they could barely practice their right to vote in many states, not to mention that interracial marriages were not recognized, and even considered as illegal, in some states. Nothing was handed to them on a silver platter—they had to fight for their rights. Some even sacrificed their lives so Blacks could attend any school or university, sit anywhere on buses, use any public toilet. True, there are not as many Native Americans, thanks to an unheralded genocide that took place when the White Man came here from Europe and moved west, but there are places like New Mexico and Arizona, for example, where you have a lot of political power that can be used wisely."

Blossom was silent for a long time before saying, "Do you have any practical suggestions?"

Le Docteur relaxed visibly, "I need to go to Washington, DC, as I told you. But when I return in a couple of months' time, I would like to speak about this to your father and, with his help, to leaders of the Native American community in this state."

She smiled because she knew that he would be returning

to her. "Come to bed, Jacque. I need you to explain in detail what you want to do."

He answered, "I just need to have a quick shower." He entered the bathroom and dialed the number of the cellphone inside the green trolley. He then whispered, "Allahu Akbar," and took a long, hot shower. He then made another phone call that would send his prerecorded message to the mass media after a delay of twelve hours. The message was short—NEMESIS claimed responsibility for the attack on the powwow.

Blossom was waiting in bed, wearing nothing but a big smile. Le Docteur's smile matched hers, but he had an additional reason that she was unaware of. He had some unfinished business in New Mexico—something so grand that going to Washington would have to be postponed, perhaps indefinitely. He couldn't share this with Blossom, and that raised some qualms, but he kept his eye on the big issue—instigating the war of civilizations. Blossom would be one of its many victims.

***

The explosion at the cinema disrupted the festivities. The organizing committee of the powwow met for an emergency meeting. Some of the members demanded that they continue with the program according to schedule while others insisted that they must cancel the event and mourn the victims of the heinous crime. The death toll reached eleven people, including nine tourists and two Native Americans, who happened to be in the restrooms or at the part of the cinema near the restroom at the time of explosion. There were two dozen people who were injured, most of them maimed by beads of glass that ripped through vital organs.

The members of the organizing committee were in a heated discussion of this matter when one of the tribe's elders raised his hand, cleared his throat, and said, "You have probably forgotten the attack on the Israeli athletes at the 1972 Olympic games in Munich. Several athletes were murdered, and others were held as hostages by Palestinian terrorists who belonged to the Black September group. A few of the terrorists, and all the hostages, were killed when the German police forces bungled an operation to take down the terrorists and free the Israeli hostages."

The youngest member of the committee rudely interrupted, "So what's your point?"

The tribe's elder looked at the young buck and nodded his head. "The international committee of the Olympic games decided to continue with the games according to schedule. They only held a short memorial ceremony in honor of the dead athletes. We should follow suit and do the same."

One of the other elders said, "I recall that the Israeli Mossad hunted down the terrorists who were involved in the planning and execution of this attack. Should we do the same, once the perpetrators are known, of course?"

As he was speaking, several of the committee members simultaneously picked up their cellphones and quietly read the flashing news item. Then, all hell broke out in the room. The tribe's elder said, "If the Muslims want to start a war with us—then they'll regret the day they were born."

The young buck said, "I'll organize a posse, and we'll hunt for Muslims. The first one we'll catch will be skinned alive, just as our ancestors would do to people who cheated them and murdered their brothers and sisters."

He rose to leave the room when one of the elders stopped him, "We cannot start a war against all Muslims because of an act carried out by some extremist."

The young buck wouldn't have any of this. He shook off the elder's hand and said, "We need to catch and skin one or two to save our honor and restore the self-respect of our people." He paused and added, "Anyone want to join me?" He was disappointed when none of the other committee members joined him, and he stormed out of the room.

The tribe's elder, the one who spoke first, said, "I suggest that we issue a statement that the Native Americans will not bow their heads to terror. That the powwow will continue as planned, after a ceremony of mourning the dead is carried out according to our tradition." He saw the looks on the faces of the other members and continued, "Yes, I know that most of them were tourists and not of our Nation. Yet this horrendous act was carried out on our territory and the ceremony will be by our custom. I want us to stand united behind this decision. Any objections?"

One of the others, who was a lawyer by training and was an activist for the cause of his people, said, "I think that we should use our political strength in the state and in other states in which we have a significant presence to support rules against the Muslims who perpetrated this dreadful deed."

The tribe's elder was shocked, "Do you mean that we should lend our support to the racist, Senator McCorey, just because he is a Muslim basher?"

The lawyer shrugged, "The dire enemy of my enemy can be my friend. I believe that the senator is a bigot, but if we can use him to exact revenge on the people who harmed us—then so be it. I think that we should issue our support for his proposal to lock up all Muslims in internment camps. This would be a more sensible step than lynching a couple of innocent Muslims, as our young friend wants." He looked around and was pleased to see that most of the committee members nodded in assent.

***

The media was having a field day. Here was an event that contained all the elements of a good story: Muslim terrorists performing a dreadful act in a peaceful gathering of Native Americans, disrupting the show of unity of a population who has been mistreated by the White Man for centuries. Native Americans, photographed in full tribal regalia during the powwow, were very picturesque and evoked memories of movies and books in the minds of most people in the world. The fact that most of the victims were tourists from the United States and abroad also added an element of nationwide and global interest, in what would otherwise be considered as a rural event, in the corner of New Mexico—a state famous mainly for Billy the Kid and visits by aliens.

The junior senator from New Mexico, the Honorable

James McCorey, received the media attention he yearned for. The list of TV networks, national newspapers, and international press agencies that requested interviews, preferably an exclusive interview, was very long. He reiterated his programmatic approach for dealing with Muslims: those in the United States would be sent to internment camps for an indefinite period, while all those requesting to enter the US would be denied a visa. There were few exceptions to the latter clause, which included members of the royal families of Saudi Arabia, the United Arab Emirates, and a few other "desirables," like the president of Egypt, the king of Jordan, and other rich Arab nobilities. When he was asked if keeping all American Muslims in internment camps wouldn't be expensive, his answer was curt, "They'll be forced to work and earn a living. Those unable or unwilling to work will not receive any handouts."

Finally, the interviewer asked the prearranged provocative question, "Senator, do you think that the American public can rely on the Department for Homeland Security and the FBI to provide the protection it needs?"

Senator McCorey seized the opportunity and, in fact, started his election campaign for the office of POTUS, "Obviously, the administration has failed miserably in that respect. If Americans cannot feel safe when they attend a public festivity, when they see their cultural heritage denigrated and destroyed in a museum, when the greatest symbol of American democracy is attacked by radioactive substances—then it is time to replace the people who are in charge of our protection by someone who is capable of providing the most basic components for happiness—security and safety. When Muslims raise their dirty heads and claim responsibility for dreadful acts against innocent Americans—then it's high time to transfer them to places where they can cause no more harm and damage. I guarantee that if you give me the power, I'll put an end to those horrible attacks that threaten to tear to pieces the fabric of our society. I declare that I'll be running for the office of the president of the Unites States in the next election. Until then, I vow to do everything in my power as a senator to pass laws that will put an end to these terrorist activities on US soil. My motto is 'Give me the power, and I will curb terrorism and bring back security and safety.' Remember this day of infamy, when our dear Native Americans and good people who came to join their celebrations were slaughtered by worshippers of a false prophet and a fake God."

The interviewer had a follow-up question, "Senator McCorey, have you just officially announced your intention of running for the office of the president?"

McCorey looked at him, "I think I was very clear. Let me repeat my motto so no one can doubt my intentions—'Give me the power, and I will curb terrorism and bring back security and safety.' I trust that the great American people will know that they can rely on me to fulfil this promise. God bless America. Thank you all."

***

His personal assistant passed him a note that Professor

Jacque Deleau wished to speak to him. The senator asked the representatives of the press and everyone else to leave the room and picked up his phone. "Jacque, good to hear from you. You have performed a miracle."

Le Docteur answered, "I just saw your impressive announcement. Good things happen to good people. You deserve everything that's happening. I have received some inside information that you have been endorsed by the council of the Native Americans as their champion. They will support you in the upcoming election and will help you pass the laws regarding the treatment of Muslims."

The senator was overjoyed, "Jacque, this will help me here in New Mexico. I have bigger things in mind, as you know. Do you have any ideas for something that will get me nation-wide support?"

Le Docteur's smile could almost be heard over the phone. "Jim, what I have planned will win you the presidency of the United States." He hung up, feeling that he had the senator in his pocket—he could raise him to unprecedented heights or bring him down in infamy.

CHAPTER 7

Yankee Stadium, New York

The fifty-thousand-strong crowd filled the Yankee Stadium to the brim to watch one of the most important games of major league baseball. Many spectators were busy eating hot dogs, drinking overpriced beer and sodas, and studying their cellphones for news or messages because in the eighth inning the score was still 0-0, and the game turned out to be a real bore. A few spectators had already started to make their way to the parking lot to get a head start before the masses began to pour out of the stadium. Some of the spectators tried to follow the action, or rather, lack of it, on the field, but most of the people watched the large-screen TV monitors that showed the action and facial expressions of the players more clearly. Others went about their favorite pastime at a ball game—swearing at the players and their incompetence, giving unsolicited advice to the coaches and owners of the teams, and casting serious doubts on the maternal ancestry of the umpires and the alleged profession of their mothers. Some of the more aggressive spectators were busy searching for like-minded people willing to pick a fight and vent their frustrations—better yet, to find some nerd, preferably with round, rimless glasses and a mousey girlfriend, and provoke them into starting a fistfight or scare them off.

The crowd cheered when the batter hit a high ball but, seconds later, jeered when the right fielder, who went for an easy catch, dropped the ball. "Butter fingers" was the most civil thing shouted at him. The poor player tried to point at the sun, to indicate that he had been blinded by it, but this only increased the volume of the jeers. The pitcher rubbed his aching shoulder, chewed on a wad of tobacco, and sent it in a well-aimed stream of spittle in the direction of the right fielder. No words were needed to tell how he felt about his teammate.

No one paid attention to the middle-aged couple in row six of the main level section 210 who rose from their seats and headed toward the stairs leading down to the exit. Their neighbors thought that they too wanted to beat the crowd to the parking lot. No one noticed the yellow backpack that they left under their seats. The couple knew that all hell would break out in a few minutes and wanted to be in a safe spot to watch the stampede that was sure to come. They lingered by the parking lot, keeping their distance from the ambulances and police cars that were there on standby.

***

A ten-year-old boy who was sitting next to the now vacant seats noticed a plume of smelly, black smoke coming out of the yellow backpack. He started coughing, and when his father looked at him anxiously, he complained that something smelled bad. His father, a long-time fan of the Yankees, sniffed the air and found that it indeed had a familiar, foul smell. He had served in the US armed forces in Iraq and recognized the smell of cordite. His post-traumatic stress disorder set in, and he vividly recalled the smell that preceded the blast from the bombing incident that took the lives of his sergeant and best friend in Baghdad. He grabbed his son's hand, rose from his seat, and shouted, "There's a bomb! Get away!" He pulled his son to the end of the row and started running down the stairs to the exit.

The people around him watched his strange behavior, and then the gravity of the situation hit them. Panic set in like fire in a forest after a long dry season, and instantly hundreds of people in the section 210 rushed to the exit. People in nearby sections, especially those in the sections at the higher levels, saw the commotion, and they too made their way toward the exit, understanding that something dangerous was taking place. Old people, women, and children were trampled by the rushing herd. Anyone who fell to the floor or, worse yet, on the stairs was immediately crushed by the stampeding mass of frightened people.

The umpire saw that something unusual was going on in the stands and noticed that the players had stopped playing ball and were watching the crowd. He blew his whistle and stopped the play. The public announcements were confusing because no one knew how to respond to the wave of panic that spread through the stadium. Finally, the manager of the stadium grabbed the microphone and said, "Please stay calm. Remain in your seat until we sort out what's going on." This had the opposite effect and only added to the panic. One experienced reporter said that the crowd's behavior reminded him of the Fiesta of San Fermin in Pamplona, Spain, where throngs of people, mostly young men, run along the boarded narrow streets, chased by a herd of large bulls. Another reporter, who had obviously been raised on a farm in Texas, said that it was more like a cattle stampede, where the herd instincts take control and the mass of frenzied animals run blindly, crushing everything in their path.

First responders who were on standby at the stadium tried in vain to figure what was happening. The head of the police unit forcibly stopped one of the men who rushed past him and asked him why he was running. The man struggled to get away from the grip of the police officer and shouted, "There is a bomb," and slipped away to continue running away from the stadium. The first responders tried to enter the stadium but were pushed back by the fleeing crowd. Only after most of the people left the stands were the teams of police, medics, and firefighters able to make their way up the stands. The medics stopped to attend to the people lying in the corridors and on the stairs, while the firefighters skipped over the victims and searched for the cause of the panic. With the help from the police officers, they spread out and checked one row of seats after the next. The head of the emergency forces sent the firefighters to the top of the stands to work their way down, row by row, while the police officers worked their way from the bottom up. This was no easy task, because the escaping crowd left behind many backpacks and shopping bags that had to be individually inspected.

Finally, one of the firefighters, who inspected section 210 spotted the yellow backpack with a thin plume of smoke still lazily drifting out. He noticed the foul odor and immediately shouted to attract the attention of his supervisor, who told him to keep the others away from the backpack. Shortly, the bomb squad arrived. The bomb removal technician suited up in his protective gear, crossed himself twice (just to be on the safe side), and placed the remote-controlled robot thirty feet from the yellow backpack. He then stepped back and guided the robot closer, aimed the shotgun the robot carried, and discharged it. A barrage of metal balls shredded the backpack, and that resulted in a fresh gush of smoke that bawled out of the backpack. After thirty seconds, when nothing else happened, the bomb-squad tech gingerly approached the backpack, and a moment later, he raised his hand holding what looked like a can of soda. On closer observation, the shredded can, painted like a can of Coke, had a screw-cap top, was thicker and heavier than a normal soda can, and contained some black residue. Later, at the laboratory, the substance was found to be a sticky, tar-like compound to which slow burning gun powder was added to create the effect of burning cordite. This created the smoke and odor that so scared the people.

***

The middle-aged couple who planted the bomb walked to their car, got in, and joined the line of cars waiting to leave the stadium's parking lot. The driver turned on the car's radio, and they both listened to the report from the stadium, delivered by an overly excited male reporter. The reporter said that the preliminary assessment of the police was that there were twenty-three dead, about fifty people in critical condition, and over two hundred people who suffered minor injuries. The report continued, mentioning that most of the victims were children and their parents who tried to shelter them, but there were many old people among the dead and critically injured. Almost all the victims were trampled by the stampeding crowd. The reporter added that the police had found a yellow backpack in row six of Section 210, which they believed started the stampede. The woman held her husband's hand and smiled at him, "The will of Allah has been done. Our son is smiling down on us from heaven. We have avenged his murder by the American 'advisers' in Homs." She was relieved that their mission was successfully accomplished and that they could now head to the airport to catch their flight to Paris.

The police were busy viewing the footage from the CCD cameras that were installed in the stadium. Thanks to the discovery of the backpack, they focused their attention on section 210 of the large stadium. Within a few minutes, they saw that among the people leaving the stadium at the bottom of the eighth inning were several spectators from section 210. They zoomed in on row six and saw the middle-aged couple getting up and leaving the stand. Just before they got up, the man was clearly seen opening the yellow backpack and fiddling with his right hand inside, before placing it under the seat. They also saw the young kid saying something to his father, and the father standing up and shouting as he rushed his kid out of the row. The relevant footage was copied and sent to the FBI, DHS, and police departments nationwide.

***

The major TV networks managed to get a hold of a copy thanks to a friendly police lieutenant who wanted to be promoted to captain. Minutes later, a "Breaking News" banner flashed across the screens, and it was repeatedly shown. The networks didn't wait for the police's permission to screen the footage. The anchors, men and women alike, issued a request for information on the middle-aged couple and the man who started the commotion.

A few minutes later, the man, who recognized himself in the footage, called CNN news and identified himself as Pete Mitchell. He asked for legal help and protection in return for providing CNN with an exclusive interview. The network's legal department was alerted, and the head of the department cautioned the anxious head of the news department that the man may be prosecuted under the law that dealt with a person responsible for inducing panic by shouting "Fire, fire" in a theater. The news guy couldn't care less about the man's fate—he had a hot scoop in his hand, so he told the law-guy to do his best for the man.

CNN news told Pete Mitchell that they would provide legal counselling but couldn't promise him immunity from prosecution. Mitchell accepted this and agreed to come to the studio for a live interview, providing that it wouldn't be announced beforehand. The network wanted to run a large-scale promotion and suggested that Mitchell would be interviewed in his home or at a hotel near his house. Mitchell agreed to the hotel interview and said he would drive there immediately. The head of the news department said that a van would be waiting outside the hotel. Mitchell said he would try to change his appearance and would be wearing a hoody and a baseball cap drawn low over his face. CNN news ran another "Breaking News" banner, promising an exclusive interview with the man who was the first to point out the dangerous backpack, starting to build the legal case to help Pete Mitchell avoid prosecution.

The interview was quite dull, despite the buildup it got. Pete explained that he was a veteran of the Iraq war and had seen firsthand what a bomb could do when he lost his friends. He said that he shouted a warning to the people who were near the smoking backpack and had no intention to cause widespread panic in the stadium. The head of the news department who sat next to the reporter suggested that Pete should receive a medal for his help in preventing a disaster. Over 75 percent of the talk backs were strongly opposed to this suggestion, and some even blamed Pete for the death toll and said that he should be prosecuted for starting the deadly stampede. CNN news offered Pete legal assistance, just in case he would be indicted for causing the deaths and injuries.

***

The middle-aged couple watched the news on one of the

TV monitors in the terminal and were glad that they took precautions before going to the ball game. The bald man patted his closely shaved head and watched his image in the footage, in which he appeared to have a full head of curly hair. His dark-haired wife watched the overweight blond woman on the screen and noted that she appeared to carry at least twenty pounds of extra weight, thanks to the girdle she had put on when going to the ball game. Both had been wearing sunglasses throughout the game, so the cameras didn't get a view of their eyes. Le Docteur had warned them that the eyes were the key feature that facial recognition algorithms used. Their flight was announced, and they boarded the plane to Paris without looking back.

Le Docteur had waited for their departure before releasing his prerecorded video clip. "NEMESIS has demonstrated once again that there is no place that is safe for Crusaders and the colonialists. The new Yankee Stadium, the pride of New York, the home of one of the most revered ball teams in the world, with its fifty thousand spectators, was hit by our brave people. Our supporters come from all walks of life. In this case, an elderly couple that lost their only son, who came to Syria to help his besieged brethren as a paramedic and died at the hands of American soldiers in Homs when he was twenty-two years old. Like the Al Qaeda suicide attacks that were carried out on 9/11, no weapon was used, nor was one needed to sow death and injuries. A simple canister the size of a soda can with nothing more toxic than some tainted tar-like substance was enough to start a stampede of thousands of people. These people, obviously, had no regard for the weak, the young, and the elderly, and in their rush to safety, trampled over their fellow Americans. NEMESIS is only indirectly responsible for the death toll and maiming—after all, the panicked mob did the damage." He paused to let this sink in and then continued, "When NEMESIS began to operate in Europe just a few years ago, it warned the colonialists that they would never be safe in public places and should stay away from public events. I now issue a similar warning to the American people—stay home, don't go out, avoid crowds. I know that this will affect the economy—the capitalists stand to lose a lot of money. But, good Americans, do you care about their profits or about the health and well-being of your family and friends?"

***

Washington, DC

Senator McCorey watched the video clip and the TV coverage of the events that took place in Yankee Stadium. Personally, he had no affection for New York liberals and left-wingers who time and again voted for the Democratic party in New York. His opinion didn't waver when a Republican from New York beat a New York Democrat to become president of the United States in the November 2016 elections. Nevertheless, the bold attack presented him with another opportunity to gain the attention of national television with his anti-Islamic rhetoric.

He gladly accepted an invitation from CNN news to participate in a debate that was defined as "The future of Islam in

America." He asked who would be representing the other side and was not really surprised when he was told that it would be Sheikh Ibrahim Salah, the Imam of the Islamic Center of Washington. The narrator was one of the most respected news anchors, John N. Newman, who was regarded by the older members of the audience as the new Walter Cronkite—someone who was not involved in any scandal, financial or sexual, someone whose word could be trusted, someone who reported news items that were confirmed and substantiated. He was someone who was far removed from fake news and alternative facts.

Newman opened the debate, "Today, we'll discuss the future of Islam in America from two opposing viewpoints. On my right is the junior senator from New Mexico, the fiery Senator Jim McCorey, and on my left is the Imam of the Islamic Center of Washington, Sheikh Ibrahim Salah. I'll address my question first to Sheikh Ibrahim. Sir, what is your opinion on the recent terrorist attack at Yankee Stadium and the fact that NEMESIS claimed responsibility for it?"

Sheikh Ibrahim kept a solemn expression on his face and spoke in a low, slow voice. "First, let me offer condolences to the victims and their families on behalf of the Muslims in this great country. Muslims in America condemn this attack, and all acts of terror against civilians in this country and in the world. The fact that the obscure, extremist organization of NEMESIS claimed responsibility doesn't mean that Muslims were the perpetrators. Let me remind you that the man who started the stampede was Pete Mitchell, not an Islamist radical or a Jihadist. Therefore, any attempt to attribute the heinous terrorist attack against innocent American civilians to Muslims is uncalled for. In fact, we are considering taking legal action against the media and press who blamed Muslims for this dreadful incident."

The sheikh would have continued with such platitudes, but the narrator intervened, "Thank you, Sheikh Ibrahim. I see that our other guest is impatiently waiting for his turn. Senator McCorey, the floor is yours."

The senator took three deep breaths, following the advice of his media consultants, before answering. He controlled his temper and started in a quiet tone, "The curveball the sheikh tossed here, placing the blame for the terrorist attack on Mr. Mitchell, the poor man who was the first to identify the potential danger, is the height of hypocrisy. Mr. Mitchell called attention to the bomb left in the stadium by Muslim radicals. He wanted to save the lives of his son and all other good Americans who were out to see a ball game and support their favorite team. We must take the declaration of NEMESIS at its face value—the radical Islamists are responsible for the loss of life and limb, and wriggling and wiggling by the sheikh will not change that." He was working himself into a frenzy and continued, "Mr. Newman, please ask the sheikh to open his mouth and show you his tongue. I am sure that you'll find that he has at least two tongues—the one he uses to address the American people is sugar-coated and moderate, but the other he uses in his mosque, the so-called Islamic Center, is as venomous as that of a king cobra."

Newman intervened, "Senator, let's not turn this into a personal duel between you and the sheikh. Look at the large picture—do the Muslims who live here pose a danger to the American people and our way of life? Please, keep your answer short."

McCorey was now all heated up, "All Muslims regard our way of life as something that is fundamentally opposed to theirs. Their representatives in this country, like Sheikh Ibrahim, try to disguise this and say that they want to live side-by-side in peace with us, here in our country. Secretly, they preach for imposing the Shariya, the rule of Islam, on the entire world. Do you know what this means to the American way of life? Look at Saudi Arabia. For example, a woman is not allowed to drive a car, to go out without the escort of her husband, brother, or other member of her family. Hands of thieves are chopped off, and I hate to think what happens to adulterers." He paused to allow the audience to imagine that and then continued in a harsh, loud voice, almost shouting, "We need to treat the Muslims in this country as double agents, as traitors, as a fifth column, and to protect ourselves, we must place them under guard in internment camps or send them away, willingly or not, to the twenty-two countries the Muslims have. The further away, the better."

While he stopped to pick up the glass of water that was placed in front of him, Newman said, "Thank you Senator McCorey for your candid opinion, so eloquently expressed here. Now, let's hear what Sheikh Ibrahim has to say about the issue and about the senator's words."

The sheikh had expected the fiery outburst from MBJ—Muslim-Bashing Jimbo—so was in full control when he answered. "I am sorry that the honorable member of the senate does not know that Islam is a religion of peace and love and tolerance. There are one and a half billion Muslims in the world today, and only a very small minority are involved in what you call terrorism. Even fewer are actively trying to force people to accept Islam. We believe that anyone who studies our religion will realize that it allows its followers to live in peace and respect one another and that it provides answers to all the questions and queries of the modern world. Here, in America, we are grateful that we can integrate with the mainline of society and yet maintain our religious dictates. Our religion has five pillars: testifying to God's one-ness, prayers five times a day, preferably in public, giving charity, fasting during daylight hours in the month of Ramadan, and making a pilgrimage to Mecca. None of these are unacceptable or meant to impose on non-Muslims. Don't all monotheist religions—Christians and Jews alike—believe in the one-ness of God or in the need to pray? Is there anyone who is against giving charity to the people who are less fortunate? Don't you have your version of fast, or partial fast, during special periods? And, finally, don't you all have sacred and holy places you would like to visit?" Newman looked at him to determine if he was done, but the sheikh continued, "The senator wants to deport all Muslims or force them into internment camps. What will be the next stage? Gas chambers and cremation ovens? Are you like the Nazis you fought against? Do you want to be responsible for the next genocide? I bring you a message of peace and love and you respond by threatening us with concentration camps and deportation?"

Newman thought that the debate was getting out of hand.

"Gentlemen, please address the main question—the future of Islam in America. Sheikh Ibrahim, you go first."

The sheikh was brief, "I'll repeat what I have said, that Islam is a religion of peace and love and tolerance. Muslims will continue to be part of the mosaic of the American society and will be valuable citizens who contribute to the economy, culture, science, and technology. We will help make America great."

Senator McCorey was enraged by this last statement. "How can you claim to be productive citizens when you are continually supporting terror and providing help and shelter to terrorists? Your religion is one of belligerence, hate, and intolerance—the direct opposite of what you claim it to be. If you had your way here, as you did in Asia and Europe centuries ago, then all Americans would be either Muslims or dead. Let's not forget that Islam spread by sword and by conversion—those that converted were spared the sword. If the American people want to survive, want to maintain our way of life, there is no place for Muslims in this country, and given the power, I vow that they will have no future."

Newman concluded, "We have heard two orthogonal opinions of the future of Muslims in America. I would like to thank Sheikh Ibrahim Salah and Senator McCorey for candidly sharing with us their thoughts and beliefs." He was grateful that the debate ended without any physical violence. He had seen that debates of this kind on Egyptian, Jordanian, and Lebanese TV often ended when one participant tried to punch or strangle his rival. This made good rating but was not suitable for an American major TV channel.

CHAPTER 8

Holloman Air Force Base, New Mexico

The flight of the two F/A-22 Raptors took off from runway twenty-five, heading almost due west. On this routine exercise, both single-seat, twin-engine, tactical fighter aircraft were configured for stealth mode. That meant that all their armament was in the internal weapon bays, greatly reducing the plane's radar signature and aerodynamic drag, thus improving its maneuverability. The secondary mission of the two-plane flight was to be on alert in case they would be needed to intercept aircraft trying to cross the US-Mexican border, which was only about seventy-five miles to the south. This was the reason that they were carrying live munitions, something that was not routinely done in exercises of this sort. At supersonic speed, even without the afterburner, the F-22 (few people persisted in calling it F/A-22) could cover the distance to the border in five or six minutes. With the fuel-inefficient afterburner, the pilots could easily shave off one minute and dive down on the intruder like an eagle on a dove, or more appropriately like a velociraptor on a plant-eating, timid, Apatosaurus. Therefore, each Raptor carried air-to-air missiles in each of the two internal side bays and air-to-surface ordnance in the main bay, just in case they would be directed to carry out a combat mission against a real enemy. However, all red-blooded pilots preferred to use the Vulcan rotary gun to shoot down enemy aircraft and thus relive the good old days and legendary stories narrated by the veterans of the Vietnam war. The Raptor's rotary gun was concealed in a bay in the plane's wing to maintain its stealth profile. This little routine exercise would cost the American taxpayer about $60,000 per hour, per plane. However, this sortie would cost the taxpayer much more, and not only in dollar terms.

Major Arnie Buchanan was the leader of the two-plane flight, and his number two, or wingman, was Captain Lara Wayne. Lara was one of the few female pilots who flew combat missions on the F-22 and was very proud of this fact. She insisted on being designated as wingwoman and hated to be called "number two" in anything. Her short marriage to Air Force Colonel George S. Wayne ended when he tried to behave like his namesake, but no relation, John Wayne. Although the actor was never shown, or ever accused of, striking a woman, Colonel Wayne tended to use Lara for a punching bag when he was drunk. This happened more and more frequently since he was passed over for promotion. One night, Lara showed him that her lessons in Krav Maga, the Israeli version of a self-defense fighting system, were not wasted on her. Although he outweighed her by sixty pounds, his movement was slowed down by excessive alcohol consumption, and with great speed and strength, she punched him in the solar plexus. When he bent over in pain, she lifted her right knee to his exposed face and broke his nose. She walked out of the apartment and only saw the results of her handiwork, or more precisely her legwork, when her lawyers won the divorce settlement that left the poor colonel as a poor man.

Few people knew that Lara's full name before her unfortunate marriage to Colonel Wayne had been Layla Maysun Mayor. In Arabic, her first name literally meant "born at night" and middle name meant "of beautiful face and body." As a third generation Palestinian, she had a longer surname, typically Arabic, which her father dropped when he became a Christian. She didn't mention that fact when she enlisted in the US Air Force. Her grandparents left their home in Haifa in 1948, believing Arab propaganda that they would soon return with the victorious Lebanese army to claim their home back, as well as the property belonging to their Jewish neighbors. However, after the state of Israel was founded, like hundreds of thousands of other Palestinians, they ended in refugee camps in the neighboring Arab countries. The then young couple, with no children of their own at the time, managed to obtain visas to enter the United States and did quite well for themselves with their fruit and vegetable store that they opened in New Jersey. They made sure that their only son, Badi, whose American name was spelled Buddy, who was born in the USA, received proper education and became a respected physician. Buddy moved away from his parents and Arab heritage, changed his surname to Mayor, converted to Christianity, and married a woman of Swedish ancestry. He opened a medical practice in the small city of Solon in

Iowa, with a population of less than twenty-five hundred. His only daughter, Lara, or Layla, as her paternal grandparents insisted on calling her, grew up like a typical Midwest girl. She excelled in athletics, competed with the boys in her class in science and technology, and joined the national guard for pilot training. She turned out to be one of the natural pilots, those that were considered by their peers as stick jockeys and joined the US Air Force as a career move. Her unfortunate encounter with Colonel Wayne left her scarred but more determined to succeed in her chosen vocation.

Yet somewhere deep within her blood and genes, the last words of her grandfather on his deathbed kept haunting her. He said "Layla, never forget where you came from. Haifa, my dear, is our home, and we shall return there one day to claim our birthright as the owners of the place."

***

Lara revved up both engines and took off thirty seconds after Major Buchanan's Raptor, and within a minute, she took up her position to his left and slightly behind. They climbed rapidly to ten thousand feet above ground (that was about fifteen thousand feet above sea level), the altitude assigned to them by the controller. As the exercise was to be conducted in stealth mode, they had switched off all electronic systems—including their radios, friend-or-foe transponders that identified them, as well as their active radar system. The controller could not see them on his radar screen, and it was his responsibility to ascertain that no other aircraft entered the airspace assigned to them for the exercise. The plan was for the planes to break off and head out, Buchanan to the north and Lara to the south, for one minute and then come flying toward each other and start the mock dogfight. The winner would be the one who managed to capture on video the other plane in the gun sights for a period that was long enough to assure a hit. In their six previous exercises, each pilot had won three times, and this was to be the decisive encounter. The loser would stand a round of beer for the winner, and everyone else who happened to be in the club at that time (and of course all the other pilots would make sure to be there). Buchanan was pretty sure that he would win—he had just seen a video of a dogfight between an Israeli F-15I and an American F-18 taken at the latest Red Flag joint exercise. The Israeli performed an unconventional maneuver that placed him on the tail of the F-18, and Buchanan had studied that and practiced it whenever he was flying with other wingmen. Lara knew that this exercise would be anything but a routine one and knew that no one would be buying a round of beers at the club that evening and that it would probably be closed that night.

***

Cloudcroft, New Mexico, Three Months Earlier

Several months before the events at the powwow took place, some other significant act occurred in a remote part of New Mexico. This involved Le Docteur and Lara, and its repercussion were sure to shake the whole world, not only the United States.

On one of her weekend leaves after her messy divorce, Lara drove up to Cloudcroft to give herself a short skiing vacation. The ski slopes of the small village, only twenty-two miles from the base, were a good place to meet young men and not-so-young men, especially during the apres-ski hours at the bar after a long, strenuous day on the slopes. She noticed that a handsome man in his late thirties or early forties was paying close attention to her and following her every move. When she was sitting at the bar, nursing a beer, he finally moved and stood next to her. In a quaint, slightly French accent, he asked her if he could buy her a drink. She looked him up and down, reminiscent of the way a predator looks at prey, and liked what she saw.

She said, "I am Lara. Are you Dr. Zhivago?" referring to the 1965 British-Italian romantic film.

Le Docteur smiled, "Are you referring to Boris Pasternak's novel or to the overly sentimental film? I can be Omar Sharif, if you are Julie Christie." Lara laughed. There were not many young men that had an idea what she was referring to. She had seen the movie at least a dozen times after her divorce and cried her heart out every single time. Of course, she never allowed anyone to see her tears—so unbefitting a tough, strong-minded fighter pilot. Encouraged by her reaction, Le Docteur continued, "My name is Jacque Deleau, and I am a doctor and a professor, alas, not of medicine but of political science and European history."

Lara was intrigued, "So, Professor, what's a man like you

doing in a place like this?"

"Please call me Jacque. I could ask you the same question." He looked around the bar and continued, "I see that a table with a nice view of the mountains is available. Should we continue our challenging conversation over there and get some inspiration from the view?" Without waiting for her answer, he picked up his drink and headed to the table, arriving there a couple of seconds before some other patron got there. The other man stared at him and decided to avoid a confrontation, much to the disappointment of Lara, who observed the whole scene with interest.

Le Docteur waited for Lara to sit beside him so that they could both face the magnificent, snow-covered mountains. He told her that he was teaching a course on colonialism and European history at the University of New Mexico in Albuquerque and wanted to do some skiing, away from Taos, the more popular site that was favored by the Santa Fe jet-set crowd. He asked Lara what she did and, much to her pleasure, showed his great surprise and admiration when she told him that she flew jet fighters out of Holloman Air Force Base.

Le Docteur was now truly intrigued. His mind was racing at supersonic speed, toying with the possibilities of using this piece of information to advance his own objectives. He said, "You must be something special. What do you fly?" He paused for a moment, trying to tread carefully on the slippery slope, "If it's not classified, of course."

Lara laughed, "I don't think you are a spy—or are you?" When she saw his grin, she thought that he liked her joke. She had no idea that he was way beyond being a spy—he was a terrorist, responsible for countless deaths and for disrupting life in Europe and elsewhere. He was literally inches away from becoming a mass murderer on an unprecedented scale, had his plot to detonate an atomic bomb in the heart of London not failed. She continued, "I fly the best fighter jet in the world, the F-22 Raptor." This was arguably a true statement, although some pilots thought that the more advanced F-35 Lightning was better because of some of its technical features, but the real stick jockeys would prefer the Raptor in a dogfight every day of the week. Then she added, "I am proud to be one of the handpicked pilots, let alone women, who can sit on the tiger's back and make it jump through the hoops of fire."

Le Docteur sensed that she meant every word. He wanted to know more about her, so he asked, "Is your father also a pilot? Or anyone else in your family?"

Lara's face broke into a huge smile, "Far from it. My father is a physician and has a private practice in Iowa. My maternal grandfather grows corn there and still works the fields with his tractor, although he is over eighty years old." When she saw that Le Docteur looked at her expectantly, she hesitated before saying, "My paternal grandparents used to own a fruit and vegetable store in New Jersey and worked together sixteen hours a day. They used to send the money they managed to save to refugees in the Middle East—that's where they came from. Unfortunately, my grandfather passed last year, and my grandmother followed suit a month later."

Le Docteur couldn't believe his ears, and his luck. He pried gently, "Do you mean that they supported Syrian refugees?"

Lara said, "No, they came to this country from Haifa. They donated their money to Palestinian refugees in Lebanon because my grandfather thought that some of his family's descendants were still in refugee camps over there."

Le Docteur thought that he had heard enough and decided to proceed cautiously and very slowly. He said, "Let's go and get some dinner. Is there any place around here that you can recommend?"

Lara said, "Jacque, tell me about yourself. I must know who is buying my dinner."

"There is not much to tell. As you can hear, I am a French-Canadian. In fact, I feel more French than Canadian. As I told you, my specialty is European history and political science. I have no permanent academic position and prefer to be free and have no long-term obligations. You could call me a 'teacher for hire' because I like to express my opinion on European colonialism and on the evils of the Crusaders and the communists. Have you heard about the difference between capitalism and communism?" When he saw her blank expression, he continued, "Under capitalism, man exploits man. Under communism, it's just the opposite." She gave a polite smile, and he saw that this type of talk would not gain favor with her. He quickly said, "This is attributed to John Kenneth Galbraith. I am much more concerned with colonialism. You said that your grandparents came from Haifa—this must have been because of the Jewish colonialists." He saw that he was now on the right track, "Yes, many people consider Israel as another type of colonialism, not greatly different from the classic European usurpation of the people in Africa, Asia, and

America. Here, in Cloudcroft, New Mexico, a place that has seen one colonialist nation, the Americans, fight and expel the Spaniards who were another colonialist nation."

Lara said, "Enough politics. Let's go and eat."

***

During the meal, they talked a little about themselves, completely avoided speaking about the political situation, and discussed the safe topic of tourist attractions in New Mexico. Lara had been posted at Holloman AFB for the last two years, and after her divorce from Colonel Wayne, she lived off base in the small community of Alamogordo. She said that she liked to spend her weekends in winter on the ski slopes and in summer at the swimming pool. Occasionally, she would go to the typical rural celebrations, like the rodeo and the Great American Duck Race in Deming, New Mexico, or the chili festival in Hatch, where she bought a ten-pound bag of hot chilies that were roasted on the spot. She told him that she greatly enjoyed the Whole Enchilada Fiesta in Las Cruces, in which a gigantic enchilada was prepared and then cut to manageable portions that were sold to the expectant crowd. She also attended the Cinco de Mayo Fiesta on the plaza in Old Mesilla and other cultural events, although they had become less authentic and more of a show for tourists. She said that being in those places gave her a better understanding of the people who lived in New Mexico. Le Docteur was impressed by her enthusiasm and the way her eyes glittered when she described some episode that happened at the duck race when she rented a feisty duck that kept biting her hand but refused to budge when it was time to race. Finally, she said, "Jacque, here I am telling you stories like an adolescent girl from Hicksville. I want to know more about you."

Le Docteur said, "There is nothing to know. I told you that I like to travel and meet people, and I think that you also like that. How about joining me on a day trip to the Valley of Fires, near Carrizozo? I heard that the place is like being on Mars or some strange planet."

Lara was pleased that he wanted to see her again and that he wasn't trying to get her into bed just hours after their meeting. She didn't suspect that he had much more ominous plans for her. They left the restaurant and arranged for him to call at her home early the next day. She returned to her apartment in Alamogordo, and he spent the night at the hotel near the ski lift in Cloudcroft.

***

The next morning, Le Docteur showed up at her apartment exactly on time. Lara was ready to go but invited him in for a glass of iced tea, which he politely declined. They left the apartment, and he offered to drive in his rental car, but she laughed and said that she would drive. She led the way to a convertible, black Porsche 718 Cayman and motioned for him to take the passenger's seat. The roar of the engine and vibrations of the car transformed Lara from a quiet, even docile, young woman into a wild-eyed, Formula 1, driver. Within seconds, they were moving at sixty miles per hour, and once they hit the highway, they passed one hundred miles per hour. Lara handled the car with the skill and confidence of a racecar driver, weaving in and out of the slower traffic. Le Docteur sat on the edge of his seat and clung to the door handle as if his life depended on the support it gave him. Lara saw his reaction from the corner of her eye and laughed. "Jacque, don't worry. I am used to much higher speed in my Raptor."

Le Docteur stuttered, "Yes, but there are no other crazy drivers in the sky."

Her laughter grew stronger, "*Au contraire*, I beg to differ. There are many crazy pilots who ended their life in the sky." Much to his relief, she slowed down a little, and he began to enjoy the ride. His appreciation for this exceptional woman grew by the minute. The sixty-mile drive to Carrizozo took them less than forty minutes because Lara slowed down when she saw a police car in the distance. Le Docteur didn't see the patrol car until they approached, but she spotted it instantly. She said, "When you are a fighter pilot, searching for threats in the distance becomes second nature."

They reached Carrizozo, and she turned left, toward the northwest, and headed to the Valley of Fires recreation area. She parked the car near the strange, black formations that were created when the flowing lava cooled and froze. They took the short, circular footpath that meandered through the porous boulders formed by the lava. She told him to close his eyes and count to fifty. He did as she requested, and when he opened his eyes and looked around, he didn't see her. He scanned the area, and all he could see was black lava with a few bushes, an occasional cactus, and some strangely twisted and gnarled tree trunks with few green leaves. Then he heard her laughter coming from somewhere below the surface. He looked closely and saw that Lara was hiding in one of the cracks in the lava field and beckoning him to join her. He saw no one else on the circular path and gingerly climbed down the crack in which she was hiding. She stood up and, when he approached, wrapped her arms around him and rose to her toes to kiss him. He was surprised at her boldness for a moment, but then recalled that she faced the world on her own terms. His body responded to her embrace, and their bodies soon melded together. Their idyll was rudely interrupted by the shouts of a mother calling her three children to stop climbing up the lava boulders.

Lara smiled at him, "Jacque, I have always fantasized about making love in this lava field. When you suggested that we come here, to the Valley of Fires, I felt that you read my mind and were here to fulfil my fantasy." She paused before continuing, "I know that I came on to you very strongly and perhaps scared you a little. But you must understand that since my divorce, I have not found a man I wanted to be with until you appeared like a God-sent angel from heaven last night. I sense that there is something sinister about you, and I know that I may be hurt by falling for you, but I am attracted like a piece of iron to a magnet."

Le Docteur was aware that he had this effect on certain women but had never seen it work so forcefully after such a short time. Once again, he was reminded that Lara was not one of his female students who were twenty years younger than him, but an independent-minded woman who had no inhibitions in getting what she wanted. For the first time in his adult life, he began to worry that he would not be able to satisfy the needs of a woman who wanted him. He managed to say, "Lara, we need to get to know each other better. Let's not rush things. Before returning to Alamogordo, I would like to go to Roswell and see where the urban legend of aliens landing had originated from."

Lara was a bit disappointed that he wasn't feeling the same burning urge that she did. "It's about ninety miles from here, and then we have to return to my apartment, which is another one hundred and twenty miles. Are you sure that you want to go there just to see a field in which alleged aliens allegedly landed seventy years ago?"

Le Docteur saw that she was not keen on the detour he suggested, so he yielded, "I guess that Roswell can wait. Perhaps, next weekend, if you are free, we'll go searching for aliens. Let's have something to eat and go home."

She liked this, especially when he referred to her apartment as "home." She planted a kiss on his cheek, "You won't regret this."

***

Their lovemaking was passionate but also exploratory in nature. Lara took the initiative and guided him to do all the things she liked. She did this in an uninhibited fashion, and he could tell that she had been yearning for the touch of the right man. He got the impression that even before her divorce from her colonel, she didn't enjoy the physical part of their relationship, and probably no other aspect of it. In his mind, he thought that her response to his every touch was like that of a flower in the desert to the first drops of rain. Her responsiveness, he thought, was like the response of her Porsche 718 when she touched the gas pedal—only her purring was louder than that of the powerful motor and her wild vibrations outdid those of the car. Lara's world of images was slightly different—she felt that her body was like the F-22 accelerating on the runway and ready to soar to skies, when the stick is pulled back a fraction of an inch. Le Docteur was unaware of her thought process and therefore surprised when he felt her hand squeezing his manhood and pulling on it.

Afterward they both cuddled and melded together as if they had done this many time before. The fit was just so perfect that they fell asleep in the same position. He woke up when she started stirring, still asleep, and he got out of bed silently and went to the bathroom. He showered, trying not to make any noise, and found a large, pink towel in which he wrapped himself. He looked in the bathroom cabinets and saw nothing that indicated that anyone else regularly stayed in the apartment or used the bathroom.

When he exited the bathroom, he was surprised to see Lara holding a large mug of aromatic coffee and wearing a Cheshire cat smile and nothing else. He smiled back and took the mug from her outstretched hand, patting her gently on her butt as she passed him on her way to the bathroom. A few minutes later, wearing a silk bathrobe, she joined him at the kitchen table and took a sip from her own coffee mug.

Neither of them had to say anything about the sex—both felt elated and satiated—and each knew that they had a special connection of body and soul, even without talking.

Le Docteur felt that he could confide in this exceptional woman who he had met for the first time less than twenty-four hours earlier. Yet he decided that it would be wise to do so slowly. "Lara, we don't need any words to express how unique our feelings for each other are. We know this instinctively, at the very basic level of our minds, that we have created something special. I need to tell you a little more about myself and my views."

He saw her nodding, "From the first moment you spoke to me, I knew that you were more than meets the eye. Jacque, I figured that you are not a French-Canadian, or at least were not born and raised as one. I promise that whatever you tell me will not be divulged to anyone without your approval."

Le Docteur said, "You are very perceptive. I was born in France to an Albanian mother and French father. My father, like yours, was a physician. He joined Doctors Without Borders and worked in many places in which medical care was needed. He was murdered by members of a Serb militia while assisting a Muslim woman giving birth in Kosovo. My mother perished in Paris when she was trying to save the children in a Muslim kindergarten from a fire that was started deliberately by French racists. This made me hate the people who sent these murderers—the colonialists and the Crusaders, as well as the communists who oppressed and exploited our people, the Muslims, in the countries they control, like Chechenia and Afghanistan, or the Uyghurs in western China." He didn't yet tell her that his real name was Albert Pousin or that the name his parents gave him was Anwar.

Lara was surprised by the passion in his voice. "What about the Americans?"

Le Docteur had to make the most important decision because the examples he had given so far would not be objectionable to any patriotic American, and he was sure that Lara regarded herself as one. "The Americans have given military and political support to Israel—the very same people who took your grandparents' home and sent them to rot in refugee camps. You were lucky because they received a chance to a better life in this country and raised a small family and have given you the opportunity to fulfil your dream of becoming a fighter pilot. I admit that this could not have happened in Palestine, or any Muslim country. Yet you must always bear in mind that the presence of American troops on Arab soil and their support of the corrupt regimes, while pumping out the oil given to our people by Allah, shows that traditional colonialism was replaced by modern capitalism." He looked at her, before continuing, "Lara, the Americans have been good to you, personally, but are the direst enemies of the true Islam. I am sure that your grandparents, who probably faced the dual loyalty conflict between their own fate and that of their fellow Palestinians every day, would have considered that their prime loyalty lay with their people."

Lara had tears in her eyes, "Jacque, you sound as if you were present when my grandfather told me to never forget that Haifa is our home. He believed that we shall return there one day to claim our birthright as the owners of the place."

Le Docteur realized the terrible struggle that was taking place in her mind. He looked at her expectantly, waiting for her to reach a conclusion about her loyalty. He placed his hand on hers and patted it gently. Lara's eyes were still filled with tears, and she raised her head, stared at him for a long moment, and quietly said, "Jacque, what do you have in mind? I can tell that you have already worked out a plan that involves me."

Le Docteur took the plunge from the high diving board, not knowing if there was water in the pool. "Lara, I have a vague idea of hitting the Americans where it will hurt them the most. I need you to help me plan it and then to execute it. It will involve considerable personal risk—and even if it succeeds and you survive, there is a chance that you'll never be able to return to this country. Worse, the authorities are sure to hunt you wherever you try to hide, just as they are after me. The only reason that I am still alive is that they are looking for me everywhere, except under their own nose. I cannot even promise you that we'll be able to live together, as much as I truly want to do so more than anything else in the world."

She interrupted, "So why don't we just go and live somewhere quietly. Why do we have to risk the happiness we've just found?"

Le Docteur reacted, "Because I'll never be able to settle down and forget about the plight of my people. I am willing to sacrifice my personal happiness for the sake of the cause." Lara was taken aback by the short outburst. He saw that he had reached the point of no return and told her everything about NEMESIS and the acts that were carried out by his organization in Europe. He concluded, "True Islam will only succeed if all Muslims unite in the struggle against the colonialists, Crusaders, communists, capitalists, and Jews. The Islamic State, ISIS, is passé. Its war against the colonialists in Iraq and Syria has antagonized the Shiites. Carrying out the fight to European cities and terrorizing civilians is more effective in unifying Muslims because the Europeans regard us all in the same way, not understanding the undercurrents of our society. Their reaction to terrorism has endangered Muslims on the one hand but has brought us all together against the common enemy of racism and prejudice. This is what I have been trying to do, until the failure in London that forced me to escape from all the intelligence agencies of the world—the West, the Russians, the Israeli Mossad, as well as those of Arab countries."

She regarded him for long moment and then smiled and said "Come, Jacque, I need a little more convincing." As he rose from the kitchen table, she stretched her hand and grabbed the pink towel that he had wrapped around his midsection. "You won't need that where we are going," and laughed while taking off her bathrobe.

***

When they were done, she said that she was famished and ordered pizzas from the nearby café. They quickly showered and got dressed, and when the pizzas arrived, they washed them down with a couple bottles of beer. So, after satisfying their hunger and thirst, they continued their conversation.

Lara said, "I am ready to hear your plan, although I am not fully committed to it."

He said, "First, let me tell you that my real name is Albert Pousin, and the intelligence services would pay you a fortune if you tell them where I am. My parents called me by my Albanian Muslim name, Anwar, but to the world, I am Albert. It is best if you continue to call me Jacque, just in case someone overhears us talking. Second, I have a general idea for a plan, but I need you to fill in the details. Third, and perhaps most important for us, I think we can devise a way for us to stay together after we execute the plan."

"What do you have in mind?"

Le Docteur outlined the most daring and audacious plan that was beyond imagination. They discussed the details for hours, went back to bed, ate the reheated remains of the pizzas, and washed them down with another couple of beers. On Monday morning, she returned to Holloman Air Force Base and Le Docteur returned to Albuquerque after collecting his gear from the hotel in Cloudcroft. Before parting, Le Docteur said that he had to take care of some loose ends and that he would be in touch.

CHAPTER 9

Albuquerque, New Mexico

Le Docteur returned to Albuquerque after his very close encounter with Lara. He knew that he had to make a difficult choice: Blossom or Lara. He couldn't continue with both relationships. Blossom was an important lynchpin in his plan to enlist the Native American population of New Mexico to support the cause of NEMESIS, while Lara was essential to his most ambitious and audacious plan ever executed by NEMESIS on American soil. Both were deeply in love with him and willing to do whatever he requested, but both made it clear that they expected exclusivity in return. He loved them both, in return. Normally, he would have tried to juggle both relationships, but the stakes were too high. What was even worse from his point of view, he would have to eliminate one of them. He had done that before, in France, when he had to terminate his affairs with two of his former lovers and would have to do so in a way that they wouldn't endanger his identity or organization.

After much deliberation and a few sleepless nights, he made his choice—Lara was vital for his plans, while Blossom could possibly be replaced by someone else. After the weekend at the powwow in Gallup, he told Blossom that he had to return to Washington, DC, the following day and suggested that they spend their last night together doing something they had never done before—take a night hike up to one of the peaks of the Sandia mountain range, from which they would get a great view of the city lights and, when dawn broke, would watch the sun rise from the top of the mountain. Blossom readily agreed, and when they drove up the narrow, winding road in the dark, she was thrilled and excited.

When they reached the end of the road, Le Docteur, took a rough blanket out of the car's trunk, took a backpack in which he had put a couple of wine bottles, and headed up the trail. The trail led further up the mountain and was quite slippery. Blossom held his hand and he guided her, warning her to watch her step whenever there were loose stones on the trail. After climbing for half an hour, they reached a small clearing from which they could see the magnificent view of valley and the city lights. Le Docteur spread the blanket, sat down, and patted the space next to him. Blossom sat down, and he opened the first bottle of wine. He filled two glasses and made a toast, "May we meet again soon."

After they drank the wine and he refilled the glasses, she said, "Do you mean when you return from Washington."

He said, "Close your eyes, and you'll see what I mean." As soon as she closed her eyes with a smile of anticipation on her lips, he took the second wine bottle and struck her left temple with great force. She passed out instantly. After kissing her unresponsive lips, he took a nylon bag and placed it around her face. He averted his eyes as he didn't want to watch her body convulse. After everything was silent, he carried her body to a deep ravine on the east side of the mountain and pushed her down. He knew that few people ever came to this place and that the chances that her body would be discovered were very slim. He packed the blanket, wine bottles, and glasses and headed back to the car.

***

The Airspace Above Holloman, AFB, New Mexico

Lara looked out of the cockpit of her F-22 Raptor and scanned the horizon for Major Buchanan's plane. She knew that her reactions and actions in the next sixty seconds would be the culmination of the preparations of the last three months. Her affair with Le Docteur, she preferred referring to him by that title rather than call him Anwar or Albert or Jacque, was even more hot and heavy than at its beginning. They had started planning their future together, although they knew that after today's events, they would both be at the top of the most wanted list of the American authorities, as well as on other similar lists.

Lara decided that diving down to the deck, in this case to an altitude of three hundred feet above the ground, would make it much more difficult for Buchanan to spot her plane, while she could eliminate all threats from below her. She controlled her breathing and continuously scanned the horizon, looking upward for the other Raptor. She spotted a black speck at her eleven-o'clock position, and to her surprise it was only slightly above her own altitude. She figured that Buchanan had the same great idea of flying close to the deck to avoid being attacked from below. She turned directly toward Buchanan's plane, slowed down, and briefly opened the left side internal bay, thus allowing the active sensor of the heat-seeking air-to-air missile to acquire Buchanan's plane. The ground clutter made it difficult for the infrared sensor of the missile to pinpoint the other F-22, even with the sun behind her back. Nevertheless, she heard the clear signal from the air-to-air missile, mentally crossed her fingers, and pulled back the stick to gain some altitude to safely launch the missile. She whispered to herself, "Allahu Akbar," and pressed the button that launched the live missile. She felt it accelerating ahead of her plane and managed to follow it with her eyes for several hundred feet. The unsuspecting Buchanan had no idea that a live and armed heat-seeking missile had homed on the tailpipe of his left engine. By the time he saw it, it was too late for him to do anything about it. In a desperate attempt to evade it, he tried to fire a flare, but the missile rode right up his tailpipe and exploded before he touched the release button. Due to the plane's low altitude, the poor major didn't have a chance to eject himself and plunged straight down to the unforgiving soil of the New Mexico mesa.

The entire episode lasted less than one minute. Lara raised her hand in a silent salute to her commanding officer, climbed to an altitude of forty-five thousand feet to save fuel and to stay above the commercial airline routes. As planned, she directed her plane to the southwest, on a trajectory that would take her to Puerto Penasco in Mexico. The control tower at Holloman AFB was unaware of what had transpired. The exercise called for total radio silence and stealth configuration until the series of dogfights was completed. Lara had hoped to cover the distance of about five hundred miles before the controller started searching for the two planes. Le Docteur had asked her to find a target along the flight path and bomb it, but she thought that was not a good idea as it would be a giveaway of the direction she took. In any case, the only attractive target that had symbolic significance without killing too many people was the Pima Air and Space Museum on the outskirts of Tucson. She easily spotted Tucson and knew that the museum was located southeast of the city center. She saw the almost endless lines of planes that had been put out of commission, as there was a huge storage area, or graveyard for aircraft, adjacent to the museum. She deliberated whether to drop some of the air-to-ground munitions on the museum but decided to avoid doing this.

***

Puerto Penasco, Gulf of California, Mexico

Half an hour after shooting down Major Buchanan's F-22, Lara approached the Wagner Basin in the northern part of the Gulf of California, which separated mainland Mexico from the Peninsula of Baja California, and saw the small airfield at Puerto Penasco. The airfield had a single runway, heading directly north-south, and was eight thousand feet long - more than enough for her jet fighter. She approached it from the north and saw that the prearranged signal for a safe landing—three long strips of red canvas arranged as a triangle—was in place. She gently eased the jet down and landed. She taxied to the small makeshift hangar at the southern end of the runway. When the doors opened wide, she easily taxied inside and switched off both engines. The sudden silence was deafening. She removed her helmet and peeked out of the canopy. The sight she saw brought tears to her eyes—a metal stepladder was pushed by a couple of mechanics to the cockpit and Le Docteur, wearing a face-splitting smile, was standing at its top rung.

Le Docteur had driven from Albuquerque in New Mexico to Puerto Penasco in Mexico a couple of weeks before the arrival of Lara and her F-22. The drive was long because after entering Mexico at Ciudad Juarez, the border town across the Rio Grande from El Paso in Texas, he stayed on Mexican soil. The highways leading west in the United States' side of the border were far better than those south of the border, but Le Docteur didn't want to leave any tracks that he was travelling to the west, just in case his disappearance was linked to Lara's. He figured that if there was a record of him entering Mexico at Juarez, then it would be difficult for US authorities to guess which way he headed in Mexico or if he left the country to seek sanctuary elsewhere. He sold his US-registered car for a ridiculously low sum, knowing full well that it would be dismantled within the hour and sold as spare parts in the garages of El Paso. He purchased a three-year-old car with Mexican registration and drove it to Puerto Penasco. When he arrived there, he bought the cooperation and silence of the airfield's small crew in preparation for the arrival of Lara's jet fighter. He thought that money could buy you anything in Mexico, but there was always the chance that even more money could "unbuy," if there was such a verb, the silence and cooperation he paid for. His plan was therefore trying to minimize the period that he needed silence. He had yet to discuss this with Lara, as this was part of the plan that he devised on the long solitary drive from Albuquerque.

***

Control Tower, Holloman, AFB

The air traffic controller, Top Sergeant Morris, looked at his watch and then checked the time at the bottom corner of his computer screen to verify that he had it right. He picked up the phone and called his superior, Major Chuck Harden, "Sir, the two Raptors exercising dogfights have not checked in. They are five minutes overdue and have not responded to my repeated calls."

Major Harden, the duty officer in charge of the control tower, asked, "Who are the pilots in this exercise?" and when he heard that they were Major Buchanan and Captain Lara Wayne, he kept his cool and added, "Perhaps they decided to go for best of three. You know that both are excellent pilots and the other pilots are placing bets on who will win. The loser will have to buy drinks for everyone at the club tonight. Give it another five minutes."

Morris continued to call Buchanan and Lara, and when

there was no reply, he called his boss again. "Sir, you'd better come here. Their failure to respond is not typical. Also, they are still in stealth mode, so I cannot see them on the radar."

Major Harden followed the standard operating procedure. He called all aircraft to return to base, declared the exercise area a no-fly zone, and sent a couple of helicopters to search the area. The worst-case scenario that played through his mind was that in the heat of the dogfight, the jets collided in midair. In that case, both pilots could be dead instantly without getting a chance to call for help or transmit a Mayday signal.

Twenty minutes later, one of the search pilots radioed that he had spotted the smoldering remains of what had been a jet fighter. He hovered over the crash site and transmitted live video photos. The formation of the debris that were scattered along a straight line indicated that the plane had crashed into the ground almost intact and refuted the possibility of a high-altitude midair collision or explosion. The helicopter pilot added that there were no signs that the pilot survived the crash and that the canopy was still attached to the cockpit, indicating that the ejection seat had not been operated. Major Harden asked for the tail number of the crashed plane. The helicopter pilot said that the left-side rudder was completely missing as was most of the engine, and the tail number on the right-side rudder was only partly readable. He read out the numbers and letters he could decipher, and Major Harden recognized that it was Buchanan's plane. He got the exact coordinates of the crash site and ordered the search pilot to continue looking for the other jet. He then informed the base commander, General Earl Lancaster, about the incident and the findings and said that he would continue to investigate the matter.

Major Harden quickly assembled a team of mechanics and safety investigators and summoned the medical officer to join them. He sent them all in another helicopter to the crash site after cautioning them that the two Raptors were equipped with live munitions. The pilots of the first two search helicopters reported that they were low on fuel and had to return to the base to refuel, so Major Harden sent another couple of search teams to look for the second jet.

The safety investigator jumped out of the helicopter and approached Buchanan's plane. He gingerly circled the plane and saw that the two side weapon bays and the main bay were still closed, meaning that the munitions had not detonated when the plane crashed. When he looked at the plane's tail section, he saw that the left engine was shattered, and the left-side rudder was missing. He looked closely and could still see the remnants of the tail fins of an air-to-air missile. He was an experienced investigator and had seen what happened to drones that were used for aerial warfare practice when they were hit by such munitions, and he understood what had happened. He returned to the helicopter that brought him to the crash site and contacted Major Harden. He said, "Major, there certainly was no midair collision. It looks as if Buchanan's jet was shot down by an air-to-air missile. I cannot tell if it was an accident or a deliberate act. Have you received any news about the other plane?"

Harden replied, "This is the weirdest thing I have ever

encountered. How can a thing like this happen by accident? Surely, if it were accidental, then the other pilot, Captain Wayne, would have reported it. I'll issue a nationwide search for her plane. A Raptor cannot disappear into thin air—it must land before it runs out of fuel or it will crash somewhere." He quickly called the base commander and gave him the startling news. General Lancaster ordered him to instruct everyone involved to keep a tight lid on the incident and not discuss it with anyone else.

The general called the air force headquarters and was told to inform the Department of Homeland Security about the incident. He could imagine the headlines in the media, "Holloman AFB is searching for a lost F-22 Raptor. Please contact the police or FBI if you find it." He shuddered when he thought of the implications to his career. He opened the bottom drawer of his desk, poured himself a large glass of whiskey, gulped it down, and poured another. Then he called the base's public relations officer, Lieutenant Sara Stone, who also happened to be his lover.

She entered his office with the usual big smile she reserved for him alone, but when she saw the expression on his face and the empty glass, she said, "General, what's the problem?" She circled his desk and started to massage his shoulders.

The general impatiently removed her hands from his shoulders and, in a formal tone, told her to sit down. When she was seated across the desk from him, he said, "Sara, we are facing a public relations catastrophe," and then related the story of the Raptor that was shot down by an air-to-air missile and of the missing plane that was flown by Captain

Lara Wayne.

Sara said, "Do you suspect foul play by Captain Wayne, or do you believe that an accident of this type could occur? Perhaps Captain Wayne freaked out after the accident and tried to fly her plane far away from the site." When he said that an accident could be ruled out, Sara, who was a clever woman, immediately proposed that they read Lara's personal file and search for any irregularities. The general pulled up Lara's electronic file from the human resources department, swerved his computer monitor so Sara could watch, and they both studied the personal details. They saw that she was a divorcee, and Sara mentioned that the gossip on the base was that her husband had abused her until she had had enough and got back at him, physically and financially. The file noted that her maiden surname was Mayor and that she was raised in Iowa. Lara excelled in everything she did and had received the highest grades from her flight instructors. One of them commented that she was a "natural pilot and a born stick jockey" and that he considered her as one of the best pilots he had ever trained. Sara suggested that they dig deeper into her family history and found that in one of the forms she submitted when she joined the national guard, she listed her full name as Lara Layla Maysun Mayor. The name triggered an alarm in the general's mind—he had served in the Middle East and knew that Layla Maysun was an Arabic name. He kissed Sara on her cheek, patted her back, and said that he had to pass the information to the FBI and ask for a thorough background investigation. He said that he badly needed relaxation and said he'd come over to her apartment in the evening.

***

Solon, Iowa

Dr. Mayor was attending to a patient at his clinic when his receptionist knocked on the door of his office. She apologized for the interruption and in a shaky voice asked him to step out for a moment. He told the patient to relax and said he would be back in a minute.

He was surprised to see two clean-cut men in business suits. Both held out badges that identified them as FBI agents. The senior agent asked him if he could spare a moment in a formal tone that left no doubt that he meant business. The doctor asked them if they could wait until he finished attending to his patient. The senior agent agreed reluctantly, so the doctor returned to his office and gave the patient the prescription she had requested for anxiety attack symptoms. He thought that perhaps he should take some of the medication himself because he had no idea why the FBI agents wanted to speak to him.

He knew that if something had happened to his only daughter, Lara, then air force personnel or local police would come over to break the news. He invited the FBI agents to his office, and as they sat down in the two chairs across his desk, he poured himself a glass of water and offered coffee to the agents. They declined, and the senior agent opened, "Dr. Mayor, we apologize for intruding, but we need to talk to you urgently. Do you know where your daughter is?"

Dr. Buddy Mayor had not expected that question. "I think she is at Holloman Air Force Base in New Mexico."

"When last did you hear from her?"

"She called me a couple of weeks ago and said that everything was well."

"Have you noticed any change in her behavior, attitude, politics?"

"You know, she is thirty-two years old and has always been very independent minded. Since her divorce from that no-good colonel, she has distanced herself a little from our family. She calls every week or two and speaks mainly to her mother."

"Doctor Mayor, can you tell us a little about your background?"

"My parents came to this country nearly sixty years ago. They settled down in New Jersey and worked hard to enable me to go to medical school. While at school, I met my wife at a party. After graduation, we moved here to her hometown, and I started my own private practice. Lara is our only daughter, and we are very proud of her achievements and career as a fighter pilot in the United States Air Force."

The FBI agent hesitated before asking the next question because he knew that it was not politically correct and could be considered as intrusive. He searched for a way around it, "Doctor, did Lara belong to any youth organization, community center, or attend any church activities?" He really wanted to know if she had any ties to Islamic organizations or radicalized religious activists.

Dr. Mayor, who was no fool, knew what the agent was asking, "Lara was interested in athletics and science, and let me tell you, she excelled in both. These activities kept her busy. She was very popular socially but had little interest in boys her age and had little time for dating. She married that colonel because he represented the tough guy that she was aspiring to be."

The FBI agent decided that he should be more direct. "Was Lara close to her grandparents?"

The doctor hesitated, "She adored my parents and respected them tremendously. She spent many holidays with them in New Jersey. She also loves her maternal grandparents who still live here, in Solon. When she was young, she used to dine at their house, quite often, when my wife and I were busy at work."

The junior agent didn't like this waltzing around the topic of interest. He said, "Doctor, I understand that your parents lived in Haifa until 1948, when they were forced into exile by the Israelis. Did they express resentment to Israel? To Jews? Or, perhaps, to the United States that supports Israel? Were they active in any Muslim community?"

Dr. Mayor couldn't evade the questions any longer. "My father kept the key of his apartment in Haifa, hoping to return there one day. But, as you know, I have converted to Christianity and Lara was raised as a typical Midwestern girl, without any connection to Islam. I don't know what you are after, but please speak frankly."

"I understand that her full name was Layla Maysun Mayor and that your name was Badi, before you Americanized it to

Buddy."

The doctor was not happy. "So what? We gave Lara an Arabic name to honor my father's wish that she also carries a name to remind her of her heritage. I changed my own name to be accepted in the community here. The people in Solon, Iowa, are not used to strangers, and we wanted Lara to lead a normal life, so no one used her other names."

The senior agent exchanged a glance with his partner and, in a formal tone, said, "Captain Lara Wayne is missing. She had not returned from a routine exercise in which she flew as number two. Her flight leader's F-22 crashed, and he was killed. Lara did not report anything, and her plane has disappeared. The entire area around the crash site had been inspected by planes, helicopters, satellites, and on the ground. Nothing was found."

The doctor interrupted, "How can that be? How can a plane vanish?"

"It was a Raptor, flying in stealth mode. There have been no reports of a crash or of a plane landing in any known airfield." He shrugged and added, "The plane could have crashed in some remote place or plunged into the ocean or some lake. There have been no signs of life from Captain Lara Wayne."

Doctor Mayor's ashen expression left no doubt in the agents' minds that he had no idea of the incident. The agents thanked the doctor for his time and cooperation and left his office. The junior agent said, "Sir, the good doctor was trying to hide something. I think that her grandfather had a great influence on Lara. This was probably dormant until her divorce. We need to report back to Holloman that they should investigate her recent social contacts. I am quite sure we'll find that she had undergone some changes."

The senior agent said, "I think you are correct." He proceeded to call his superiors and relay the information and reservations.

***

Puerto Penasco, Mexico

Le Docteur had to make the long drive from Albuquerque to Puerto Penasco in the Baja California Peninsula on his own. He amused himself with the thought that Lara would be arriving by air, although by no official airline. The drive was uneventful, and he was glad to arrive there.

After three weeks of being apart, Le Docteur and Lara celebrated their reunion in their room in the small hotel in the village of Puerto Penasco. After the adrenaline rush had dissipated, they just lay still, cuddling in the bed. The air conditioning was not functioning properly, but they didn't mind that their perspiration-soaked bodies stuck to each other. He lazily got out of bed and entered the shower. There was no hot water, or for that matter, really cold water, but the tepid water was refreshing. He shaved, showered, and walked back into the room to put on his bathing trunks. Lara watched his body and, with a smile, said, "Jacque, you have lost some weight." She still called him Jacque in public, although she knew that his real name was Albert Anwar Pousin, and in her mind, he was forever Le Docteur. "Please, pour me a drink while I shower. Then we'll go down to the beach."

He said, "After that, we'll talk about the future."

***

Le Docteur was having a real dilemma: on the one hand, he was deeply in love with Lara. He truly admired her professional skills as a fighter pilot and her strength of character, in addition to her ability to execute, literally, a maneuver that few people in the world had done—to shoot down an F-22 Raptor. On the other hand, the F-22 that she brought and landed so beautifully at the remote airfield in Mexico was an asset to NEMESIS, which he still had to figure out how to cash in on. He could try to sell it to the highest bidder—the Russians, Chinese, Iranian, and North Koreans would all pay a king's ransom for this perfect piece of American high technology with a myriad of top-secret super components that could be reverse-engineered by skilled technological personnel.

Le Docteur liked money just as much as the next person, but he wanted something that money cannot buy, at least on the open market, and probably not even on the black market. The thing he really wanted was an atom bomb, preferably two or three nuclear devices. Exploding an atom bomb, even something as modest as a Hiroshima-sized device, in Times Square in New York would probably result in hundreds of thousands of fatalities or seriously injured people, millions of people contaminated by radioactivity, immediate losses of billions of dollars in real estate and property, and trillions of dollars vanishing into thin air when the global markets react to the bombing of New York.

Le Docteur was not a physicist, but he had gained some knowledge about nuclear forensics and gathered that modern analytical science would be able to trace the bomb back to its place of origin. Thus, Russia, China, and Iran would fear that the US would retaliate disproportionately against whomever made the atomic device, regardless of the fact that it was delivered by NEMESIS. So, although he figured that trading the F-22 for an atom bomb would be attractive to the four countries mentioned above, only the North Koreans were likely to allow him to use it.

An alternative was to send the Raptor on a one-way mission to take out a select target within the borders of the United States or even an aircraft carrier in, or near, the naval base in San Diego. Although he was initially disappointed that Lara had not bombed a target, like the Pima museum, on her way from Holloman AFB to Puerto Penasco, he now realized that he could do so much more with the asset she had delivered to him. He told her, only half-joking, that the Raptor was her dowry and that he could now marry her. She didn't find this funny at all and said that he is the one who should be bringing her the bride price or bride service.

Lara saw that her man was deep in thought. "A penny for your thoughts, Jacque."

"Thanks to you, I am thinking in terms of billions of dollars, not pennies." He decided to share some of his deliberations with her, "I am thinking of what we can do with this wonderful gift you delivered. You know that we can sell it for a fortune to any of the enemies of the United States.

The Russians would give us the plane's weight in gold, not to mention the Iranians or the Chinese. We can also consider the North Koreans as an interested party."

Lara said, "It is a terrible risk because if word gets out that such a plane is on the black market, the interested parties would stop at nothing to lay their hands on it. I fear that we would not be able to maintain our safety when the stakes are so high. We would be eliminated as soon as word about the 'Raptor for sale' gets out. I would rather destroy the plane and go as far away as possible from this place before the FBI or others find out where the plane is."

Le Docteur said, "I agree. Negotiating directly with any of those countries is extremely dangerous, even suicidal. There is another option, but I hesitate to bring it up because it involves a great personal risk to you."

"What do you have in mind? I can assess the risks. I am willing to do anything for the cause, and for you."

"Lara, do you think you could penetrate the US aerial defenses with the Raptor, take out a target in the US, and return here safely?"

"Jacque, do you want to use this airfield in Puerto Penasco as a clandestine base for strikes against the US? You must be out of your mind! In any case, there are only a few air-to-surface munitions in the plane's internal main bay, limited fuel, and no skilled technicians to carry out maintenance."

"Fuel we can get here, for an exorbitant price, of course, but affordable. As things are now, you have enough fuel and munitions for at least one effective strike at a close target like San Diego, for example. When you return here, you can ditch the plane in the gulf and eject safely from it before it crashes and sinks."

"Crazy, but brilliant. Jacque, this would be my grandfather's revenge for losing his home in Haifa and for the suffering his family endured in the refugee camps in Lebanon. I am willing to do this." She thought about this daring proposal for a few more moments and finally spoke up. "Jacque, we can have the best of both worlds. I can fly on a mission to the US, return safely to the Gulf of California, and ditch the plane in shallow water. We can then negotiate its sale to the highest bidder or perhaps trade it for an atom bomb. The buyer will have to salvage it from the Gulf's seabed, of course, and that will give us an insurance policy because no one else will know where the plane is. It is much safer than returning to the airfield in Puerto Penasco, where anyone who enters the hangar where it is hidden can make a deal for cash."

Le Docteur hesitated, "Doesn't this place you in harm's way? I think it's too dangerous."

Lara smiled, "I am an excellent pilot, and I already told you I'll do anything for you and the cause."

***

Holloman AFB, New Mexico

General Earl Lancaster, the base commander, received the report of the FBI agents who interviewed Captain Lara Wayne's father in Iowa. He had already asked his PR officer, Lieutenant Sara Stone, to find out what she could about Lara's private life. Sara entered his office, "Sir," she never addressed him differently when on formal duty, "I have discovered that Lara had been in a close relationship with some academic professor of political science. One of her neighbors told me that she spent most of her free weekends with this man. When she met Lara with the man, she introduced him as Professor Jacque Deleau—the neighbor wasn't sure about the spelling or pronunciation of the name. He spoke with a slight accent, which she thought was French. She also said that the man was handsome but couldn't provide a detailed description. Lara's colleagues on the base said that she looked happier than she ever did since her divorce and thought that a man was responsible for this but knew nothing about him. One of the pilots said that she had behaved a bit differently, a little more reserved and distant, during the last few days. He added that Lara appeared to be under some stress but that she didn't share her problems with anyone in the squadron. As she was the only female pilot among a group of macho men, she wasn't close to any of them, and since her marriage to Colonel Wayne turned sour, she seemed to avoid any emotional involvement with her colleagues. She was heard saying that male pilots were like peacocks—walking about as if someone stuck a pole up their backside."

The general, who was a pilot himself, took offense from the description. "Sara, thanks, you have done wonders. We need to locate this Professor Deleau and find out more about him. I'll update the FBI and see whether they can add anything."

Sara nodded and walked out of the office with what she considered as a sexy move, shaking and wiggling her shapely backside as she left. The general smiled and then picked up the phone to call the top FBI agent in the region and update him about Professor Deleau.

***

The FBI didn't need more than a few minutes to discover that Professor Deleau had taught political science and European history at the University of New Mexico in Albuquerque and that he had left the city after the semester ended. His present whereabouts were unknown. The FBI agents in Albuquerque interviewed some of his colleagues on the department's faculty, and all stated that he was a very agreeable guy, popular with his students, and well respected in his field of expertise. Students who were questioned said that he had delivered his lectures in a way that inspired them to think independently and not accept anything without checking the facts. Most female students spoke about him with enthusiasm that was not due solely to his professional presentation of the subject matter, and evidently many had crushes on him. The agents wanted to know if he spoke about Islam but quickly learned that the word was not mentioned once in his lessons. One of the more conservative students said that he had described European history as being driven mainly by the colonialist forces who wanted to expand their empires and that he depicted the Crusades as part of the imperialist movement, not as a religious undertaking set to liberate the Holy Land. The FBI agent in charge of the investigation noted this but didn't find it as anything exceptional that required in-depth enquiry.

One of the female students mentioned the fact that the professor had a special relationship with one of the students. She only knew that her first name was Blossom, but that was enough for the agent to find out that her full name was Blossom Bearskin. He also discovered that her father was of Native American origin and on her mother's side she was Palestinian. Both her parents were outstanding scientists and worked at Sandia National Laboratory. However, when he tried to contact Blossom, he was told by her father that she had disappeared several months previously, shortly after the school year ended. Dr. Jonathan Bearskin was bereft with sorrow and said that his daughter's mysterious disappearance in the prime of her life had crushed him and his wife. He said that she was so happy to be in love with a man somewhat older than her when they both vanished and had not been heard from since. The agent was surprised to learn that the man in question was none other than Professor Jacque Deleau.

He immediately called his supervisor, and the information was relayed to General Lancaster. The description given by the professor's colleagues, his students, and by Jonathan fit the vague description of Lara's neighbor. The FBI issued a nationwide search for the professor, for Blossom, and for Lara—saying that they were wanted for questioning related to a sex scandal. However, there was no information on the current whereabouts of the threesome.

CHAPTER 10

Naval Base San Diego, California

Commander Lewis, the commander of the large naval base, was fast asleep, in the middle of a dream that he was on board a coast guard helicopter as an observer.

The mission was to raid an unidentified ship that refused to answer all calls from the shore. Suddenly, the helicopter executed a sharp left turn, dropped three hundred feet, and fired a couple of decoy flares. The pilot managed to issue a warning that a surface-to-air missile had been launched at them and he was taking evasive action.

The explosion of the missile sounded like thunder and was accompanied, almost simultaneously, by a bolt of lightning, causing the helicopter to disintegrate instantly. It was the sound of the explosion that woke the base commander from his sleep.

When he opened his eyes, he realized the explosion was real, and through his window, he could see flames rising from one of the piers. While trying to determine which of the thirteen piers had been hit and what hit it, his phone rang.

The duty officer tried to control his excitement. "Sir, the USS Boxer and the USS Dewey have been hit by missiles.

We have not identified the origin of the missiles—they could have been launched from the ground, the sea, or the air."

Commander Lewis interjected, "Give me the damage report."

The duty officer stuttered. "Sir, all I know is that the guided missile destroyer, the Dewey, has received a direct hit on the bridge and is on fire and some of its ammunition is exploding. The flight deck of the Boxer, the amphibious assault ship, was hit, and several of its helicopters are on fire. Emergency measures were taken to extinguish the fires where possible, and the crew is trying to push burning aircraft from the deck into the water. One problem is that intact craft had to be pushed over the side to clear a path for the burning machines."

"I am on my way to the pier. Try to find out what type of missiles hit us."

***

The Gulf of California, near Puerto Penasco

Lara was ecstatic after the successful air raid she carried out. She saw that she scored two direct hits on two naval vessels moored to one of the piers in the San Diego Naval Base.

She would have preferred to take out an aircraft carrier, but none were within the range of the Raptor. Even after being refueled at the small airfield in Puerto Penasco, the operational range of her plane was only four hundred miles, so she had to find a suitable target within that radius.

San Diego was about three hundred miles from the airfield, and she wanted to make sure she had enough fuel to return to the Gulf of Mexico and ditch the plane in shallow water, as planned. She had not fired the rotary gun because she didn't want to waste fuel doing a strafing pass over the burning ships. In addition to the full stock of ammunition for the rotary gun, she still had air-to-air missiles in her internal side-bay, and that gave her insurance in the unlikely event she was chased by other planes. She was confident that if the occasion arose, she would be the winner of the dogfight, if it got to that.

She knew that every radar station near San Diego would be searching for her plane, and hoped that in full stealth mode, she would remain invisible. She was particularly worried about low-frequency radar that may be able to track her, so she kept low until she crossed back into Mexican airspace, hoping the ground clutter would eliminate her plane's radar signature.

She rechecked the weapon bays to ensure they were closed after most of her armament was deployed. So far, she had not been spotted, to the best of her knowledge, and she hoped this wouldn't change when she would eject from the plane. She would have to do this at a relatively low altitude to ensure the plane went down in a shallow spot and at a low speed to increase the chances of her survival and keep the plane relatively intact.

Le Docteur would be waiting in the area with a speedboat. They would have to refrain from using their radio and rely on flares for visual contact during the meet up.

She brought the Raptor to an altitude of three hundred feet above the dark waters of the Gulf of California, just a few miles west of the lights of Puerto Penasco. She saw the flickering red and white light from the beacon on Le Docteur's speedboat, switched on the F-22's landing lights for two seconds, and then turned them off. Her air speed was just above stalling speed, so controlling the Raptor was not easy. With difficulty, she managed to maintain a straight and level approach as she passed over the speedboat and pulled the lever that initiated the ejection sequence.

She prepared herself mentally and physically for the kick in the butt, just as she had done in training but never in practice. First, the cockpit's canopy flew away—the sight and sound of the pyrotechnics charge made Lara shut her eyes tightly. So, a fraction of a second later, when her seat was shot up in the air, she barely grasped what was happening, but training set in, and she clutched the parachute that brought her softly down to the warm waters of the Gulf.

She didn't quite see as the pilotless Raptor glided over the water at a flat angle and slowly sank down in the murky waters. When she had discussed this part of the plan with Jacque, he raised his concern that the plane would stay afloat, like the U.S. Airways Flight one five four nine in the miracle on the Hudson incident. Lara had laughed at him and said that the weight-to-volume, or floatability, of the F-22 was nothing like the Airbus-A320 and that miracles of this type didn't happen twice.

She suffered some bruises, more from the brutal ejection than from the landing in the water. But in any case, her adrenaline rush was so great she felt no pain. When she was helped on board the speedboat by Le Docteur, she was shaking from joy, not from cold as Jacque had thought when he hugged her tightly.

She was in full control of her faculties when she reminded him to mark the coordinates of the speedboat's exact position and the direction in which the plane plunged into the water. He confirmed he had done so and headed toward the lights of Puerto Penasco.

They knew they would have to wait until morning to view the crash site and determine if the plane could be spotted from the air. Le Docteur suggested they do this by carrying a quadcopter equipped with a camera to fly over the site and not just rely on the view from the water surface afforded by the speedboat.

***

The next morning, they took the speedboat out to the crash site and tried in vain to see the submerged F-22 on the seabed floor. They also launched the quadcopter and viewed the photos taken by its built-in camera. On very close scrutiny, and, of course, knowing exactly what to look for, they could barely see the outline of the plane. As far as they could judge, it was in one piece, possibly with some minor parts, which could not be distinguished, lying nearby.

***

San Diego Naval Base

Commander Lewis almost had a cardiac arrest when he received the report his two ships were hit by air-to-surface missiles as well as by two one-thousand-pound bombs. The investigation of the remains showed that the missiles were launched by American made LAU-142/A launchers, which could be fired from a distance way beyond visual range, but the use of the bombs proved beyond doubt the plane from which they were dropped was very close to the naval base, probably right over head.

Commander Lewis consulted with the senior aviators on the base, and they said these were typical of ordnance carried by the FA-22 Raptor. They added that this could also explain why the plane was not detected before, during, or after the attack on the base. One of them, who had experience in flying surveillance and combat mission over war-torn Syria, said that in stealth mode, the Raptor could go undetected even by the Russian integrated air defense system (IADS) and could, therefore, operate in areas that were defended by the deadly S-300 and S-400 Russian missile systems. He wasn't sure whether it could evade low-frequency radar, but in any case, none were operative near the base at the time of the attack.

The enraged base commander recalled a top-secret message he had received a few days earlier that one F-22 crashed in a training exercise in New Mexico and a second plane was suspected as being responsible. He remembered the weird comment at the end of the message—the whereabouts of the second plane and its pilot were unknown.

At the time, he took no special notice of this message, believing the strange things that always happened in New Mexico were more like an urban legend than real news. Now, the pieces of the puzzle seemed to come together. He called the Pentagon and shared his suspicions with the chairman of the Joint Chiefs of Staff, who happened to be an admiral under whom he had served decades before as a lieutenant junior grade.

***

The disaster that occurred at the San Diego Naval Base couldn't be hidden from the media—there were too many casualties and too many people had heard the explosions and seen the fires.

At first, a statement was issued that an accidental explosion had severely damaged the USS Boxer and the fire had spread to the USS Dewey, which was berthed nearby. However, this didn't hold water for more than thirty minutes, so a clarification was added that the cause of the initial explosion was unknown, and a second explosion may have occurred at the same time. The reporter from Fox News asked if terrorists were suspected for causing sabotage, and the spokesman denied that categorically, as instructed by the Pentagon.

Commander Lewis thought that holding terrorists responsible for the attacks would be less destructive than admitting it was probably carried out by a renegade pilot who managed to steal one of the most advanced and sophisticated planes the United States owned and then used it to shoot down another plane and bomb one of the most important naval bases on the West Coast.

This was a public relations fiasco of unprecedented proportions. He didn't think that he shared any part of the blame or had any responsibility, yet he thought the honorable thing to do was to submit a letter of resignation. Much to his dismay, the Secretary of the Navy accepted his resignation. Commander Lewis wondered if the commander of Holloman AFB, General Earl Lancaster, had also resigned and was told the general was about to face a court-martial.

This pleased him because he considered General Lancaster as being at the root cause of his problem. He was informed that many heads rolled in the FBI, the Department of Homeland Security, and in the CIA, but that was at best minor consolation for his own fate.

***

Ensenada, Baja California, Mexico

Le Docteur and Lara rented one of the small beach houses on the sandy shore of the Baja California Peninsula, a few miles south of the village of Ensenada. They spent their days riding on horseback along the beach, the evenings drinking margaritas on the deck, watching the sun set over the Pacific Ocean, and the nights making love and getting to know each other better.

A couple days after they had arrived at the beach house, Le Docteur drove up to Tijuana and purchased a video camera to record another message about the acts of NEMESIS against the colonialists, crusaders, communists, capitalists, and Jews (C4J, for short).

Lara asked him why he didn't simply use the camera on his cell phone, and he answered that everything spoken, photographed, or recorded on the cell phone could be picked up by the NSA. He said that after Snowden's revelations, he was sure the National Security Agency kept tabs on every electronic transmission, and words such as NEMESIS, attacks, and so on were sure to be on the short list of trigger words.

Lara caught on quickly and asked him how he intended to send the video, and he explained he would go back to Tijuana, or perhaps even cross into San Diego, and send it through a chain of servers on the dark web.

***

Le Docteur was filmed as a dark silhouette on an extremely bright background, and his voice was electronically distorted. Despite the distortion, the smugness could not be misinterpreted. "Citizens of America, today you were given a taste of your own weapon systems—this time on the receiving end. We have attacked a purely military target—a naval base in one of your most secure cities, thousands of miles from your closest enemy. Perhaps now you can begin to imagine what happens when peaceful civilians are targeted. Once again, NEMESIS is not trying to impress you by the number of casualties, we could have just as easily attacked a shopping mall, a hospital, or a stadium in which a sporting event was being held. We just gave you a small demonstration of our ability to hit you hard where you feel safest and to select quality targets. Next time, we may change our policy and select a nuclear power station, a crowded air terminal, or perhaps the White House, and there is nothing you can do to stop us."

He paused to allow his words to sink in and then changed track. "You have not heard much about NEMESIS recently, and that is because the organization is now operating on a C4J agenda. You may wonder what C4J stands for, so allow me to enlighten you—it means that we will be fighting the colonialists, crusaders, communists, capitalists, and Jews—the individuals responsible for the oppression of people around the world. The natural resources of the poor people in Africa, Asia, and the Western Hemisphere have been plundered by the colonial nations of Europe, who ruled their colonies with an iron fist until they were forced to let go of their prey. They were replaced by the Neocolonialists—the United States and Russia—but the system has not changed very much. Exploitation of cheap labor, robbery of oil and minerals, spreading diseases to promote sales of expensive medications, using the impoverished countries as dumps for industrial waste and pollutants—these are but a few of the Neo-evils brought about by the Neocolonialists. War mongering to create markets for weapon sales is the new version of the old divide-and-conquer policies. If you look closely, you can see the dirty hands and clear fingerprints of the C4J I mentioned."

He paused a moment for dramatic effect. "NEMESIS is basically an organization set on avenging the wrongdoings the C4J entities had done to the Muslim people. Any intelligent person who has followed the news recently and read history books knows the evils of the C4J against Islam have intensified. Foreign infidel forces are present on holy Arab soil in Saudi Arabia, Qatar, Iraq, Syria, and Afghanistan, to mention just some of the more blatant examples. They must be removed, or NEMESIS will continue to exert its revenge on these forces and instill terror in the hearts of the governments and people that sent them there. Any acts against the Muslims living in your countries will be answered by increased waves of terror. If you try to deny these guests of yours their lawful rights, you will be punished severely by NEMESIS."

Now he raised his voice and stated, "History is on the side of Islam—you know that within less than one century, Muslims will rule most of the world, especially the European countries, which were formerly the main colonialist countries and are now the place in which modern slavery is practiced."

In a voice that was barely audible, he continued, "You are probably curious to know what happened at the San Diego Naval Base recently. The base was attacked by a brave pilot, to whom I will refer by her real name, Layla Maysun. In Arabic, it means *born at night* and *of beautiful face and body*—a true description of this exceptional woman who is a third-generation Palestinian. The attack on the naval port at San Diego is a reminder that her family was deported and sent into exile from the port city of Haifa. The weapon she used was one of your very own F-22 Raptor jet-fighter planes. It is ironic, isn't it, that it was one of your most sophisticated war machines used by American crusaders to attack Muslims and is now used by a Muslim to attack crusaders."

He now could barely suppress the smile that was evident in his speech. "You may remember *Catch-22*, the book and movie that described life in a World War II bomber squadron. In one of the episodes, the bombers are sent on a mission to bomb their own base—for money, of course. Irony at its utmost—the number twenty-two designates the F-22 Raptor that was used to attack an American base."

He was now reaching the conclusion of his speech. "American citizens, ask not what you can do for your country, but what your government is doing to you. Do you feel safe in your home, knowing that military bases can be attacked so easily? Are you proud of your democratic institutions, knowing the seat of your Congress and Senate, your Capitol building, have been attacked by radioactive material? Do you think your president can guarantee your safety? Do you believe that words will deter us from exacting revenge?"

Lara turned off the camera and walked up to him. "Jacque." She still called him by that name. "You were fantastic. Now let the press and public tear apart their government and president."

***

CIA Headquarters, Langley, Virginia

The director of the Central Intelligence Agency, the DCI, heard the latest news with mixed feelings. On the one hand, he was flabbergasted the entire intelligence community of the United Sates was so completely blind. How could such an unprecedented attack on one of the most important and supposedly well-defended naval bases occur, literally and figuratively, under the radar?

On the other hand, the responsibility of the CIA in this fiasco was limited. Other federal agencies were to bear the brunt of the debacle: the DHS for allowing the head of NEMESIS to enter the country and carry out such an operation, the FBI for not being able to find the man, the vetting procedure of the military for letting the radicalized Islamist go unnoticed, and the air force for giving such a person full control of one of its most sophisticated, secret, and expensive weapon systems.

The NSA, which was supposed to know everything that was sent by e-mail and about every telephone call in the country and abroad, showed great negligence in performing its duty. And then there were all the police departments, military and civilian, that couldn't lay their hands on the perpetrator, who, he was quite sure, was out of the country. No, he mused, there is no way the CIA, and certainly its director, were answerable to this sordid affair.

The director of the FBI, a political appointee whose main task was to shut down any investigation of POTUS and his family members, didn't worry too much about the events and their repercussions. He knew he would always find a scapegoat, preferably outside the bureau, to take the blame. Accountability, he believed, was for fools.

As a skilled manipulator with vast experience in interdepartmental politics, he already explained to the president that the FBI was not involved and it would do its best to arrest the perpetrators when, and if, they set foot on American soil. So long as they were outside the U.S., the FBI had no jurisdiction, and in any case, the FBI was not responsible for restricting the entry to the U.S. of terror suspects.

Similar thoughts passed through the minds of the directors of the other federal and local law enforcement departments across the nation. A cynical columnist in one of the major East Coast newspapers wrote that the people in charge of the White House archives should search for the little sign on Harry Truman's desk that said: *The buck stops here.*

He added that since Truman's presidency, many bucks passed over that desk and underneath it, and he believed that some of those found their way to the deep pockets of some of the Oval Office tenants. He concluded his column by asking who was responsible for bringing the perpetrators to justice and for providing assurances to the American people that such attacks, or even larger ones, would not recur.

***

The White House, Washington, DC

The atmosphere at the press conference held by the press secretary of the president of the United States was like that of a lynch mob getting ready to hang a man caught raping a ten-year-old girl in the Deep South.

The press secretary tried in vain to complete reading the statement carefully drafted by the top political advisers of

POTUS. He managed to say, "The pilot of the F-22 Raptor was probably temporarily insane when she shot down her wingman and later bombed our naval base in San Diego. We are checking her medical history–"

The tall reporter from Fox News jumped up and blurted out, "How did the air force allow a person who was obviously a radicalized Muslim to control a fully armed jet-fighter? Who missed the signs there was a traitor in our midst?"

The press secretary tried to answer, but then a reporter from Breitbart network shouted, "How many more Muslim traitors are there in the military? How many in the State Department? How many in the government?"

Senator McCorey watched the press conference on the large screen TV in his office. He picked up his glass of bourbon, closed his eyes, and imagined he was back in the 1950s playing the role of his idol, Senator Joseph McCarthy. He knew he would now be invited as the guest of honor to talk shows, and not just on TV networks that were notorious xenophobes, but on the more respectable networks. He had already asked his own secretary to draft an article for the New York Times, in the senator's name, of course, and repeatedly remind the readers of this "left-wing, liberal" publication that he had been the first to warn the nation about the dangers the Muslims posed to the American way-of-life.

The press conference continued. "The President of the United States condemns these acts of terror and mourns the deaths of service men and women and innocent civilians. He has issued a directive that all Muslims and people of Muslim descent who are presently in government service, or in the military, be vetted. This is not a racist decree, but measures taken for the safety and security of the public."

Senator McCorey laughed to himself, raised his glass in a toast to POTUS, and mumbled, "Let's rebuild for the Muslims the internment camps we built for the citizens of Japanese descent during World War II."

***

Mossad Headquarters, Tel Aviv

David Avivi followed the news from the United States and kept shaking his head in frustration. He saw the TV clip released by NEMESIS and had no doubt the very same perpetrator, Le Docteur, whom he had followed across Europe a few years earlier, was back in business. He called his close team of operators for a meeting.

He took his place at the head of the table in the Mossad director's conference room and waited for the select team to show up.

Edna Rieger was the first to enter. She had long passed the compulsory retirement age and served as a special consultant. He appreciated her comprehensive knowledge of every terrorist attack that occurred since the assassination of Tsar Alexander II in Saint Petersburg in eighteen eighty-one and regarded her as a living database. She could see connections and associations between events that no computer relying on artificial intelligence could.

The human chameleon entered the room a step behind

her. The man was so nondescript that one could look straight at him and forget him a moment later. He went by several names—Joe or Joey, Joseph or Iosef, Yusuf or Youssef, Sepp, Jojo, Josephus, Jose, and even as Osip.

Next to come was a petite woman, Miriam, who was better known by her nickname of Mata due to her resemblance to the legendary spy Mata Hari.

Last to join them was the Fish, the cool and efficient representative of the Israeli Security Agency, ISA, who knew more than anyone about the radical Islamic movements in Israel and their ties to international terror organizations.

When everyone was seated, David knocked on the connecting door of Haim Shimony, the head of Mossad and David's long-time mentor. Haim entered and personally greeted each member of the small group of operators. Introductions were not necessary, so he got right to the point. "Ladies and gentlemen, I am sure you have all heard about the recent terrorist attacks on our closest ally and friend. David here strongly believes the organizer, and perhaps the perpetrator, is the same man you all chased in London and Paris. You know how smart, daring, and elusive he is. Based on our previous experience and involvement with the man, the Americans have asked for our help. Your task is to find the man and his partners and stop them before they spread havoc in the United States as they have done in Europe."

He paused as he looked around the table. "David will oversee the operation and be responsible for coordinating everything with the Americans. Due to the confusion and blame game played by the different federal authorities in the U.S., David will work closely with his long-time colleague and associate, Dr. Eugene Powers. Eugene, as you know, is a senior member of the National Nuclear Security Administration. The NNSA has not been involved with the theft of the F-22 Raptor and the attack on the naval base, but based on Le Docteur's history in London, we have reason to suspect that nuclear material will be involved sooner or later. The American president himself asked our prime minister for help, and he sanctioned our presence despite any interdepartmental rivalry in the U.S." Haim left the room.

David said, "Any ideas or suggestions?"

Edna spoke up, "The attack with radioactive substances on the Capitol building a few months ago also has Le Docteur's fingerprints all over it. I wonder if he lay dormant between that attack and some other acts of terror that seem to have their focal point in New Mexico. I propose that part of our team start the search over there."

David thought about it for a moment and agreed. "We'll fly out to New York tomorrow with the El Al midnight flight. We'll arrive at JFK airport at the crack of dawn, local time. Edna and Joe will catch a flight to Albuquerque and try to follow the footsteps of Le Docteur. The Fish will fly to San Diego and try to find out what he can on the aerial raid on the base. I'll go with Mata to Washington to meet with Eugene Powers and receive an update, and then we'll decide where to continue the search. Go and pack and we'll meet at the check-in desk."

CHAPTER 11

Embassy of the Democratic People's Republic of Korea, Mexico City

Le Docteur stood on the street corner in one of Mexico City's nicer neighborhoods, just outside the embassy of the Democratic People's Republic of Korea (DPRK, for short) and studied the building.

The building looked well kept, with its clean white and brownish-yellow exterior, the arched deck, and decorative windows. There was a small sign above the door stating it was the embassy of the DPRK and a flagpole with the national emblem could be seen on the roof.

He had found the address—Calle Hally No. 12, Colonia Anzures, Delegacion Miguel Hidalgo, on the web, and knew it was one of the few embassies the country possessed. Not many people applied for visas to travel to the DPRK, and only a handful of those received permission to visit. People who have been there testified in public it was a fascinating place and worth a visit, but in private complained they were constantly watched and strictly forbidden to speak to the local people.

One cynical tourist said it reminded him of a tour of

Universal Studios—you were shown the polished façade but had no idea what lay behind it.

Le Docteur remembered the fate of the young American who removed a poster from the wall in his hotel, supposedly to take it back home as a souvenir of his visit. He was arrested, punished severely, forced to confess to crimes against the DPRK, and only after intensive diplomatic efforts, official and unofficial, was freed to return home. Alas, by then his physical condition was so bad he died shortly after arrival in the U.S., despite the medical treatment he received.

Le Docteur was glad he didn't intend to travel to North Korea, only planned to meet with representatives on relatively safe ground in Mexico.

Gingerly, he walked up to the solid-looking dark door and knocked on it. He didn't have to look around to know his every move was recorded on a surveillance camera, so he kept a straight face with a small smile. He had altered his appearance in such a way that even his Lara wouldn't have recognized him. In fact, she was anxiously waiting for him at a nearby café to which he intended to bring his North Korean contact.

The door opened and a rotund man, who was obviously Korean (Le Docteur couldn't distinguish between men from South Korea and the DPRK), with a solemn expression, asked, "Are you Don Alberto?" The name Le Docteur used when he called the previous day. When he nodded, the Korean added, "I am the Cultural attaché of the DPRK in Mexico. Would you like to come in to discuss the business you alluded to?"

Entering the embassy was the last thing Le Docteur

wanted. He looked over his shoulder to be certain no one was behind him, and said, "If you don't mind, I prefer to go to a public place. I have had some unpleasant experiences entering heavily guarded buildings in the past."

The shadow of a smile crossed the Korean's face, and he nodded. He stepped on to the sidewalk and shut the door behind him.

The two men strolled down Calle Hally, crossed a wide avenue and took Calle Eucken toward the busy district on General Mariano Escobedo Avenue. Le Docteur led the way as if he was a native of Mexico City, although he had familiarized himself with the area around the embassy only a couple hours before the meeting. He led the way to a small café.

The Korean diplomat, who was obviously an operative of the MSS counter-intelligence agency, spoke little Spanish, but his English was very good. After all, he had been trained at an 'American' village and school, run by the Ministry of State Security, the much feared and hated MSS, on North Korean soil.

The choice of the meeting place put Le Docteur in the role of host. He said, "How would you like me to address you? Calling you Mister Cultural Attaché is a bit cumbersome, isn't it?"

He was glad to see the Korean had a sense of humor. He answered, "Call me Kim—you probably know that almost one quarter of the people in the DPRK, and south of the border, are called Kim. So, this will do until we get to know each other better. I'll call you Don Alberto for the time being. I see you are perspiring a little under your wig—don't worry, I think I know who you are, and honored to meet the man who was, and perhaps still is, a thorn in the side of the enemies of the DPRK. *Our enemy's enemy is our friend*, as Kim Il-Sung used to say."

Le Docteur was quite sure the founder of the DPRK was not the first to use this truism but refrained from commenting. Overall, he found 'Kim' to be intelligent and with a quick mind, so he cut to the chase. "Kim, I have something your country can use as an ace-in-the-hole against your dire enemies." He saw that Kim was unfamiliar with the expression, so changed the wording. "I can give your country a weapon system that will put your air force in a superior position against your enemies from the south, on par with the United States and the envy of your Chinese neighbors."

Kim was skeptical. "I'll be glad to learn more about it. But please tell me what you want in return?"

Le Docteur didn't hesitate, he had been prepared for the question. "Something that would give your enemies and mine a taste of hell."

The two men continued the negotiations like two swordsmen probing each other's defenses and seeking weak spots, or, taking an example from the animal kingdom, like two porcupines getting ready to make love. Finally, the Korean was given to understand that his country could receive a slightly damaged F-22 Raptor jetfighter in return for a small, primitive, atom bomb. The exchange would take place in Mexico, far away from the more populated areas that are closely controlled by the central government.

Kim rose from the table, smiled, and shook hands with Le

Docteur. "Please call me in three days' time. I need to clear the proposed deal with my government."

Both men knew the final decision would be given by none other than the young, brash leader of the DPRK. Kim added, "I think you wouldn't want me to call you, or even know how to reach you. So, call me."

As soon as he left, Lara, who had been watching the exchange from a safe distance, approached Le Docteur's table. She knew him well enough to realize all had gone well and according to plan.

***

Ensenada, Baja California, Mexico

They returned to their little house in Ensenada and passed the time like all the other tourists in the area—enjoying the beach, the food and the drinks—and getting to know each other better. After three days, Le Docteur used one of the burner-phones he had purchased to call Kim at the embassy in Mexico City. Kim was delighted to hear his voice and treated him like an old friend. "Don Alberto, I am glad to tell you that our revered leader has approved the deal and would like to proceed. He is sending one of his uncles—a man who has his trust—to finalize the details. Where and when would you like to meet with him?"

Le Docteur was thrilled by the warm response. "I suggest we meet in the same café where we met last time. Frankly, I feel safer in a public place than at your embassy, as I told you last time. Would he be available for the meeting in two days from now?"

Kim answered, "He is already on his way. Would four pm, the day after tomorrow, be convenient for you?"

Le Docteur looked at Lara and smiled. "Yes, that is fine."

The couple made some preparations that would strengthen their negotiation point. Lara had some photographs in which she was seen seated in the cockpit of her F-22. They made copies of the photos and deleted any signs that would identify her—her face was covered with pixels as was the tail-number of her plane, and, most importantly, the tag on her flight-suit with her name was scratched out of the photos.

Le Docteur was quite sure the North Korean intelligence service knew about the missing plane and pilot, and probably were aware of the pilot's identity. After all, the U.S. authorities had been searching for the plane and the pilot and even published her photo in the media, requesting assistance from the public.

They hoped that the changes in Lara's appearance would disguise her. Her long, brown hair and dark black eyes were replaced by a short haircut, dyed to dark red, and she wore blue contact lenses. She also tried to dress in a way that seemed to add twenty pounds to her lithe body.

Le Docteur still thought she was the most attractive woman he had ever seen and told her so. She shrugged at the compliment and said she felt like an ugly, fat woman. Le Docteur, who knew quite a lot about women, from personal experience one might say, thought that as usual, almost no woman he had ever met was pleased with the way she looked.

***

Café near the Embassy of the DPRK, Mexico City

The two North Korean men who entered the café attracted the attention of the regular patrons. They were used to seeing people with round faces and slightly slanted eyes—many of the descendants of the ancient Mexicans had similar physical features—but the Koreans were evidently different. They wore solemn expressions, rarely smiled, and always seemed to be looking behind their backs as if they were followed by enemies.

This was uncalled for in Mexico, which was one of the few places in which North Koreans were welcome. The main reason for this, was the animosity many Mexicans had to the Gringos from the north, something that was shared by the people of the DPRK.

Two Korean bodyguards sat at a table near the café's kitchen to keep a close watch on the back door, and two others remained seated in a car with tinted windows illegally parked on the sidewalk outside the café. All four bodyguards were wearing poorly tailored light jackets, despite the heat and humidity, that badly failed to conceal the weapons they wore.

Le Docteur arrived a few minutes late at the café. This was intentional and intended as a sign he was not desperate to make the deal with the Koreans. He immediately noticed the bodyguards but ignored them as he made his way to the table where Kim and an older Korean man were seated, drinking beer directly from the bottle.

Kim rose from his chair to shake hands and to greet Le Docteur. “This is Uncle Chong. He is a very important man in our country.”

Le Docteur bowed. “It is an honor to meet with one of the most influential and wise people. I have heard a lot about you and your distinguished nephew.”

The infamous nephew’s name was not said aloud in foreign public places, or for that matter, neither in the Democratic People’s Republic of Korea.

Chong smiled. “The honor is mine. Your reputation precedes you. You are something of a legend, and something of a hero, in our country. The strikes that you orchestrated against the enemies of our country are taught in our schools.”

After Kim’s initial report of the meeting with Le Docteur, Korea’s MSS had gathered intelligence about the mysterious ‘Don Alberto’ and knew who they were dealing with.

Le Docteur was taken aback by Chong’s response. He had been hoping he would be able to maintain his anonymity while dealing with Kim and the representatives of the DPRK in Mexico. He managed to say, “I am flattered, but you probably have the wrong man.” He stopped denying when he saw the smiles on the faces of Chong and Kim, and added, “Well, these were exaggerations of the press. I have done a little to promote my cause. I am sure you understand that we have common interests, common enemies, and a common urge to show them we will not lie down quietly while they trample all over us.”

He was encouraged by the reaction of the two Koreans.

"What I have in mind will dwarf everything we had done previously."

Chong nodded. "Don Alberto, I have heard the general outline of the proposal you made. I like it, our leader likes it, and we'd like to discuss the matter a little further and work out the details, before we go ahead. What, exactly, are you offering to give us?"

Le Docteur smiled. "As I told Mr. Kim, I have an F-22 Raptor, only slightly damaged, I am willing to trade for something you have. Possession of the plane will enable you to do some reverse engineering and learn about the secret materials the Americans use to obtain the stealth capability. This will allow you to make all your planes practically invisible to the radar facilities operated by your dire enemies in South Korea. You will also have access to the software that controls the plane's weapon systems and defensive capabilities as well as its flight and outstanding maneuverability."

Le Docteur sat back and crossed his arms. "This will give you an option to surprise their air force in all their bases and destroy their planes on the ground. This will help you understand what you may be up against if an open conflict begins. If you master the technology, you can counteract it. And, last but certainly not least, just imagine the great propaganda achievement—the intelligence service of the small DPRK has outsmarted and outmaneuvered the great CIA, DHS, FBI, U.S. military, and its president! There are other financial benefits—you can sell the technology to the rich Iranians, donate it to the poor Pakistanis, and, of course, win the favor and eternal gratitude of your Chinese allies."

Chong and Kim were markedly impressed. "What do mean, when you say that the plane is slightly damaged? Is it airworthy and capable of flying? Or is it a collection of parts that are fit only for the junkyard?"

Le Docteur hesitated before answering, " I cannot guarantee that it is airworthy, although it may be possible to get it to fly again. That depends on the skills of your scientists, engineers, and technicians. It is certainly more than a collection of junkyard-worthy parts."

Chong looked worried. "So, Don Alberto, you want to sell us, for a formidable price, I may add, a cat in the bag? We would have to check the merchandize before we can set the price. When can we carry out a close examination of the plane?"

Le Docteur knew that this was the moment of truth. "I can allow one of your experts to examine the merchandize. I emphasize that I mean 'one'—a single representative to accompany me to the site where it is at present. You may pick your man, but I must caution you it must be someone with expertise in avionics as well as being physically fit."

He saw the curious expression on the Koreans' faces, so continued, "You must understand the plane is well hidden in a place that is not easily accessible." He added, as an afterthought, "Your man will not be allowed to communicate freely with you, after the inspection. He will only be allowed to send you a short message with the results of his inspection, phrased in a language that I understand, not in Korean. After that, I will have to keep him in isolation until the deal is sealed. If there is no deal, then the man will never be heard from again…"

Chong nodded his agreement. He would have done things the same way, had their roles been reversed. "What do you want in return?"

Le Docteur repeated his demands. "I want a small nuclear device, based on highly enriched uranium. I don't know if you have developed 'suitcase' size atomic munitions, that would be my first choice, of course. But I would settle for a device that can be packed in a box, half the size of a standard shipping container. The device must be well shielded so it cannot easily be detected by standard radiation monitoring systems."

Chong shrugged. "Possible. What explosive yield do you want? We can give you something like the bomb the hateful Americans dropped on our even more detestable Japanese enemies. Is that big enough?"

Le Docteur said, "Perfect for my purposes." He saw the expectant stares of the Koreans. "I won't specify the target—just think of any big city in the United States as a possible target."

Kim spoke up, "Where do you want the device delivered?"

Le Docteur laughed. "Preferably at 1600 Pennsylvania Avenue, Washington, DC." He saw the uncomprehending look on Chong's face. "This is the address of the White House."

In a serious tone he added, "I would like it delivered anywhere in the United States, of course, from where I can easily transport it to my target. But I understand this would be unacceptable to you, because of logistic difficulties and because it would tie the DPRK directly to the attempt to use atomic weapons on U.S. soil."

The gentlemen at the table nodded, understanding and appreciation evident in their faces. Le Docteur stated, "No, I'll make life easier for you. Anywhere in the Western hemisphere is fine. I'll take possession and make sure it is transported safely to its destination."

He smiled to himself when he thought how closely the words 'destination' and 'destiny' were related in this case.

Chong said, "These are reasonable and acceptable terms. All we need now is to examine the merchandize. Kim will be in touch with you to arrange the inspection. We'll need another week to make the arrangements, so call Kim in seven days' time. It was a pleasure meeting you—the most wanted man in the world."

***

Puerto Penasco, Gulf of California

Lara and Le Docteur returned from Ensenada to Puerto Penasco, on the eastern shore of the Gulf of California. During the long drive, Lara commented that the American imperialism was evident in the name of Baja California, that was a peninsula fully located in Mexico as was the Gulf of California, that separates the peninsula from mainland Mexico.

Le Docteur smiled and replied that the name of California itself was also 'stolen' from the Spanish occupiers of Mexico. He then added, "Do you know that one of the versions for the origin of the name 'California' stems from Queen Calafia, who fought alongside the Muslims against the Spanish. It implies that California was part of the Caliphate, meaning that it is ours to claim."

Lara laughed and said, "I wonder what would happen if Muslims demanded that it be returned to the Ummah," referring to the Nation of Islam, "and require all infidels to have visas and permission to reside in California."

Le Docteur answered, "This would be the counterclaim to Senator McCorey's cry for legislation to send all Muslims to internment camps. Perhaps there should be two types of internment camps—one for Muslims and one for non-Muslims. The Native Americans could then reclaim the land of their ancestors."

They both fell silent, contemplating the ironies of history.

After driving for close to seven hours, mostly on rickety highways, they were glad to check in to the small hotel they had stayed in previously. The representative of the DPRK, Chun-hee Choi, was due to land at the small airfield later in the evening, and a room had been reserved in the same hotel.

Le Docteur drove out to the airfield to greet the man from the DPRK and waited at the arrivals gate, searching for a Korean man. He was surprised when a lithe woman, obviously Korean, approached him and in British English said, "Don Alberto, I am so glad to meet you."

Le Docteur recovered from his momentary shock. "I thought Chun-hee Choi was an expert in avionics, and naturally expected a man." He took another good look at the woman, and added, "I am very happy I was so totally wrong. I hope you are not offended."

She stared at him, gave him the up-and-down thorough scan that he had given her, and said, “No offense taken. I am sure we’ll get along wonderfully. Let’s get my luggage and go to the hotel. I am looking forward to meeting your colleague.”

He said, “Please call me Jacque—that’s the name everyone here uses. Don Alberto is for my formal friends, like Mr. Kim and Mr. Chong. I am sure we won’t be formal with each other. Lara will surely be as surprised to see you, as I was.”

Chun-hee picked up her bag and they headed for the hotel.

CHAPTER 12

Washington, DC

Dr. Eugene Powers didn't want to meet David Avivi and Mata at his office in the NNSA headquarters in the Forrestal Building, that was the home of the Department of Energy.

He, correctly, thought that an official meeting in full view of his colleagues, would raise eyebrows and awkward questions. He did have Presidential authority to consult with the Israeli Mossad agents, but doing it on federal property would be like sticking a finger in the eye of the U.S. intelligence agencies. So, he walked down Independence Avenue and entered the cafeteria of the Air and Space Museum, that he knew was one of David's favorite sites in Washington. He saw that David and Mata were already having coffee and busy studying the brochure of the museum. He got his own coffee and joined them at the table.

David and Eugene greeted each other like old friends, and Mata was introduced. Eugene eyed the attractive woman he had heard so much about, and couldn't get over the apparent discrepancy between her petite stature and the legendary operations she had been involved in. He said, "It is a great honor to meet the woman David has praised so much."

She blushed, knowing that her reputation was not a great asset in her line of work.

David broke the growing awkwardness and said, “We need to get down to business. Eugene, have your people traced Le Docteur and your renegade pilot?”

Eugene coughed to cover his reaction to Mata’s presence, looked at David and said, “We have reassigned some of our satellites to cover the area between the Holloman Air Force Base in New Mexico and San Diego, and to survey a wide strip of three hundred miles on each side of the line connecting these two points. The National Reconnaissance Office (NRO) and the National Geospatial-Intelligence Agency (NGA) that is responsible for providing world-class geospatial intelligence, are directing their efforts to finding the missing plane. We have also sent unmanned drones to take multispectral photographs of the same area, and to search for any anomalies. In addition, our intelligence agencies have called in their assets on both sides of the Mexico-U.S. border and promised an award of five million dollars to whoever will supply information on the whereabouts of the two perpetrators and the missing plane. This is a very large area to cover, and a large part of it in sparsely inhabited.”

David said, “We have analyzed the situation and viewed the data we had, and we believe that we can narrow the search area. Our analysts have drawn two circles: one with its center at Holloman AFB and the other with its center at San Diego. The radius of each corresponds to the range of the F-22, considering it had used up most of its fuel during the training exercise and after it. We also assumed, and I admit this is speculative, they would stay away from U.S. territory. If you take a good look at the map." He switched his Tablet to Google Earth. "Focus on north-western Mexico, you can find a number of airfields suitable for operating a Raptor. Remember, the plane must have landed on the day of the exercise, and then taken off a couple days later to carry out the raid on the naval base. We have no idea if it returned to the same airfield after the raid or not."

Eugene intervened, "The area is full of small airstrips used by drug gangs and by smugglers. Most of them are not even marked on any map."

David nodded. "Sure, but the jet had to land without suffering any damage and then had to take off again. I think that a clandestine airstrip wouldn't fit the operational requirements. I believe they must have used an official or semi-official airfield, and there are not too many of these in the limited search area."

Mata added, "We don't think the plane returned to the same airfield after the raid on San Diego."

Eugene rose from the table. "Thanks for your input. If you are correct, then the job of searching those airfields is for the CIA on the ground and for the National Reconnaissance Office from above. I have Presidential authority to make sure these two agencies cooperate, and I am sure they will. However, if we locate the airfield, each would claim success, and if we don't each will blame the other. I hate office-politics. Please, call me tomorrow and, meanwhile, enjoy the museum."

***

David looked at Mata. "He is really one of the good guys. We have helped each other before, and I am sure he'll do his best. Let's wander around the museum. Perhaps we'll get some useful ideas from seeing the exhibits. After all, we are trying to find a plane."

Mata smiled. She saw that David was as excited as a child with the prospect of walking around the museum. Personally, she couldn't care less about planes, aviation, rockets, or spacecraft, but decided to humor her boss and tag along.

They wandered around the exhibition. David had seen the full-size planes and models that represented the early stages of aviation several times previously and was not interested in the rockets and spacecraft. Instead, he went to see to the World War II exhibits.

Mata noticed that he looked around as if missing something, and then he asked one of the members of the museum staff where the *Enola Gay* exhibit was. The elderly woman, who was a volunteer at the museum, gave David a long look, and reluctantly said it was now at the Udvar-Hazy Center, an annex of the National Air and Space Museum and is at Washington Dulles International Airport.

David told Mata he had read about the controversy involving the B-29 Super-fortress bomber that dropped the atom bomb on Hiroshima on August 6, 1945. Apparently, there was a public outcry to remove it from the Smithsonian because of the controversy regarding the way it was displayed.

Veterans didn't like the photos of the Japanese victims of

the atomic bomb and wanted to emphasize the surrender of Japan that ended the war, in the aftermath of the bombing, saved numerous American and Japanese lives. Opponents splashed red paint over the gallery's carpeting and others even threw ash and human blood on the fuselage. Eventually, the plane was fully restored and presented to the Udvar-Hazy Center.

Mata asked, "David, do you think atom bombs will be used again?"

He looked at her. "You know that terrorist organizations have been trying to get their hands on improvised nuclear devices and detonate them in the center of Western cities. Just a few years ago, NEMESIS and Le Docteur, almost succeeded in doing this in London. I would be surprised if he had given up his hope of carrying out such an attack. Fortunately for us, the F-22 that Lara stole didn't carry any nuclear weapons. Or else, San Diego would have probably been in nuclear ashes by now. Mata, I wonder if he isn't after something like this right now. I want to call Eugene and share our fears. Let's go."

***

The next day they met with Eugene. He informed them that the CIA and NRO had gone all-out to search all airfields in north-western Mexico from which an F-22 could land and take off. The NRO has spotted close to a dozen possible places and the CIA asked permission of the Mexican authorities to visit them and check recent activities.

The Mexicans were not happy with the request, saying

it interfered with tourism and caused undue alarm, so the U.S. had to promise to compensate the government. Eugene said that he was sure the compensation would end up in the pockets of the government officials involved, and none of it would reach the areas affected.

David said, "I am impressed by the actions taken by your government. Yesterday, at the museum, we wondered whether Le Docteur had devised a plan to get his hands on a nuke and, now that he has a qualified fighter-pilot with him, and perhaps even a plane, he might wish to deliver it by air."

Eugene was taken aback. "What are you saying, David? How can he get a nuke? And I doubt whether the missing plane is anywhere on the face of the earth. Are you imagining the unimaginable?"

David shrugged. "Yes, this is exactly what I am suggesting. Let's assume that he can find a buyer for the F-22. Not just someone who is willing to pay money for it, but someone who is willing to barter. In view of Le Docteur's history, he would be willing to beg, borrow, or steal a nuke, and use it. Who, do you think, would be willing and able to make such an exchange?"

Eugene's reply came rapidly, "Willing—there is a long list of countries, organizations, and individuals willing to explode a nuke right here in Washington, or elsewhere in the United States. Able—that is a much more limited group. There are, supposedly, only nine countries that have nukes. Of those, some are allies of the U.S., or at least not dire enemies. That leaves China, Russia, North Korea, and perhaps Iran, if it has obtained a nuclear device, which I doubt. If any of these countries want to use NEMESIS as their agents to deliver a nuke to the U.S., then they are playing a very dangerous game, and I doubt if they would take such a risk. On second thought, the rash, irresponsible leader of DPRK might think he can get away with such a plan. David, if you are right, then we are facing a nuclear war, because the United States of America would retaliate with all its might if a nuclear attack occurs on its soil or citizens. I need to go to the top with this. Thanks for the input, but I pray you are wrong."

"Eugene, we'll be in town for another couple days. Let me know what the NRO and CIA discover. I also suggest you call on all your assets in North Korea and try to find out what's going on there. Anything that looks out of the ordinary—a heightened state of alert, special actions regarding the known nuclear facilities, scientists and engineers travelling abroad. Everything. Then call us. Good luck."

Mata waited for the American to leave. "David, I don't like the idea of sitting here in Washington, doing nothing. Perhaps we should go to Mexico and sniff around. I think if the rest of our team has not found any leads, then they should join us."

David nodded. "Let's get the reports from our guys and decide what to do next."

***

Edna and Joe were sent to Albuquerque to try and discover everything they could about Le Docteur. Edna met with the FBI agents who had already done some groundwork and heard from them that he was a faculty member at the University of

New Mexico and was well liked by his colleagues and by his students.

He used the name Jacque Deleau and claimed to be a French-Canadian and that explained the slightly French accent he had. One of the FBI agents alluded to the fact that many of his female students had a crush on him and mentioned he probably had been involved in a relationship with a student whose name was Blossom Bearskin.

Edna asked the agents whether they had searched his room and were told that nothing of interest was found there.

Joe spent his time interviewing some of the faculty members who had worked with Le Docteur, or Jacque as they called him. They said he was friendly and cooperative but kept his distance from them, and they had no social interactions with him. They said that as they knew he was a visiting professor for a semester they weren't bothered by his remoteness.

One of the scientists from the chemistry department mentioned in passing the last social affair that Jacque attended was the retirement party for a faculty member held at the National Museum of Nuclear Science and History. Joe remembered that one of the historical exhibits was destroyed and that caused quite a big scandal; made the international media.

When he checked the dates, he saw that the museum was vandalized during the night after the party. His sensitive antennae immediately suspected a connection between Le Docteur and the incident. Motive, opportunity, and means were all there: Le Docteur would enjoy destroying a historic exhibit connected to one of America's greatest technological achievements. He was at the site of the attack, at the right time, and the means to destroy were on hand. Furthermore, the motto inscribed on the wall was a classic 'red herring'—so suitable for the *modus operandi* of the sophisticated man.

He met with Edna and told her about his suspicions. She agreed that Le Docteur was the prominent suspect. Edna told him about Blossom and suggested they try to find and question her about her relationship with Le Docteur. However, when they turned up at her apartment, they were told by the neighbors she was gone and left no forwarding address.

Edna suggested they find her parents and interview them but would have to wait until they returned from work in the evening.

They called David and updated him. When David heard about the events at the museum and Joe's suspicions, he agreed it must be Le Docteur's doing. He wondered why NEMESIS didn't claim responsibility or this act but figured Le Docteur didn't want to draw attention to his presence in Albuquerque.

Edna then said there may be a tie between Le Docteur and the attack on the powwow in Gallup. She said New Mexico seemed to be the new hub of NEMESIS—the nuclear science museum, the powwow, and the F-22 at Holloman AFB.

David thought these events couldn't be a coincidence and Le Docteur's presence in the area was not accidental.

At the end of the conversation he shared his own thoughts about Mexico being the new center of operations for NEMESIS and the possible involvement of North Korea. He instructed them to meet him in Mexico City and try to pick up Le Docteur's tracks over there.

***

Next, he called the Fish in San Diego. The Fish had nothing to report. He had visited the naval base and saw the damage inflicted by the air raid. He was a bit surprised there was no trace of the plane—not where it came from and neither where it flew to after the attack.

He was disappointed they couldn't even give him the general direction, because it had evaded the radar systems. When he asked if they could tell what vector the plane used to carry out the attack, he got conflicting answers. One of the witnesses said it came from the south, while another swore that it came from the ocean in the west.

David heard all this and was convinced the Fish was wasting his time, so he instructed him to fly to Mexico City, and meet with the rest of the team.

CHAPTER 13

Puerto Penasco, Mexico

Lara and Chun-hee eyed each other, and Le Docteur got the impression they were like two lionesses getting ready to fight over the privilege of spending time with the alpha-male lion.

During the short drive from the airfield to the hotel he managed to overcome his surprise the North Korean intelligence service had sent a female agent. Perhaps his reputation preceded him, and they knew he would find good-looking women as irresistible as they find him.

Chun-hee cautiously stretched out her hand and offered to shake Lara's hand. Lara automatically took Chu-hee's hand and shook it firmly. After all she had been raised in the American Mid-west where good manners were ingrained in the minds of young, sociable girls.

Chun-hee said, "So you are the famous pilot, and I understand the one and only woman fully certified to fly the top-secret F-22. You know in the Democratic People's Republic of Korea there are many female pilots. I am accredited to fly the most advanced jets of the DPRK, as well as being an accomplished diver and deep-sea salvage expert."

Lara and Le Docteur were impressed by her credentials, although they had no way to verify her claims. Le Docteur knew it wouldn't take long until they found out if she was just boasting to impress them or if she truly was this kind of 'superwoman.'

He said, "Chun-hee you are probably very hungry and tired after your long flight. Let's go out and eat, and tomorrow we'll get down to business. I'll give you a few minutes to freshen up and we'll meet you in the hotel's lobby."

The Korean nodded and said she would be down in five minutes.

Lara and Le Docteur slowly made their way to the lobby. They were speaking in hushed tones to avoid being overheard. Lara said, "Jacque, I don't like her. I think she is a phony, sent only to discover where the plane is. I doubt if she is a pilot, a diver, and marine salvage expert. I don't doubt she will try to seduce you—she is fully equipped to do so. Be careful, and never, I repeat, never find yourself alone with her. I know how your mind works and you are confident that you can out-manipulate her, but I have heard the DPRK has highly trained female agents for this sort of a job."

Le Docteur was taken aback by her outburst. His initial impression of two lionesses was reinforced. "Lara, is this jealousy speaking or is this an objective assessment of Chun-hee? You should adopt an analytical approach. We need the DPRK and they need us, so at present it is in the interest of both sides to play level and honest. I am aware of the stories about honey-traps set by beautiful, enticing, sexy Korean agents, and can assure you I am immune."

Lara thought that every man, or woman for that matter, who was the victim of a honey-trap maneuver was just as confident they were immune. This is the main reason honey-traps worked so well. She answered, "Here she comes. Let's go out and see how things develop."

***

Chun-hee looked at the assortment of Mexican dishes. She eyed the yellow rice with suspicion, the burritos and tacos with obvious dislike, the *caldo de queso* soup curiously, and the pork chorizo sausages with a disgusted look on her face. Finally, after hearing the explanation of the dishes she settled on a guacamole dip and *arroz con pollo* (rice with chicken).

Le Docteur and Lara ordered the same to avoid embarrassing the Korean. Chun-hee looked with amazement when Lara took a tortilla chip and dipped it in the guacamole paste and put the whole thing in her mouth. She glanced at Lara's reaction to the green stuff that she thought was like the extremely spicy green dip used in Korea (something like the Japanese Wasabi) and when there was no reaction, she emulated Lara's action. This was the first time that she had tasted an avocado—something nonexistent in Korea—and she nodded approvingly. The rice with chicken offered no surprises to the Korean woman, except the flavoring was not familiar and the size of the dish was about three times larger than she had in Korea, although it was about half the size of the same dish in Texas.

Le Docteur had ordered a pitcher of local beer, and when

that was consumed, the thirsty trio ordered another one, that disappeared just as quickly as the first. By the time they were ready for dessert, the three of them were behaving like old friends, laughing and telling tall stories.

Chun-hee tasted the flan and made such a funny face of disgust that sent Lara and Jacque in hysterical laughter. When they were done, the proprietor offered them all a shot of tequila. Le Docteur couldn't resist telling Chun-hee about the worm that was traditionally, according to the urban legend, placed in the tequila bottle as proof of its authenticity.

Chun-hee challenged him and he had to admit that it was a myth created for marketing purposes. Lara added that she had seen plastic worms in tequila bottles, but said it was always in bottles that had already been opened.

Le Docteur saw that the tequila went down well with both women and purchased a bottle. When the sealed bottle arrived at their table, the trio ogled it like three morons trying to see if there was a worm at the bottom. They walked unsteadily back to the hotel.

Chun-hee said that she wanted to have another taste of the tequila and refused to leave them when they tried to retire to their room. She insisted on sharing the bottle, saying it was a Korean custom to finish dinner with a stiff drink.

Le Docteur and Lara were sure she was making this up, but were slightly intoxicated, so after exchanging a glance with each other, opened the door and invited her into the room.

Le Docteur sat on the armchair and the two women sat on the bed—each holding a shot-glass filled with tequila. When the bottle was drained dry, Le Docteur pulled another bottle from the minibar. This too disappeared in no time.

Lara was exhausted and very drunk from all the alcohol she had consumed. She lay down on the bed, staring at the overhead fan that rotated slowly and moved the air around, creating an illusion of a breeze.

Le Docteur watched with glazed eyes when Chun-hee lay next to Lara and gently placed her hand on Lara's shoulder. Lara turned her head and smiled at her, then moved Chun-hee's left hand toward her breast and slowly moved it to caress her erect nipple.

Le Docteur had no idea that Lara was interested in women—he was even slightly offended she allowed a stranger to touch her in such an intimate fashion. Chun-hee moved closer to Lara, to make room and patted the bed by her side. Le Docteur didn't need another invitation and joined the two women. Chun-hee was now between the two lovers. She stretched her right hand and moved it along Le Docteur's chest, pulling him closer to her.

He turned toward her and started to stroke the Korean woman's face, and then slowly moved down her neck and chest, lightly touching her breasts and then moving further down between her thighs.

Chun-hee moaned softly and continued her exploration of Lara's body until she, too, groaned in a throaty voice. Le Docteur started to undress Chun-hee, but her hand gripped his and stopped it. She pulled him over her body, so he now lay between the two women, and motioned to Lara to start undressing him slowly from her side while she did the same from the other side.

Le Docteur thought he was in heaven. His imagination ran wild. He thought that if two experienced women could drive him crazy with desire then the seventy-two virgins awaiting him in heaven would certainly drive him right out of his mind.

Chun-hee turned out to be exactly what Lara had warned against—a highly trained North Korean female agent, with greatly advanced skills in sexual encounters. This wasn't the classic honey-trap, unless you could embarrass a couple who did a trio together, but it left an unpleasant mental aftertaste (not physical, of course, that was fantastic).

***

The next morning, Le Docteur was the first to wake up. He had to climb over one of the sleeping women to get to the bathroom, but had a hard time deciding over which one. He looked to his left and then to his right—both nude women were a sight for sore eyes—and carefully crept over the curved body of Lara. She felt him stirring, and still half asleep, pulled him toward her, trying to hold him.

Chun-hee also felt that Le Docteur was awake and stretched her hand to stop him from getting up. He managed to wriggle free and made his way to the bathroom. When he returned to the room, after relieving himself and brushing his teeth, he saw that the two women were locked in an embrace. He wasn't sure if it was love, desire, lust, jealousy, or rivalry that brought them together, so he quietly sat on a chair and watched.

Lara was larger and locked the smaller, but well-proportioned, Korean woman in a tight hold, as if trying to strangle her. Chun-hee didn't try to resist, she brought her face close to Lara's and kissed her on the mouth. Lara was so surprised by the move, that she loosened her hold.

The Korean quickly moved and straddled Lara, pinning her to the bed with her body. Lara started laughing and that surprised Chun-hee, who joined in on the laughter. Then the two became aware of Le Docteur ogling them, and without a word both women got up and pulled him to the bed, one of them holding his feet and the other pinning his hands to the bed. They met no resistance but were glad to see that his body reacted to their none too gentle maneuvers. They exchanged a glance, and in an instant left him lying on the bed, and giggling loudly, entered the shower together.

Le Docteur could only imagine what went on in the shower, behind the closed door. He looked down at his body, considered finishing on his own what the two gorgeous women had started, but then decided to wait for their return.

***

After breakfast in a nearby café and several cups of terrible coffee, the trio returned to the hotel room for a serious discussion.

Chun-hee was now all business. "I am here to verify you have the merchandise you alluded to, and to examine its condition. I understand it is submerged somewhere, not too far from the coast, and I need to inspect its condition, as well as assess the necessary means to retrieve it from the seabed."

Le Docteur answered, "You know our terms: we'll have to blindfold you when we take you to the crash site. After you inspect the merchandise, you'll be allowed to send the short-prearranged message, confirming the deal is on. If you think that the goods are damaged, then you'll send the other prearranged message. In both cases, you'll be under 'house arrest' and won't be allowed to leave Puerto Penasco, until we make arrangements with the other buyer we have contacted."

This, of course, was not true. If Chun-hee reported that the deal was off she would have to be eliminated, as she, too, fully understood.

Chun-hee replied, "This was agreed upon with Uncle Chong. Let's go to the site."

Lara was surprised to see this tough-minded Korean woman was showing signs of emotion, even of anxiety. They all knew what was at stake.

Lara said, "We have prepared everything for your inspection. You'll have to abide by our rules, or you'll be putting us all at risk. Please, get your bathing suit and follow us."

They got into Le Docteur's car and he drove to the pier. The speedboat was moored there, but before getting into the boat, they checked the scuba-diving equipment. There was scuba diving gear for the three of them, including three pairs of fully charged compressed air tanks, each with a pressure regulator, a mask, snorkel, and fins. Despite the mild water temperature, they had wet-suits because they wanted to maintain their body temperature during what they expected to be a long dive.

Finally, Le Docteur pointed to a couple additional items, and said, "This is a state-of-the-art underwater camera. It will provide you, and your people, with irrefutable evidence we are offering the real thing. This is a powerful light, that we may need if the water becomes murky. We don't have the fancy stuff like a diving computer or equipment for underwater communications." He took another look at the slim Korean, and added, "Here's a weight belt, although you probably don't need it."

Le Docteur headed away from the pier, and when they were less than a foot from the shore, Lara said it was time to put on the wet-suits.

Chun-hee removed her clothes unashamedly, stretched out, making sure that Le Docteur noticed her pert breasts, before donning the two-piece bathing suit, if one could call the small triangles of cloth with short strings, by that name. Lara and Le Docteur followed suit, and then all three put on the wet-suits.

Lara said, "Chun-hee, I need to blindfold you. You'll be able to remove it once we are under water. We don't want you to get the boat's bearings by marking our position relative to the shore."

The Korean shrugged and allowed Lara to tie the piece of thick cloth and cover her eyes. She was a little intimidated by the feeling of being blind and helpless in the company of these two people, who, she knew, had already killed numerous people.

After sailing for about thirty minutes, the boat stopped. Le Docteur dropped anchor and shut off the outboard motor.

The couple helped Chun-hee strap the compressed air tank to her back, helped her put on the fins, and guided her to the side of the boat.

Le Docteur placed her mask in her left hand and took her by her right hand. He said, "We'll all dive together. You'll be breathing from my air tank using the duo air supply piece until we reach a depth of two feet. Then I'll hand you your mouth-piece and we'll go further down. Lara will remain at that depth and keep an eye on us, while we explore the plane. Do you understand?"

Chun-hee laughed. "I told you that I am an accomplished diver. I can easily go down to five feet without an air tank and stay there for almost two minutes."

"You'll probably want to stay down much longer to inspect the plane. Just remain calm. Follow me and note my signals. Don't rush ahead, unless I give you permission."

They descended quickly to a depth of two feet and Lara removed the blindfold from Chun-hee's eyes. Le Docteur was not really surprised to see she didn't ask for his mouthpiece even once. He pointed at his depth gauge and signaled for her to use her own air supply.

She put the regulator's mouthpiece in her mouth, made the okay sign with her hand, and followed him down.

Once they were down to twenty-five feet, the silhouette of the plane was clearly seen about twenty-five feet further down. Le Docteur noticed that Chun-hee emitted a stream of bubbles when she spotted it. He thought it was a sign she was excited by the sight of a real-life, full-size F/A-22 Raptor. They carefully circled the plane.

Le Docteur was worried it may have become the temporary residence of dangerous denizens of the sea, like sharks, giant octopuses, or deadly rockfish. When he thought the wreck was clear, he signaled to Chun-hee that she could roam the site freely.

Lara wanted to see the results of her handiwork, so she disobeyed her instructions, and joined the other two divers. They all saw that the plane was almost intact. One of the internal wing-bays was open, and the Vulcan rotary-gun could be seen.

The shells were also clearly seen, with their shiny tips. Lara glided to the cockpit and tried to see what happened to the instrument panel after she ejected with her seat. She noted there appeared to be very little damage, except for the gaping space where her seat had once been.

Le Docteur observed Chun-hee's excited behavior, and snapped a few photos of the plane, switching on the diving light to add clarity to the photos.

They ascended to the surface slowly, obeying the decompression routine, to ensure that all dissolved gases were safely released from their fatty tissue. The last station was at two feet from the surface. The stopped. Le Docteur placed the blindfold back on Chun-hee's eyes. With some difficulty, they climbed back on the speedboat.

Lara helped Chun-hee remove the air tank from her back, and suggested she remain in her wet-suit. When they returned to the pier, Chun-hee removed her wet-suit, allowing Lara and Le Docteur to get another look of her body.

She smiled, "Well, I must admit the merchandise you had

advertised is everything you promised. Salvaging it from a depth of fifty feet will not be easy, or cheap, but it can be done with proper equipment. I am ready to send the prearranged signal that all is well."

Le Docteur looked at Lara. "Chun-hee, I hope you are not entertaining any idea of cheating. We both like you very much but won't hesitate to stop you if you try anything."

Chun-hee laughed. "Why should I try anything. I understand that I'll be having a paid vacation here on the shore of the Gulf of California. I can go swimming and diving during the day, have good Mexican food that I am beginning to the enjoy in the evening, have some good drinks later, and enjoyable sex with the two of you at night. I am ready to send the message to Uncle Chong and tell him I like the merchandize. However, you'll have to conclude the second part of the deal with him. I suggest that you take some of the photos with you, when you meet him. They are pretty convincing."

Le Docteur was suspicious that her enthusiastic words were a trap but had no evidence to that effect. He now had to solve another difficult problem: keep Chun-hee under constant guard in Puerto Penasco or elsewhere while negotiating the delivery of the nuclear device with Uncle Chong.

He wondered if he could leave Lara on her own to keep an eye on Chun-hee. Perhaps, he could restrain the Korean woman and keep her locked up in an improvised prison until he completed the deal. The alternative was something he detested doing to the beautiful Korean, especially as it would possibly infuriate her boss. He had to think about it.

Lara knew nothing of what was going on in her lover's

mind. She felt she was not properly appreciated. "Perhaps we should first return the scuba gear and the speedboat, and then have dinner. I am famished after the dive, and I could use a little alcohol to calm my nerves. It was quite pleasing to see the plane glided down to the sea-bed without disintegrating. I think the two of you," she looked at Le Docteur and Chun-hee with a noticeably offended expression, "don't appreciate the excellent flying maneuver I performed. I am sure it should be studied in military flight-schools all over the globe, if it could be published. As far as I know, no pilot has ever landed a jet-fighter so smoothly. I wonder if anyone will make a film about me, like they did for Chesley Sullenberger who landed his Airbus-320 on the Hudson River."

Le Docteur wanted to make amends. "Lara, you did a magnificent piece of flying, and you did that voluntarily at a risk to your own life. You were not forced to do it—that makes it so much more an act of bravery." He hugged her tightly and planted a huge kiss on her lips.

This seemed to appease her somewhat, although she had expected a spontaneous round of applause.

***

By the time they finished their excursion and dive, it was time for dinner. They returned to the same restaurant in which they had dined the previous evening. Chun-hee was now an aficionado of Mexican food and ready to try new things so they ordered an assortment of Mexican dishes that they all shared. A few pitchers of beer followed by chasers of tequila helped settle the mood.

They straggled back to the hotel and Chun-hee sent the prearranged message. Soon after that, Le Docteur called his contact at the Korean embassy. “Kim, I think you are satisfied with the results of the inspection. We now need to proceed with the deal. When can we meet with Uncle Chong?”

Kim was very practical. “Upon receiving the news, he booked a flight. He’ll be ready to meet with you in two days. Same place as before, at noon.”

Le Docteur had come up to a solution for his problem regarding Chun-hee, so he said, “Kim, let’s make it in three days. I need to attend to something first.”

He then spoke to Lara and Chun-hee. “Girls, we leave tomorrow morning for Ensenada. There Chun-hee can do everything she dreamed about—mornings on the beach, good food and booze, and wild, unrestrained sex at night. There is no fear that she’ll go exploring the seabed and search for the plane, because she’ll be hundreds of miles from here. Lara, you’ll make sure she has no cell phone or access to any phone, so her colleagues do not attempt to take her away. In addition, no one will know where to look for us. I’ll fly down to Mexico City and work on the details of the deal. You two, just stay at the beach house and enjoy the fun and games. When I return, I expect to see what you have taught each other.”

Everyone was pleased with the idea.

***

Ensenada, Baja California

During the long drive from Puerto Penasco to Ensenada the mood in the car was subdued. Le Docteur was driving and Lara was seated next to him, while Chun-hee sat in the back seat. There was nothing interesting to see, and the car's radio was useless because there was no decent radio station. None of the people in the car were inclined to chat, so each was adsorbed in their own thoughts.

Le Docteur was considering how to best approach the next stage. He assumed that the Koreans would try to cross him—get their hands on the plane without delivering the nuke—and sought insurance. His main trump card was that the leader of the DPRK would love to see a nuke explode in the heart of Manhattan, or for that matter in any major city of the hated United States, as much as he would.

He expected their assistance in providing the nuclear device, in transporting it to the target, and in setting it off. On the downside was the fact they must be worried they would be blamed for planting the bomb and that the U.S. would retaliate against them—returning North Korea to the stone-age.

He had seen a recent news item that quoted a CIA report on the successful development of miniaturized nuclear warheads by the DPRK. The report allegedly concerned that warheads could be placed on long-range ballistic missiles, and, therefore, could strike at the U.S. mainland.

He wondered if these miniaturized weapons were composed of components that Western intelligence didn't recognize. If that were the case, then even the most advanced nuclear forensics methods would not be able to prove their origin was in North Korea, and the U.S. wouldn't dare retaliate without irrefutable proof. He smiled to himself—yes, this was the solution. The new nuclear device would be small and light, making it easier to smuggle into the United States, and it would not be recognized as belonging to the arsenal of the DPRK.

***

Lara was also deep in thought. So far, she had carried out the most dangerous part of the plot. She had performed a feat that no one had managed to do in all human history—she had stolen one of the most advanced jet-fighters, shot down her wingman, carried out a daring and successful air-raid on one of the most secure American naval bases, and safely ditched the plane in shallow water. She felt that these heroic acts were not properly appreciated by her lover. She was pleased the North Korean woman did seem to respect her. She turned her head and saw that Chun-hee's eyes were closed and she appeared to be asleep.

Lara whispered, "Jacque, I am worried they will capture you and torture you until you reveal the location of the beach-house in Ensenada and then the coordinates of the plane."

He answered, "Lara, I have given the matter considerable thought. We share a common interest—attack the U.S. where it hurts the most, causing casualties that will make 9/11 and all previous attacks like a child's play. In an instant, we'll kill more Americans than in all the years of the Second World War. This will give the oppressed people, especially the Muslims, the signal to rise against the new colonialists, crusaders, communists, and capitalists. In New York we will surely not only kill many Jews, but we'll erode their influence on American politics and the support of Israel by the U.S. True, I recognize the danger of playing ball with the North Korean devil, but am sure there is a method in the madness of their young leader. And this method is to inflict death and pain on the U.S."

Lara looked back and saw that Chun-hee was no longer asleep—her body became rigid and it even looked as if her ears were standing erect.

Lara said, "Chun-hee, what do you think? Will your people honor the deal?"

The Korean woman shrugged. "I think Jacque is right. We do have a common interest and a common enemy. Our leader is not an insane despot, as your popular press tries to present him. He knows that our people's honor has been offended by the Americans, and that the only language the American president and people understand is that of force. The U.S. didn't dare to pick a fight with any country that had nuclear weapons in the past and will not do so in the future. Our leader has seen that the U.S. invaded Iraq twice, fought in Afghanistan for years, undermined the legal regimes in numerous countries in the Western Hemisphere and elsewhere, but refrained from attacking China or the Soviet Union or modern Russia. To answer your question, Lara—yes, the DPRK will honor the deal, as long as you uphold your end of the deal."

***

Deep in her mind, Chun-hee was not at all as confident about this as she appeared to be. She was also concerned about her own fate. She had feared that Jacque would eliminate her after she had sent the message that the plane was in good condition. In fact, she wasn't sure it wouldn't happen at some deserted spot on the way to Ensenada. There was little traffic on the road and every time the car slowed down, she worried that the moment would come. She had some concealed weapons—a pen that could squirt acid, a nail-file that had a sharp blade, and a strip of metal that could be used as a lance in the frame of her handbag. She was also a master of martial arts, but she knew the couple had the advantage. For a short while, she had even considered killing them both but wasn't sure she would be able to locate the submerged plane on her own.

***

Three worried and not very happy people arrived at the beach house near Ensenada. Le Docteur parked the car, and they all got out, stretched their limbs, and entered the house.

Lara showed Chun-hee to her room and the couple unpacked their bags in the master bedroom. Chun-hee looked at the beach and the ocean and said that it looked ideal for a vacation.

Le Docteur didn't waste any time and offered margaritas all around. After the third drink, they called an Uber and headed to a nearby restaurant for dinner. They had a few more drinks with their dinner and walked back the short distance to the beach house.

They sat for a while on the deck, looking at the full moon slowly setting down on the Pacific Ocean. Each deep in thought wondering whether this was an omen of their fate.

A few additional margaritas changed the mood, they started laughing and hugging each other, and very quickly moved to the master bedroom.

CHAPTER 14

Mexico City

Le Docteur looked at the underwater photos of the plane with great satisfaction. This was the proof of the pudding. The most expensive jet-fighter ever produced, with the most advanced technology, the creation of the most ingenious minds in the United States, and he practically owned the one and only specimen that wasn't in one of the few military bases from which this technological wonder could take off.

True, the valuable item was slightly damaged, would never fly again, and would certainly not engage in combat, but its secrets could be exposed, and copied, by a country with proper scientific and engineering skills. He had no doubt the Democratic People's Republic of Korea had the motivation and knowhow.

He smiled to himself when he thought that they would be doubly motivated—not only to have the greatest fighter-jet in the world, but to have the satisfaction of sticking their finger in the eye of their hated rival. He fantasized that one day, in a few years' time, a flight of twelve F/A-22K Raptors would fly over a grand military parade in Pyongyang, and the rotund leader of the DPRK would laugh like an insane person. In his fantasy, the letter K was added to the official name of the plane, to signify that it was the Korean version.

His daydreaming was interrupted by the commotion caused by the arrival of Uncle Chong, Kim, and four, large bodyguards. Two bodyguards occupied the table on the right and the other two seated themselves on the other side.

Le Docteur rose to greet them and Chong bowed politely. “Don Alberto, I see that you have kept your word. Chun-hee has confirmed you have the merchandise and it is every bit as good as you have claimed.”

Le Docteur passed him the photos, and the Korean’s face split in a smile. “These are even more impressive and convincing. Now we have to discuss the exchange.”

Le Docteur could only think of the American childish motto: *I don’t care if you have to beg, borrow, or steal to get it,* reflected his attitude toward getting his own little nuke to play with.

He said, “Uncle Chong, we have gone to great lengths, have risked our lives, to get this one-of-a-kind specimen. It is literally priceless because no matter how much money you are willing to pay for it, you won’t be able to lay your hands on one. And I am asking for something you can easily spare. An item, that is quite common in your country that you won’t even feel if one went missing. However, I want to stipulate that for your own protection, and mine, it must be modified in such a way that it would not be traced to your country.”

He paused and looked at Chong and was pleased to see him nodding in approval.

Chong said, “You realize that the merchandize is of no

value to us so long that it remains submerged under fifty feet of water. We need to figure a way to salvage it, clandestinely, of course, and then transport it to our country. This will take time, cost a lot of money, foreign currency that we are short of, I may add, and present a risk to our people. We are also taking a huge risk providing you with the item you have requested. We would like to change the terms of our deal, to make you an offer you cannot refuse. What do you say?"

"I have a feeling I know what that offer will be."

Chong smiled. "You are a clever man. This is the offer: you give us the coordinates of the plane, and after we recover it, we let you and your girlfriend walk away, unharmed, and we'll help you settle down anywhere in the world."

Le Docteur laughed, although inside he was terrified. "This is what I expected. I have taken out an insurance policy." He was bluffing and hoped it would impress the Korean.

Chong was experienced in reading people and didn't buy it. He said, "Don Alberto, we are much more experienced than you in brinkmanship, so don't try to bullshit us. I was only joking before and wanted to test your nerves. We have a common interest, as you have pointed out, and will support you in your effort to exact revenge on the corrupt regime and the people of the United States. We are aware of the forensics capabilities of the Americans and will make sure they won't be able to trace the origin on the device we'll give you and to hold us responsible. The new miniaturized warheads we have developed for our missiles are of a new type, unknown in the West."

Le Docteur was greatly relieved but kept his 'poker face.'

"Uncle Chong, I am glad that you and I see things eye to eye. Let's cut the bullshit and get down to business. I'll give you the exact coordinates as soon as the nuke is in my possession. I prefer it shipped to a safe address in the United States, but I am fully capable of getting it into that country with my own resources. After I verify you have delivered the real thing, and not some mock-up, then you can start with your underwater salvage operation. You have your expert, Chun-hee, and the funds, and you know that you have to carry out the operation without being detected by the American authorities or the Mexicans on their payroll."

Chong replied, "This is unacceptable. You'll get the 'toy' you want after the plane is safe in the DPRK, not one moment before."

Le Docteur had been in similar situations when he fought with the Al Qaida and Islamic State people in the Middle East. He knew how to haggle, "Uncle Chong, with all due respect, your proposal puts me at a great disadvantage. I am an individual with a small group of supporters and you represent a nation with one of the most formidable intelligence services the world has seen and the fourth largest army. Agents of DPRK are well-known for carrying out successful operations in foreign countries with impunity. Need I remind you of the untimely death of Kim Jong-Nam in Malaysia by two women, believed, by the press, to be agents of your country? I think I need to be in possession of the 'toy,' as you call it, before I give you the exact location of the plane."

Chong had expected this stance. "Don Alberto, did I tell you I like this name you assumed? Let's meet halfway. You'll get the 'toy' when the plane is on board the salvage vessel, still in Mexican territorial waters. This way, if you are not pleased with the 'toy' you can inform the Mexican authorities or the FBI about the salvage operation, and enable the Americans to retrieve their plane, or for that matter, destroy it before it can fall in to the hands of a foreign country."

Le Docteur needed to think about this proposal. He ordered another cup of coffee and took his time drinking it. Chong and Kim ordered beers and watched him. One could almost see the cogwheels turning in his brain while he pondered the suggestion.

Finally, he said, "I still need some guarantee you won't try to eliminate me after you deliver the 'toy.'"

Chong shrugged. "The only thing I can promise you is that the DPRK is as enthusiastic about your idea of using the 'toy' as you are. It is in our interest that the U.S. suffers from the attack and that we are not accountable for it. You are serving our national interests as much as we are serving yours. There is no other viable assurance that I can give you."

Le Docteur said, "I understand, and I appreciate the fact that you didn't offer me any false guarantees. Let's shake hands at this gentlemen's agreement."

Chong stretched his hand across the table and shook Le Docteur's while Kim rose and bowed. Now they started to discuss the practical aspects and timetable, when Le Docteur suddenly remembered there was something they hadn't discussed. "What do we do with Chun-hee? She is in a safe place with Lara, and we cannot hold her in this 'house arrest' indefinitely."

Chong quickly said, "You'll have to release her because we need her expertise for the salvage operation. I hope you got a taste of her 'special skills.' She is quite famous in the intelligence community, although, personally, I haven't had the pleasure."

He addressed his colleague, "Kim, have you heard about her?" When he saw the crimson shade of Kim's face, he laughed. "I see. I am sure that Don Alberto and Lara can exchange notes with you."

He sighed. "I guess I am getting too old for these things. Perhaps we should get our scientists to work on a rejuvenation elixir rather than reverse-engineering of tools of war. Let's get down to serious business."

The Koreans began an animated discussion in their language as Le Docteur sipped his coffee. Le Docteur didn't understand a single word in Korean and had no intention of learning any, but he picked up a few phrases said in English: 'dollars,' 'F-22,' and names of places, 'Puerto Penasco,' 'Mexico.'

After about fifteen minutes, when this conversation went on and on, he said he had to use the restroom. As he rose, one of the Korean bodyguards stood as well and followed him to the restroom and waited patiently while he finished his business, and then accompanied him back to the table.

Chong said, "Kim and I figure that it will take us three weeks to arrange the salvage operation and about as long to get your 'toy.' We cannot deliver it to an address in the U.S.—you will have to smuggle it in with the help of your people and supporters. We can easily get it to Havana in Cuba or Caracas in Venezuela, where we have quite large delegations at our embassies. For that matter, it can be delivered to other diplomatic missions we have in Europe, Asia, or Africa. However, we believe that you would prefer to receive it in other Latin American countries from which there is a lot of legitimate traffic to the U.S., because anything from Cuba or Venezuela is suspect."

"This schedule is fine with me. I need to leave Mexico and make the necessary arrangements and then I'll inform Kim about the preferred destination for delivery of the 'toy.' Meanwhile, I'll send Chun-hee here. I am not worried that she'll be able to find the plane without our guidance, so she'll probably be more useful to you here and will help organize the salvage operation. I am looking forward to what I consider as our joint operation against the colonialists, capitalists, and crusaders." He didn't add communists—that would have been frowned upon by one of the last bastions of communism.

***

Ensenada, Baja California

Le Docteur returned to the beach house near Ensenada. He was glad to see that the two women seemed to be in a good mood. He had feared they would bicker and fight, without his restraining presence.

They were seated on the deck, holding glasses covered with frost, watching the sun set over the ocean—just as they were the day before he left for his meeting with the Koreans.

Lara was the first to see him. She rose from the chair and

entered the kitchen to fetch another frosted glass for him. Chun-hee already had the pitcher with the chilled margaritas in her hand and filled the glass that Lara brought.

Their jovial mood was contagious, and Le Docteur caught on, downed his margarita and held his glass for a refill. Then he said, "Girls, everything has been settled and we'll proceed with the plan. Chun-hee, Uncle Chong sends his regards. He and Kim want you to return to Mexico City and help organize the salvage operation. Lara, you and I will arrange the delivery and transport of the 'toy' that our new allies will provide. First, we'll have to do some travelling to select the location. Then we'll work out the means of carrying it to the target. Meanwhile, we have another day at the beach house here. This will probably be the last time the three of us are together, so let's make it a memorable affair."

Lara and Chun-hee laughed. The Korean woman said, "Dear Jacque, do you think we sat here of the deck worrying about you?"

She patted Lara's hand. "We have become best friends and have planned a welcome party for you. I promise it will be unforgettable. Now, have another margarita and close your eyes."

Le Docteur did as he was told. His eyes were shut with a silk ribbon that was tied around his head. But he could hear the two women moving about and feel their presence as they delicately brushed his torso with feather-like touches. Four nimble hands playfully tugged at his clothes and removed them, leaving him wearing nothing but the silk blindfold.

One of them, he couldn't tell which one, gently pulled him

up from the chair and led him to the bedroom and sat him on the bed. She made him lie on his back, adjusting a soft pillow under his head and a firmer one below his buttocks. His hands and feet were tied with silk sashes to the bed's frame and he could do nothing but twist his head and wriggle his body.

He could hear the other woman followed, obviously carrying something in her hands.

Then Lara said, "Jacque, you really look happy to see us." She moved her hand up between his legs.

Chun-hee giggled and said, "I have always wanted to see if the touch of a cold object caused shrinkage." Before he could grasp what she meant, he felt something ice-cold against his manhood. Both women laughed when his midsection instinctively shot up.

The Korean woman quickly held him down while Lara wrapped his dwindling member with both her warm hand and restored it to its previous impressive posture. Then he felt Chun-hee's mouth on his manhood. Apparently, she had rinsed her mouth with boiling hot tea and the effect of the rapidly changing temperature was driving him crazy.

He hated to lose control. "Untie me *now*."

The women laughed again, and Lara removed his blindfold. "No, you'll first watch us, and then, if you are still willing and able, we'll free you and let you do whatever you want with us."

He opened his eyes and could now see that Chun-hee was standing behind Lara and cupping her breasts with both hands. Her nimble fingers squeezed Lara's erect nipples until she gasped in pain.

Lara managed to turn her head around and her lips found Chun-hee's lips and when the Korean turned her around, they engaged in a passionate kiss. They seemed to forget Le Docteur's presence and their kiss deepened and left them breathless.

He started to protest, but they ignored him, and their hands were busy exploring each other's body. The soft moaning became stronger, and he was sure he heard words of endearment and passion uttered in English, Korean, French, and even Arabic.

At last, they took notice of the man lying prone on his back and twisting and turning, trying in vain to loosen the silk sashes that firmly bound him to the bend.

Lara took pity on her man, and asked Chun-hee to bring a knife from the kitchen. The Korean returned with a sharp knife and held the eight-inch blade in front of Le Docteur's face.

For a fleeting moment, he was afraid she was going to slit his throat, or worse, cut off any offending member that protruded from his body. He wasn't sure which he feared more.

She leaned over his torso, so that her nipple brushed against his mouth, and with a swift twist of her wrist cut the sash that restrained his right hand. Then she leaned over the other side, giving him a taste of her other nipple and cut the sash pinning his left hand. Then she rolled over his body, so that her midsection rubbed against his and cut the sashes that tied his feet.

While in this position, she started to move her pelvis in

a circular motion, that would have made the most accomplished belly-dancer proud and jealous.

Lara was afraid she would miss all the fun, if this continued any longer, so she lay on top on the Korean woman, facing Le Docteur's head. Her mouth close to Le Docteur's and they exchanged a long kiss.

Meanwhile, the Korean woman's midsection was grinding Le Docteur's fully erect manhood below her and feeling Lara's weight above her. This position was getting a little too uncomfortable for Le Docteur who felt the full weight of both women, and for Chun-hee who was being squashed from both sides. Lara felt that she was not getting all the attention she yearned for, and with a quick move tried to push the Korean out of the way and get full contact with her lover's body.

Her sudden movement toppled the threesome from the bed, and they fell to the floor, laughing crazily.

They tried a few other more conventional positions, until they decided to quit dawdling and with a series of quick, focused movements all reached their orgasms. They lay on the floor in an untidy pile of limbs, torsos, and heads.

***

Mexico City

Le Docteur and the two women took the flight from Ensenada to Mexico City. They knew the short vacation they enjoyed in Ensenada was over, and now they had to get back to the dangerous world of international conspiracy and terrorism.

Chun-hee was met by Kim from the embassy and the two of them exchanged a warm embrace, which indicated they were more than professional acquaintances.

Lara watched this and said, "Jacque, this woman is something out of this world. I don't know who trained her but am sure she came top of the class." Then she became aware of the unintended double-meaning and started laughing.

Le Docteur wasn't really listening. He was deep in thought thinking of the next phase of their operation. "Lara, can you fly a private plane? A twin-engine turbo-prop or an executive jet?"

She was surprised by his question. "Of course, I can. I can fly anything with wings and a motor, but I am not certified for most general aviation planes. In any case, I cannot legally rent any aircraft under the name used in my license. Do I need to remind you that both of us head the 'most wanted' lists all over the world?"

Le Docteur waved his hand dismissively. "I am beginning to form a plan, and I need your flying skills. Let's discuss it later."

He switched on his computer and used the Google Earth website to look at the map. He searched for the closest airport to New York City that was not on the North America mainland, and was not under control of the U.S. government. He showed the screen to Lara and told her what was on his mind.

He was focused on Central America and islands in the Caribbean, but she pointed at Bermuda that was obviously much closer.

He said, “That’s interesting. There is a small problem—the Koreans don’t have an embassy or a consulate there, but possibly could deliver the ‘toy’ via Havana.”

Lara said, “Flying from L. F. Wade International Airport, BDA, in Bermuda, to New York City, on a commercial jet is only slightly more than two hours. With an executive jet, it would take about the same time, depending on the plane’s model. With a turbo-prop it would take about three hours, or so. Not difficult, at all.”

“Let’s fly to Bermuda and get to know if it’s a viable option. We’ll use our new identities to enter this haven of British colonialism.”

***

Washington, DC

Senator James McCorey, the new Chairman of the Senate Committee on Foreign Relations, replaced Senator Buckley when the media and the president demanded his resignation after the fiasco at the San Diego naval base.

McCorey opened the session. “I have taken over the position of Chairman of this esteemed committee. But before we get down to the business of the day, I would like to caution all members.”

He paused for a long moment and looked each of the committee members in the eye. “If anyone leaks anything about the proceedings of the committee, he or she, will be charged with high-treason."

He didn't need to add that he was the only person authorized, by himself, to talk to the media about the committee's activities. When he saw that all the members were watching him, he said, "The only item on the agenda today is to discuss how our intelligence community, all parts of it, and the military, mainly the air force, failed to warn us and prevent the heinous attacks that have been perpetrated against the American people. I have summoned the heads of all the relevant agencies, and they'll be permitted to enter the room in a moment. I expect all patriotic Americans, and I hope you all are, to question them about their ineptness and about the fate of the billions of dollars they receive from us every year. Each member of this committee can freely address any of the accused, sorry, this was a slip of tongue, any of the gentlemen who we have trusted with guarding our security."

He pressed a button on the intercom and asked the committee's secretary to usher the heads of the intelligence community into the room. They were guided to chairs at the bottom end of the table.

One of the older senators, who had been on the committee for two decades, and still remembered the video clips from public trials that were carried out in Communist Russia, whispered to the senator sitting next to him, "Jim would love to see the whole bunch executed summarily, without bothering with a hearing or trial. Just so he gets credit for a purge of the liberals."

McCorey didn't hear what was said, but figured they were denigrating him disrespectfully. He addressed the old senator,

"Would you mind saying out loud what you just said?"

The older man cringed and mumbled something about the temperature of the coffee.

McCorey directed his first question to the Commander of the Air Force and member of the Joint Chiefs of Staff. "General Ellington, when General Lancaster called you from Holloman AFB and informed you about the missing F-22 and the Raptor's pilot, why did you instruct him to call the Department of Homeland Security? Why didn't you call for a comprehensive search for the plane and pilot? Why didn't you enlist all the considerable resources of the Air Force? Your delay may have enabled the pilot to get away with the plane, and that led to the raid on the naval base that cost the lives of many of our good people who served this country like true patriots."

General Ellington sank back further in his chair before replying, "At the time, we were not sure what had happened, so I directed General Lancaster to the DHS. I have since, accepted his resignation, so justice has been served—"

McCorey cut him short. "Don't you feel responsible? This happened under your command, right under your nose. Allowing a woman of Muslim extract to fly one of our most secret and expensive machines. With that background, she should never have been allowed to enter flight-school, let alone be given an advanced jet-fighter."

He saw that the general was trying to answer. "No, General Ellington, I don't need your measly excuses, I need your letter of resignation."

He turned his head a little to the man next to the ashen-faced general. "I call on the Director of Central Intelligence to give the committee an assessment on the extent of the damage to our national security."

The DCI, a political nominee with no experience in intelligence and military matters, said, "Mister Chairman, I have appointed a fact-finding team to make this assessment. I expect their report next week."

McCorey sighed audibly, "Thank you for your candid reply. I now wish to ask the Head of the Department of Homeland Security what he has done to find the missing plane and pilot?"

The Head of the DHS nodded. "We have done everything according to protocol. We have examined the background of the missing pilot and found she had been vetted, just like any other candidate. We alerted all border crossings to stop anyone whose description matched that of the suspect professor."

He signaled to the technician in charge of the display to project the photos of Lara Wayne, Professor Jacque Deleau, and the Raptor, and continued, "We have asked the NRO and NGA to search the vast area between New Mexico and San Diego of both sides of the border. The NRO has redirected satellites to do that and the NGA has increased surveillance in the area. We have played this by the book. It looks like the culprits slipped through the holes in the net."

Senator McCorey was startled by the photo of the professor who looked very familiar. He said, "I thank you all for your cooperation. The meeting is adjourned. The Committee will meet again next week, and by then, hopefully, the plane and pilot will be found."

When everyone left the room, he stumbled to side table, poured himself a glass of water, then headed back to his office in the Senate Building.

His thoughts were tormented. *Could I have been duped by the professor?*

The conclusion was he had to find the professor and silence him before his role in the affair was discovered.

CHAPTER 15

St. David's Island, Bermuda

From her window seat, Lara could see strips of land, as the plane approached L. F. Wade International Airport, the main airport of Bermuda.

She didn't believe in the legends that assigned mysterious evil forces to the Bermuda Triangle, but was glad to see solid ground after flying across hundreds of miles over the Atlantic Ocean.

She thought the sailors on Columbus's ships must have felt the same when they sighted the shores of Hispaniola, the name they gave to the island that is now divided between the Dominican Republic and Haiti.

She had read that Bermuda consisted of one hundred eighty-one islands and that only eight of them are interconnected by bridges, while the others are accessible only by sea or air. She couldn't see all one hundred eighty-one islands, nor could she count them, and had no intention of doing so.

She appreciated the skill of the commercial pilot when the plane touched down so smoothly that the sleeping passengers didn't even wake up.

While the plane taxied to the terminal, Le Docteur made

some quiet comments about colonialism. He mentioned the audacity of Juan de Bermudez, the captain of the ship who stumbled on to the shores of the islands in fifteen hundred three, to claim them for the Spanish Empire, and later to have them named after him.

He added, discreetly in Lara's ear, "The very designation of Bermuda as a 'British Overseas Territory' is an affront to justice, as it is subservient to the British monarch. Their flag that combines the Union Jack with a coat of arms on a red background is ridiculous. The official coat of arms shows a red lion holding a shipwreck between his paws and a Latin motto: '*Quo Fata Ferunt*' that means in translation, *whither the Fates carry (us)*, but actually infers a degree of fatalism—*wherever the wind carries us*. The fate of the residents of Bermuda may indeed change dramatically after we carry out our plan."

Lara asked, "Do we have any supporters or contacts here?"

Le Docteur smiled. "Quite an unlikely connection. Do you remember the Americans illegally arrested some Uyghurs suspected of having ties with the Taliban and brought them to Guantanamo?"

He saw the question forming on her lips, so quickly continued, "Of course, you don't. Few people know that after years of imprisonment they were cleared and released by a court-order issued by a judge in Washington. Bermuda, in a rare display of a humanistic and altruistic spirit, agreed to offer them asylum, and that infuriated the British Foreign Office. Some of these Uyghurs remained in Bermuda and established ties with local Muslim community. The experience of torture and incarceration in Guantanamo has radicalized them, and even if they didn't care much for the Taliban and Muslim insurgence before they were kidnapped by the CIA, they are now supporters of radical Islam. They have all kept a low profile, but we can rely on their assistance."

"Jacque, it is interesting how Newton's third law of motion works in politics. The unjust action of the CIA against these Uyghurs has led to a reaction that turned them against all things American." She patted Le Docteur's hand. "You are so brilliant in finding support for our cause in the most unexpected places."

By that time, the doors of the plane were open, and the passengers slowly strolled in to the terminal building. Lara looked around and was surprised by the combination of British formality with the free-spirit, vacation-mood, of the people.

The passport control officials smiled, asked no questions, and stamped their fake Canadian passports. The customs officials waved them through and all the taxi drivers outside the terminal had welcoming smiles on their faces.

The ten-minute taxi ride from the airport to Bailey's Bay afforded them a taste of the islands' views of bridges that spanned the ocean between the islands, of the beaches and cottages and hotels built on the shore.

In Bermuda, no place was far from the ocean. So, if you were on high-ground you could get a three hundred and sixty view of the ocean, which was quite amazing for Lara that had lived the last five years in New Mexico—a thousand miles from the ocean.

As they got closer to their hotel, they could see the demographic variety of the people strolling along the streets near the beach. Le Docteur was impressed by the people whose skin color reflected the entire spectrum from dark-black to white, and said so.

Lara commented that the so-called 'white' stretched from pink to red, and that she felt sorry for those pale tourists who allowed the sun to roast them in the hope of attaining a healthy-looking tan.

Le Docteur looked at her and laughed, saying they aspired to get the shade she received as a gift from her parents.

The taxi driver had heard this exchange, turned his head and said, "I have a dark skin and wish that it were white, and these tourists are trying to change their white skin and become black. So much injustice in the world."

Le Docteur liked the comment, and the attitude of the driver. "We will be on the island for a few days and need transportation. How would you like to work for us as a driver and tour-guide for the next three days?"

The driver said, "For the right fee, certainly."

They haggled a little and agreed on a daily fee. The driver said, "Are you sure you want to stay at Bailey's Bay? There is more action in Hamilton, if that is what you are looking for. I can get you a good deal at one of the best hotels there for only six hundred dollars a night."

Le Docteur looked at Lara, who nodded, and asked, "Do you mean U.S. dollars?"

The driver laughed. "We have Bermuda dollars that are pegged to U.S. dollars, so for us a dollar is a dollar. I can assure you that it is worth every cent. The beach is beautiful, the service is fantastic, the food is delicious, and it is very comfortable."

"You sound like you are quoting something from TripAdvisor. So, take us there."

When they arrived at the hotel it looked like an outstanding hotel, so far removed from the small, rustic hotel they stayed at in Puerto Penasco, that Le Docteur squeezed Lara's hand and quietly said, "Nothing but the best for you, my dear."

He adopted a high-class British accent that made her laugh. He didn't admit, even to himself, that the present month could well be the last for both, so they might as well enjoy life while it lasted.

***

There were about one thousand Muslims in Bermuda, according to a recent Pew Research Center report, or about one percent of the population of the islands. The mosque, Masjid Muhammad, located on Cedar Avenue, held public prayers every Friday afternoon at one thirty as the sign at the entrance said.

There was no minaret, only a large white building, with some arches that implied what its function and origins were.

On Friday, Le Docteur asked the driver to drop him off at the Athletic Club of Bermuda, across the street from the mosque, and take the rest of the day off.

***

Lara seized the opportunity to wander around the market place and look at the merchandise. She had always wondered if Bermuda shorts were indeed from Bermuda and was glad to see they were on sale at the market, although worn mainly by the tourists and not the residents.

***

Le Docteur knew that Islamic centers in the U.S. and Western Europe were often under surveillance of the local police and intelligence organizations. However, he didn't think that the police in Hamilton, Bermuda, had any concerns about the Muslim community on the islands.

Nevertheless, he gingerly approached the building and walked past the gate without entering. When he saw the small crowd of devoted Muslims leave the mosque after the prayers, he entered the small courtyard, pretending to be a curious tourist, who happened to take an interest in the building. A young man came out of the building and in a polite tone asked him what he was looking for.

Le Docteur said he had never been inside a mosque and asked if he could go in. The young man said, "We don't often get requests of this kind from tourists. I'd be glad to oblige and take you to meet our Sheikh Akram. Please, follow me."

They entered the building, and Le Docteur paused to take photos of the interior. There were no decorations in the communal room, except for a few sentences from the Quran inscribed on the walls, and the floor was covered by a large mat. The young man led him to a small room in the back of the communal room.

A middle-aged man, with a full beard, rose from a stool that was placed next to a small table, and greeted the visitor, "Salaam Alaikum."

He was a bit surprised when the tourist replied in an Arabic accent. "Alaikum Salaam." Then added in English, "Sheikh Akram, perhaps we should speak alone."

The Sheikh made a gesture with his hand, and the young man bowed and left the room, closing the door behind him.

Le Docteur waited until he heard the man's footsteps receding, and continued, "I am on an important mission and need your help. I am trying to contact our brothers, the Uyghurs who found shelter here. It is best that you, and the Islamic community here, do not get involved with my mission. We need to keep this between the two of us and let this go no further."

Sheikh Akram scrutinized the man sitting in front of him. He looked vaguely familiar, and his British accent was obviously put on to disguise his real accent. He was afraid this man could be an *agent provocateur* sent by the local authorities, at the request of the British MI6, no doubt, to entrap him.

He weighed his options carefully. On the one hand, he felt he had not contributed enough to the grand struggle of Islam against the Infidels and enemies of the faith, but on the other hand, he didn't want to take any risks that would endanger his community and himself.

So, he did what anyone else in his position would do, he dodged the question. "I am not sure I know what has become of the people you speak about. Some have left the island, and some are still around. What do you want to see them for? Are you a reporter, writing a story on them?"

Le Docteur had expected this behavior. "Sheikh Akram, please respect my request for help, and no harm will come to any of our brethren on the island. If I were working with the authorities, I would have had access to the information I am asking for."

"I understand. Please come back in the evening, and I'll try to get their last known address."

Le Docteur nodded. "I'll be back here in the evening. Perhaps, it is better if we don't meet again. Please leave a note with the address behind the plaque of your mosque, that is written in Arabic. This meeting has never taken place."

He rose, bowed slightly, and left the mosque.

***

Le Docteur walked down Cedar Avenue toward the Flagpole and met Lara at the Pickled Onion restaurant. It was well after lunch time, so the place wasn't crowded, and they were immediately seated on the outside patio. The restaurant was made famous by its cocktails, and the couple sampled some of the more exotic ones, while enjoying great views of Hamilton Harbor.

They ordered a bowl of fish chowder that was delicious, and then some pasta that was not great. After that they returned to their hotel for an afternoon nap.

Le Docteur told Lara about his meeting with Sheikh Akbar, and in the evening the two of them strolled down Cedar

Avenue, as if they had no worry in the world. They made sure that they were not being followed.

Outside the mosque, Le Docteur pretended his shoelace had become undone and bent down to tie it. Lara shielded him from view and he quickly retrieved the small note tucked under the sign and placed it in his pocket.

They continued to Front Street and walked west along the beach until they reached Point Pleasant Park. They sat on a bench for a while, looking at the boats sailing to and from the Inner Harbor.

Le Docteur looked at the note that contained only one line with an address on Spanish Point Road.

Lara looked for the address on her cell phone and in an amused tone told Le Docteur that it was near Smugglers' Caverns.

He also found that to be quite funny, although they didn't plan on doing any smuggling, or at least, none of the old-style smuggling. They intended to smuggle something of much greater significance than anything previously illicitly brought to the island.

Lara asked, "What do we need these Uyghurs for? The Koreans that bring the 'toy' can load it on the plane."

Le Docteur said, "It is true that most Caucasians don't know the difference between Koreans and Chinese, but even fewer can distinguish Chinese from Uyghurs. People who will see the Uyghurs transport the 'toy' from the ship to the plane will be sure the Chinese are involved. This will perhaps shift the blame from the North Koreans to the Chinese. Uncle Chong and his friends will be pleased that the DPRK is not accountable. They'll appreciate our sophistication and extend a helping hand."

Lara was fascinated by the deviousness of her lover. Then she raised the question that had been bothering her since Le Docteur outlined the plan. "Jacque, let's say that we can rent a plane and fly it to the United States with the 'toy.' Will we fly it ourselves or will there be a pilot? Then, once we land, surely U.S. customs will board the plane and search the cargo. All hell will break lose when they see the 'toy.' And, even if we somehow manage to pass the custom's inspection, how will we get through passport control? The minute our fingerprints and retina are scanned we'll be identified, regardless of the fake passports and the changes we have made in our appearance. I am sure you have considered all those obstacles. Please share your ideas to circumvent these obstacles."

She looked at him expectantly, and he knew the moment of truth had finally arrived. "Lara, do you remember a conversation we had a long time ago, shortly after we met? I told you I would stop at nothing to avenge the injustices our people suffered from the hands of the colonialists, communists, crusaders, capitalists, and Jews, including sacrificing my own life for the cause. You agreed to come along this dangerous and slippery path."

Lara remembered something he had said about General Patton and the quote: *The object of war is not to die for your country but to make the other bastard die for his.*

She also recalled how he denigrated ISIS for sending fighters to a certain death carrying out suicide missions. She said nothing, waiting for him to continue.

"Lara, we can avoid all the obstacles you mentioned if we do not try to land on U.S. soil."

She responded, "Do you mean that we drop the 'toy' from the plane and get out of U.S. airspace? You know that is impossible. First, one cannot open a door and throw something as large as the 'toy.' This is a plane not a truck. Second, there is no way we can get far enough from the explosion that will occur when the 'toy' goes off. The pressure wave, the heat, the radiation, are sure to toss the plane out of the sky and fry us."

Then a terrifying thought crossed her mind. "Jacque, do you mean we won't even try to get away?"

Le Docteur appreciated her quick mind. "Lara, we can go out with a bang or with a whimper. If I must go, I prefer the bang—and I can assure you it will be a big bang, one that will change the world. Naturally, I would like to spend the rest of my life with you, in a quiet place, far away from the troubles and struggle of our people, but I'll never be able to do that, knowing I had the chance to avenge generations of oppression, usurpation, and subjugation. I need you for this, without you I cannot do it, and we'll be united for all eternity after that. We'll be seated by the side of Mohammad and his prophets."

Lara didn't like this. She cynically said, "If you are seated by the side of Mohammad and the prophets, I will have to serve coffee to all of you, not to mention the other household tasks expected of a woman in Islam. Jacque, this is not a decision I can make in the spur of the moment."

Le Docteur had not foreseen this coming. This sudden attack of feministic attitude. "Lara, I forgot to mention we'll arrive in paradise as a husband and wife. You won't serve coffee—you'll justly earn your seat by the side of Mohammad—and you'll be mine alone, and I'll be totally committed to you. Would you marry me?"

Lara didn't think that marriage was the solution to anything. Her own experience with Colonel Wayne proved it was more of a problem than a solution. She hesitated. "I need to think about this."

Le Docteur came up with another convincing point. "You know the effects of a nuclear explosion are optimal when the 'toy' is detonated several hundred feet above ground level. If we place it at ground level, or should I say, Ground Zero, in Times Square then the damage would be extensive, for sure, but not nearly as effective as a detonation above the sky-scrapers of Manhattan. The same, if we detonate it above the Mall in Washington, DC, rather than under the Washington Monument."

He looked at Lara and saw this argument didn't convince her. He resumed the persuasion attempts on the personal level. "Lara, let's get officially married, view our time here in Bermuda as our honeymoon, and think no further about the plan, until we receive the 'toy' from our friends in the DPRK. Then we can decide if we are going to fly over the target and detonate it mid-air, land, and try to smuggle it through customs and the passport control authorities, or perhaps try to use the commercial shipping lanes to deliver it to the U.S. Then we can set it off in the port without going through customs. The effect will be much weaker than the aerial raid, but still devastating."

***

Le Docteur and Lara found the address of the Uyghurs given to them by Sheikh Akram. They walked up to the door of the apartment, stood there for a moment, listening for any signs of life.

They could hear music that sounded atonal and even disturbing to their ears, and figured it was Chinese music, perhaps even Chinese pop. He knocked on the door and a woman's voice said something in Chinese, and then a man's voice said in English, "Who's there?"

Le Docteur said with his best French accent, "A friend, with some good news."

He saw a brown eye staring at him from the peephole, and then the door opened a couple inches. Apparently, the resident was satisfied the caller was not an agent of some American law-enforcement agency, and the door opened.

Lara, peeping over Le Docteur's shoulder could see a living-room with no furniture, except a couch covered in an old blanket with a floral design and an outdated TV set on the floor opposite the couch. There was a tiny kitchen, a kitchenette, really, and a small folding table with two folding chairs that probably served as the dining table.

The man and woman looked Chinese, but certainly different from the Han people who were the largest and strongest sector in the Chinese society.

Le Docteur said, "Salaam Alaikum." He waited for the traditional response.

Instead of answering, a look of apprehension crossed the

woman's face and the man took a step back, toward the kitchenette where a large carving knife was visible on the counter by the sink.

Le Docteur raised his hands, with a display of his empty palms, and said, "We have come to offer you and your friends some work. I promise it will pay well and is not difficult. I have heard about your plight and am trying to help. I know that you won't take charity—you are a proud people—so, you'll work and be rewarded."

The man said, "My name is Ding and my wife is Liang. How did you find us?"

"Your story is famous and there are not too many Uyghurs on the island."

Ding said, "There are only four other members of our original group. The authorities are not making life easy for us, but at least we are not persecuted, and it is paradise compared to Guantanamo. What is it you want us to do?"

Le Docteur said, "Here's a down payment of two thousand Bermuda dollars to split between you and your colleagues. In a few weeks' time, a shipment will arrive at Hamilton Harbor. We need to transship it to another place on the island. It must be handled with care and discretion. Here's another two thousand dollars to establish an import firm. The name of the firm will be *NK Import and Export Services*, and you and Liang will be registered as the owners. You will go tomorrow to this lawyer."

He took a business card out of his pocket and placed it on the stack of money. "He is a resident of Bermuda and will register the firm and become your partner. He will need to assign your address to the company's log. Is this understood?"

Ding looked at Liang and said, "I don't like it. Double the sum and I'll consider it."

"I need to think about it." Le Docteur had really expected this, so he pretended to hesitate, as if reconsidering the deal, and finally he said, "Okay. I'll double the registration fee." Le Docteur figured this was going to Ding's pocket. The man nodded in consent.

Le Docteur pulled another two thousand dollars from his pocket and placed it on the lawyer's business card and added a cell phone to the stack. "Here's a phone. I'll call you tomorrow evening to ascertain that all is well. Don't use this phone for any other purpose."

Ding said, "You'll also need to pay us ten thousand dollars for the job you want me and my colleagues to do. We have to split it four ways, so it is not much for each."

Le Docteur sighed and agreed. After all, these guys were notorious traders and expert merchants thousands of years before the people in Europe.

After they left the apartment, Lara asked him, "Are you sure they will do what you wanted without running to the authorities?"

"They have more to lose than us. It will be different once the shipment arrives, and we'll have to take precautions to discourage them from going to the police. I'll make arrangements to provide them with an incentive to do as they are told."

They returned to their luxurious hotel, that was a far cry from the humble apartment they had just left.

***

CHAPTER 16

Mexico City

The Mossad team convened in Mexico City. David explained their operation would have to be kept completely below the radar of the authorities. Mexico and Israel were quite friendly, but the government tended to align itself with enemies of the United States. This attitude had taken a turn to the worse after the new American President issued a few derogatory statements about Mexicans in general and the Mexican government. Israel was regarded as a close ally of the U.S. and, therefore, not as a favorite in Mexico.

David had received information that the CIA teams sent to investigate the airfields in northwest Mexico had not yet been cleared to operate there. Eugene told him some undercover agents were roaming the area but their access to the airfields was restricted.

He thought that David's small team, with proper guidance from the NRO surveillance satellites, could operate more freely. David agreed to carry out the footwork, but before signing off asked if the U.S. agencies had gathered anything about irregular activities in the DPRK.

Eugene stated there seemed to be some at Yongbyon Nuclear

Scientific Research Center, North Korea's major nuclear facility, about fifty-five miles from the capital, Pyongyang.

David knew it was the center for production of fissile materials for the DPRK nuclear weapons' program, and that worried him. He asked Eugene if the NSA had picked up any special communications traffic at the DPRK embassy in Mexico City, and was told that during the last few weeks there have been a couple of visits from one of the senior advisors, Uncle Chong.

David asked if the embassy was under surveillance and Eugene said it was classified information. David was upset by the curt reply, and Eugene, sensing David's feelings, said that Le Docteur was not observed entering the embassy. He added that a Mexican cleaning woman at the embassy, who was on the CIA's payroll, hadn't witnessed any meeting with a foreigner who looked like Le Docteur. David thanked him and hung up.

He conveyed Eugene's information on the DPRK and lack of any useful information about Koreans' activities in Mexico. He sent Joe to explore the embassy's surroundings and its security measures, while the Fish and Mata toured the neighborhood to see if they could find any likely meeting places.

He and Edna would go over the maps forwarded by the NRO, search for likely airfields, then draw a schedule to visit them.

***

The team reconvened in the evening to summarize their

findings. Joe reported that there were no exceptional security measures at the embassy of the DPRK in Mexico City. There were not many security cameras, or at least cameras that could be seen from the street, and the walls surrounding the building were no higher or stronger than those of the other buildings in the neighborhood.

He noted there was a tall tree just outside the embassy and could easily install a miniature CCD camera on one of its branches that had a view of the embassy's main entrance. David asked if the buildings next to the embassy were occupied and Joe said that none of them had 'for rent' or 'for sale' signs, so he assumed they were not vacant.

He added there was a small clinic that provided medical services on the street's corner, close to the embassy. The small building was busy during the day but was not used at night. He didn't have a chance to verify if it was guarded after office hours, as were many office buildings in Mexico City.

The Fish and Mata displayed a detailed map of the area surrounding the embassy, and pointed out several cafés, bars, and restaurants within a radius of a few blocks. Although it was mainly a residential area, there were many commercial businesses in the vicinity. Mata entered several of those, pretending to ask directions to get the DPRK embassy.

In most places, the proprietor said he had no idea there was even a Korean embassy in the neighborhood, but in a few places, they were told Korean patrons frequently visited the place. David asked if there was any point to return to those places with photos of Le Docteur and Lara, but the Fish thought it would draw unwanted attention to themselves and perhaps even alert the Koreans that they were under surveillance.

David agreed the risk was great, but the benefits outweighed it. He needed concrete evidence that Le Docteur had met with people from the DPRK to support his theory of a bartering agreement between these two parties.

Mata proposed she would go around with Le Docteur's photo and pretend to be his wife that suspected him of cheating on her with another woman. She would put on her best appearance of a desperate woman seeking help. This would be irresistible to most men, including macho Mexican men willing to help a beautiful damsel in distress.

David approved her plan but suggested that the Fish and Joe would keep an eye on her, in case of trouble. He was worried Le Docteur had altered his appearance and wouldn't be recognizable in the photo they had but was still the only viable plan to track him down.

Edna showed the map of northwestern Mexico where the airports and larger airstrips were marked. She said there were about a dozen possible locations, and three of those were designated as international airports: San Felipe, Tijuana, and Puerto Penasco.

Calexico international airport, which was on the border between California and Mexico, hence the name, was an unlikely possibility because it was on the U.S. side, but perhaps also worth a visit.

Edna presented the information on the runway at each airport or airfield, and this helped disqualify some of them. Finally, she proposed they first focus on the three international airports and if nothing turned up, then they could look at the others on the list.

David said they were operating under the assumption that Lara didn't take her plane to some remote, even deserted, airport within the borders of the United States. He added that he had alerted Eugene and the American had assured him the federal and state authorities would scrutinize all those airfields.

David concluded the meeting by issuing instructions to his team: Mata and the other two men would spend the next day trying to find a connection between Le Docteur and the people from the DPRK, and the following day they'd split and go to the three airports on top of the list of suspects.

Edna would try to compile more information on the airfields and focus on the three main suspects. She'd also check the flight schedules and make reservations for the team.

***

Mata dressed up for her role—wearing a short dress with a generous décolletage that revealed the top of her perfectly molded breasts, high heeled shoes that emphasized her legs and lithe figure, and most importantly a look of desperation which seemed to distort her lovely face.

Any man who could get her to smile would feel the luckiest man in the world. The Fish followed her from a distance and Joe was a few feet ahead of her as she entered each café that could have potentially been a meeting spot for Le Docteur.

In every case she entered the premises timidly and asked

for the proprietor. In each place, a man rushed from behind the counter to get a better look at the angelic woman who descended from heaven and offer his help to a 'damsel in distress.'

After visiting the third café, Mata had perfected her pitch, and gained some practice in politely rejecting unwelcome attention. She held a small photo of Le Docteur and showed it to each man she questioned.

The Fish had been on several operations with Mata in the past but had never been a silent observer before. He managed to see what was going on, without hearing a word spoken but the body language alone didn't leave anything to his imagination. Each time, he saw the proprietor taking a good look at the photo and shaking his head.

Next, followed some verbal exchange that he couldn't hear, of course, and a gesture inviting Mata to sit down and have a drink, often accompanied by an attempt to pat her on the shoulder as an act of consolation. Walking in front of Mata, Joe missed all the fun, and after stopping and waiting for the tenth time offered to trade places with the Fish, who like a good team-player agreed.

After so many negative responses, Mata was getting a little tired and frustrated. She decided to rest a little and have a cup of coffee in the next café. As usual, her entrance was met with curious, even lustful, looks from the male patrons, and critical appraisal from the few women present in the café.

She sat down at one of the tables near the large window, and when the proprietor came over to take her order she asked for coffee and a bottle of cold water. She didn't pull out the photo immediately but sat quietly seeming to mind her own business. When the patrons appeared to lose interest in her, she beckoned to the proprietor to bring her another coffee.

When it arrived, she put on her show and tears streamed down her perfect cheeks as she pretended to study the photo of Le Docteur. The proprietor looked at the photo she was holding, glancing at it over her shoulder. He asked her why she was crying, and she pitched the 'cheated wife' story and held up the photo, cursing and swearing.

The proprietor thought he recognized the man. He said that someone resembling this man had visited his café a few times. Mata smiled through her tears and asked if he was with another woman, and the proprietor vouched he was accompanied by two men, who were obviously Chinese or Japanese, or possibly even Koreans from the embassy a few blocks away.

Mata asked him again if there was no woman he was meeting surreptitiously, and the proprietor repeated his previous statement. Mata thanked him and said she was relieved he was not with another woman and left the café.

She signaled to Joe and the Fish that the search was over, and suggested they return immediately to the hotel and update the team, and then prepare for the trip to the airfields in northwest Mexico.

***

The next day the Mossad team split. Edna and the Fish got a flight to *Aeropuerto Internacional de Tijuana*, Joe and Mata flew to *Aeropuerto Internacional San Felipe*, and David travelled to Puerto Penasco International Airport.

Before they split, David directed each pair to survey the airport terminal, get a look at the runways, and most importantly look at the hangars in which the missing plane may be hidden. They had no official status, and certainly no support from the Mexican government, so they would have to devise their own way into the hangars. He added that green dollars went a long way in Mexico, especially in remote places like San Felipe or Puerto Penasco.

As soon as Edna and the Fish landed at the Tijuana airport, they realized there was no way a jet-fighter plane, like an F-22 could land and take-off without being noticed by dozens, if not hundreds, of people. Employees of the airport, tourists that travelled to, or from, Tijuana, and residents whose decrepit homes bordered on the airport's perimeter. They immediately called David and told him that Tijuana was out of the question.

San Felipe was located on the eastern shore of the Baja California Peninsula and on the western side of the Wagner Basin that separated the peninsula from mainland Mexico.

It was not a very busy airport, with an average of about twenty flights a day, and there were no scheduled commercial airlines. In fact, Joe and Mata had to hire a small plane to take them to the airport. The single runway, named after the campus directions 13-31 (close to southeast-northwest), was only one thousand feet long, which would be too close to the safety margin for an F-22. They, too, reported to David that San Felipe couldn't be the destination of the missing Raptor.

CHAPTER 17

Puerto Penasco, Gulf of California, Mexico

David arrived by a commercial flight to Mar de Cortes International Airport, as the airport in Puerto Penasco was officially called. It was located almost directly opposite San Felipe across the Wagner Basin, but was much larger.

The airport was seventy-five feet above sea-level and its north-south single runway was two miles long, so it could comfortably accommodate the missing Raptor. Although it is declared as an official entry point to Mexico the air-traffic is quite light. The runway was the continuation of the taxi-way, not parallel to it as in most busy airports. There was only a small hangar that could serve general-aviation planes but no commercial airliners.

However, it was just large enough for a plane the size of the F-22. David reckoned that an accomplished pilot like Lara could land her plane by gliding to landing quite silently and not attract much attention even in daytime. Taking off would be noisier, but if done after dark she could do it almost invisibly.

His gut feeling told him that Puerto Penasco was the most likely airport—its location was within the operational range of the Raptor, its runway was perfect, and there were very few people present at the airfield when no commercial flight was scheduled. There was no real control-tower, the air-traffic controllers used a cabin located on the roof of the small terminal building.

He was told the control-tower was manned only when a flight was scheduled to arrive, and that the single controller, Juan de Castro, lived in a small house just a few hundred feet from the airfield. He waited for the controller to sign off for his afternoon nap, the sacred siesta, and then approached him.

He tried to start a conversation, but Juan didn't want to talk to him, and nervously avoided him. David suspected the man was hiding something and decided to induce his cooperation. For that, he needed support from his team, so he decided to wait for their arrival from Tijuana and San Felipe the next day.

He rented a car and after studying the map, drove to one of the resort hotels located on the shore at Bahia Punta Penasco, and planned to wait for them there.

The hotel was large and all its rooms provided a view of the beach and the bay. David sat on the small balcony, watching the sandy beach, while sipping a cold beer. He noticed a few small boats, some with sails but most with outboard motors, that sailed up and down the shorefront, and then a larger vessel caught his eye. It was a bit further from the beach and moving slowly, as if searching for something.

He couldn't quite make out what kind of ship it was—it was much smaller than the cruise ships that sailed in the Pacific

Ocean along the western coast Baja California and larger than the fishing boats that trolled the Wagner Basin. The ship had an arrangement of derricks and masts that didn't look like any other ship he had seen.

He pulled out his cell phone, set the camera to its highest magnification and snapped a few shots. He then sent them to Mossad headquarters in Tel Aviv, asking the duty officer to consult with the naval experts about the identity of the ship and send him an answer ASAP.

David walked down to the hotel's dining room and saw that it was almost deserted. He wondered if this was due to the late hour—meaning that it was late for the large groups of elderly American couples used to 'early bird specials' and having dinner before six, or because the other patrons preferred local, authentic food.

In any case, he wanted to get a feel for the area, so he took the rental car and drove a few miles up the shorefront. He reached a bar-restaurant located on the beach, right next to the pier that stretched to the sea and served for unloading and loading small boats.

He liked the look of the place, so he sat at the bar, ordered some of the local seafood dishes and had another couple beers to wash the food down. He was focused on his food and didn't look around him.

After his appetite was satiated, he took note of the other patrons. There was the usual crowd of young people, mostly Americans he could tell by the noise they were making, and a few older people who had probably come from the hotels further down the beach. He swerved his bar-stool and saw a group of five men, in crumpled suits, completely out of place in this Mexican resort.

They had been very quiet, and even when they were joined by a beautiful woman, their mood didn't lighten. David didn't want to stare at them, so he surreptitiously studied them in the bar's mirror. From their round heads and slanted eyes, he figured they were from the Far East.

Upon a closer study of their features, it suddenly dawned on him they could be Koreans. He saw there was some exchange of words between the men and the woman. He couldn't understand the words, but from the tone of the exchange it was clear they were arguing about something.

The woman looked at him, and when she saw he had spotted her in the mirror, quickly averted her eyes.

Alarm bells started ringing like crazy in his head, and he deliberated how to verify that, when he felt the presence of someone taking the bar-stool next to his. From the corner of his eye he saw the beautiful woman he had spotted before, openly looking at him as if studying him.

In unaccented English, she said, "Could you please help me." She reticently pointed to the group of men, and added, "These men are bothering me. They think that because we are from the same country that I am here to serve their needs."

As a Mossad agent, David had been trained, even warned, to avoid striking a conversation with strangers, especially good-looking women who seemed to hit on him 'spontaneously.' He wanted to ignore the woman. But didn't want to seem rude, "Madam, I am sorry, I am waiting for my wife to join me." And he turned back to face the counter.

The woman said, "I apologize, I don't see a wedding band, so I thought you were free." She made a show of looking around the bar. "I am sorry, there is no one else I can turn to. All the others here are either very young or very old. You are the only man here that seems able to handle those men." She put her hand on his and patted it gently.

David withdrew his hand, shook his head and called for his check. The woman, unaccustomed to being rejected by men, quickly said, "My name is Chun-hee and I don't want to be alone. I have to wait until these men go."

Her name triggered something in David's memory. "Is Chun-hee a Chinese name? Are you from China?"

She laughed, and her face lit up while her eyes narrowed. "I am from Korea."

She didn't say which Korea, so he innocently asked, "From Seoul?"

"I am from a small place not far from Seoul. Will you please stay here with me until they leave? Or, if you wish, we can go somewhere else."

The suggestive tone of her last words left no doubt in David's mind that she was setting him up for something. When she asked, "Where are you from?" The sound of the alarm-bells in his mind turned in to ambulance sirens.

"I am from Portugal, but I now live in London. My name is Dawid Costa-Suarez, but everyone calls me Dave."

Chun-hee repeated his name, "Dave. Such a short name for a big, handsome man. Dave, what would you like to do, that is if you are not waiting for your wife?"

"Why not stay here and enjoy the ambience of the place.

If you wish, we can get a better view of the sea and breathe some fresh air."

He ordered a couple drinks from the bar, and when they each had a drink in their hand, he led the way to deck. From the corner of his eye, he saw that two of the men, rose from their table, and followed them. By now, he was convinced they were North Koreans, and up to no good.

He was unarmed and although he was confident he could handle two unarmed assailants, he wasn't sure that they, and Chun-hee for that matter, weren't carrying guns of knives. In any case, he didn't want to get involved in a fight that may end badly for him, or at the very least, compromise his mission.

So, he made a fast about-face, telling Chun-hee he needed to go to the restroom, and before she could answer, he turned away, pushing his way between the two Koreans before they could react.

He walked up to the bar, asked the bartender for his check and paid it, adding a twenty-dollar bill, and said, "Could you get someone to walk with me to my car, I have trouble unlocking the door."

The bartender smiled, caught on there could be a scene because of the beautiful woman, and called his assistant.

David and the young Mexican exited the bar and he quickly got in his car and drove back to the hotel.

***

Chun-hee watched the whole scene, then scolded the two Koreans who had followed them to the deck. She blamed them for letting the suspected CIA agent slip away.

She said she didn't believe his story about being Portuguese and was sure he was an American agent. She said their salvage operation, planned for the next day could be in danger, and they would be held accountable.

***

David returned to his room, and when he turned his cell phone on, saw there was a message waiting. He opened it and was thrilled to see that the strange ship had been identified as a salvage vessel.

The pieces of the giant jigsaw puzzle were beginning to fall in place. The stolen Raptor probably landed at the small airfield in Puerto Penasco and was hidden in the small hangar. This would involve a handful of people at most—the air-traffic controller, a couple mechanics or ground crew personnel, customs and passport control officials, and manager of the airfield.

Their cooperation and silence could be bought for pitiful sum—after all, they didn't get many opportunities to earn easy money of this kind. The plane could take off at night a few days later, carry out the raid on the naval base in San Diego, and never return to the same airfield. The presence of the salvage vessel in Wagner Basin could add a vital missing piece to the puzzle—clarify how the plane could disappear from the face of the earth.

If Lara crash-landed the plane in relatively shallow water the plane could be lying on the seabed, with or without the daring pilot's dead body. David knew that Le Docteur had shown no qualms in the past when his lovers stopped being useful and became a burden. He wondered if Lara made it to safety.

The presence of the salvage vessel and the Koreans, and David was sure they were from the DPRK, in this sleepy Mexican resort, could only mean that Le Docteur had made a deal with them. One part of the deal was obvious—he gave them the wreck of the F-22.

He reckoned it would be worth a king's ransom to the Koreans—it would give them access to most advanced stealth technology and provide a propaganda triumph in the ongoing battle with the U.S.

What bothered him was the 'elephant in the room'—what did the DPRK pay Le Docteur in return for this technological wonder? Money was not an issue—NEMESIS still had its supporters, despite the fiasco in London. So, he wondered, what does the DPRK have that the mastermind terrorist wanted badly? Suddenly the answer dawned on him—a nuke!

He had to share his conclusion with his boss, Haim Shimony, the head of Mossad, but had no secure line and he was sure the NSA was monitoring all communications.

He feared that if the North Koreans found him and murdered or kidnapped him from the hotel room, there was nothing and nobody who could stop them. Worse than that—no one would know about Le Docteur's plan, and he would be able to carry out the deadliest terrorist attack in the history of the human kind, and perhaps even instigate a nuclear war.

David's Mossad team was due in the morning, but he had

to survive the night. The Koreans had seen his rental car, as he drove away from the bar, and if they spread out and searched the parking lots of the hotels in the area, it wouldn't take them long to find it.

After that, finding his room would be easy. He didn't want to think what would happen once they found him. He considered his options. Staying in the room was not one of them—they outnumbered him, were probably armed and would easily overpower him, or murder him quietly in the room. He could get into his car and drive away—to another hotel or to a remote spot and sleep in the car. He could go down to the reception and change his room, but that wouldn't buy him much time.

That left three other options—he could sneak to the parking lot, steal a car and drive away. He had been trained to do that but knew that it could get him in trouble with the local police. An alternative was to go down to the hotel's bar, strike up a friendly conversation with a woman that would lead to his spending the night in the safety of her room. He had done this before as part of the Mossad training manual and with his handsome good looks he had no trouble excelling in the training exercise.

From what he had seen in the hotel lobby and dining room he knew there were several single women who would gladly play along, but he feared that if he tried that he would be spotted in the bar by the Koreans. The last option was uncomfortable and was not risk free. He could leave the hotel through one of the service doors, hide in one of the hotel's utility rooms or in the pool-house and pass the night there.

He could even stroll along the beach, find a secluded corner and sleep there.

The main risk was the Koreans posted people on all the hotel exits and eliminating him in an isolated spot would be easy. Then another idea formed in his mind—he would lock his door, go out to the balcony and climb down to a vacant room on a lower floor and break in through the balcony. He could also try to go sideways on the same floor until he found a suitable room.

He remembered watching a movie in which the hero did just that, and when he broke into a room he thought was unoccupied an elderly matron grabbed him and dragged him to her bed. He realized his brain was starting to play tricks on him, so he quickly moved an armchair to block the door, verified it was locked, turned off the lights and stepped out to the balcony and closed the door behind him.

He was on the third floor of the resort hotel, so had no problem handling the height. He bent his head around the wall that separated his room from the one next door and saw the light in the room was on. He peeped through a gap in the curtain and saw an old couple watching their TV screen and arguing about something he couldn't figure.

The room on the other side of his room was dark, and he could not see if it was vacant. Then he saw two bathing suits laid out to dry on a deckchair. He skipped from his balcony to the next one, trying not to disturb the bathing suits, and peeped around the wall to the next room. This one looked dark and empty, so he went over the railing and listened for a long moment. When he heard no sound, he jimmied the lock on the balcony door and entered the room without switching on any light.

He checked the drawers and cupboards in the bedroom and was glad to see they were empty. Next, he went into the bathroom and saw no toothbrush or personal items. He placed the security chain on the door in case someone tried to open the door it would give him enough time to escape through the balcony. He then lay down on the bed. He didn't dare use the room's phone or speak on his own cell phone.

He sent a short text message to his team, in Hebrew: *Onto something big. Send ETAs and will meet you at airport.*

He turned off the volume on his cell phone and tried to nap. This was one other item from the training manual—teach your body to relax even in the most stressful circumstances.

***

Chun-hee and her Korean thugs didn't need a long time to locate David's rental car in the parking lot of his hotel. There were not many cars parked there—the hotel catered mainly to organized tours that flew to the Puerto Penasco airfield and were taken by bus to the resort hotel.

Chun-hee told her mates to wait in the lobby, while she went to the reception desk and spoke to the night manager. After a few American dollars changed hands, and some suggestive smiles were exchanged, the manager accepted her story about being stood up by her boyfriend. He searched the list of guests and said there was no one by the name of Dawid Costa-Suarez.

She pretended to be surprised and said he may have been using a different name to confuse her and gave him a description of David. The night manager said there was someone who fit this description, but he would need a strong incentive to jog his memory. A fistful of American dollars refreshed his memory and he gave her David's room number.

She said she would like to surprise her boyfriend and asked for a key to the room. This cost her quite a few American dollars and the night manager said he should accompany her to the room to comply with the hotel privacy policy.

Chun-hee was getting impatient with this ongoing extortion technique, but grumbled it was not necessary, cursed him in Korean under her breath, and handed over the last of her American dollars.

Chun-hee returned to the lobby and issued instructions in a terse tone to her colleagues. One of them returned to the parking lot to keep an eye on David's car, one took a new position in the lobby, from which he could see the elevators and the door of the stairwell. The third man waited by the emergency exit. The two other men followed Chun-hee to the elevator.

***

After she left, without thanking him, he couldn't quite understand how any red-blooded man stand-up this delicious-looking woman could, but as his formal education in psychology was nonexistent he didn't pursue the matter.

The night-manager saw the woman being curt with her

colleagues and started to regret that he had supplied the beautiful woman with the information about the guest. He was convinced she had played him and feared she was up no good when the solemn men with her got up and all spread out. It was like they were on a mission. He considered calling the police for help, but then figured he would have to explain how he gave the woman information on a guest, and that would possibly cost him his cushy job.

***

The elevator doors opened on the third floor and the Koreans stepped out. Chun-hee immediately noticed the CCD camera in the corridor and covered the lens with a scarf she had ready, and then motioned for the men to take positions on each side of the door to David's room. She checked to see that no guests were in the corridor and quietly inserted the plastic key into the slot and tried to open the door noiselessly. The lock clicked, but she felt a heavy object keeping the door closed.

She pushed harder and it moved, but the security chain blocked the door from opening any further. She signaled to one of her companions, who came forward and pulled a hunting-knife from the sleeve of his jacket and within seconds sliced through the thin chain, almost without making any noise.

The Koreans entered the room, and as expected found it empty. Chun-hee rushed to the balcony door and realized it was not locked. She now knew for sure the man had anticipated her actions and escaped from the room. This confirmed her suspicion he was an intelligence agent of some kind. She rummaged through his belongings but couldn't find a wallet, or passport, or any kind of documentation that would reveal his identity.

She pulled the balcony door open and saw that it would be easy for someone with minimal athletic ability to climb down to the ground level, or sideways along other balconies that circled the façade of the building.

She was frustrated because there was no way she and her companions could do a room-to-room search without causing a major disturbance and alerting the authorities. Then an idea struck her. She returned to the room and asked one of her companions for his cigarette lighter. When he gave it to her, she ignited a piece of paper and held it under the smoke detector for a few seconds until the shrieking of the alarm system rang through the entire hotel.

The three Koreans stepped into the corridor and joined the mass of confused and hysterical guests that started running around in a panic. Chun-hee and the Koreans took the stairs down to the lobby and joined their colleague who had been standing there all along.

The night manager tried to calm the panic-stricken guests and directed them to the pool area to safely wait for the firefighters.

David, who was napping just two doors away from his room, had heard the slight commotion the Koreans caused when they broke into his original room, and wondered if they would find him. When the fire alarm sounded, he figured it was set by the frustrated Koreans, so remained safely locked up in his new room.

He was sure it was a way to trap him and appreciated the initiative and strong nerves of the Korean woman, who, he was sure, was in charge of the five men he had seen in the bar.

He heard the trucks of the fire department arriving, and then the sounds of the crew in the corridor just outside his door, as they checked the reason the smoke alarm went off in his original room.

A few minutes later he heard the excited guests returning to their rooms after they were assured all was well and there was no danger.

He smiled to himself—the ploy performed by the Koreans would have worked in nine out of ten cases, but he was too smart and well-trained to fall for it.

***

Chun-hee and her thugs waited in vain for David to show up. This confused her, because she thought she had outsmarted him, and she was beginning to think he may have left the hotel before they had spotted him.

She even considered he may have parked the car and then left the hotel by taxi, or by some other means, but then thought the night-manager would have told her that.

She decided that her best strategy would be to discontinue the pursuit of the CIA agent, by now she was convinced that was his identity, and carry out the salvage operation as quickly as possible.

She summoned her team and told them they would take a speedboat ride to the salvage ship, immediately, in the hope that the CIA had not yet discovered the plan to salvage the sunken plane.

The salvage ship was already over the site of the sunken plane and had positioned itself so that the plane would be raised on the side of the ship hidden from the shore.

Chun-hee would lead the divers to the plane and organize the salvage operation. Her plan was to place inflatable rubber tubes below the wings, tail, and fuselage, and then inflate them in a controlled fashion until the plane was off the seabed. Cables would then be placed in the proper positions, and the inflatable tubes would be removed so the plane remained hanging on the cables.

The ship's winches would slowly raise the plane above surface of the sea and hoist it on to the deck. This last part would be performed after dark. As soon as the plane was on board, it would be covered with a large tarpaulin, and the ship would head out of the Gulf of California and away from Mexican territorial waters.

She reckoned they would be highly vulnerable during the forty or so hours it would take them to traverse the almost seven hundred mile stretch of the Gulf of California.

They would be at the mercy of the Mexican authorities if they decided to stop the ship and search it, and there was nothing she could do to expedite the sea voyage. Even after they had escaped to the Pacific Ocean they may boarded, illegally according to international maritime law, by ships of the United States Navy.

Worse, yet, they could be sunk by a plane and disappear to the bottom of the Pacific with their prize cargo on board. The salvage vessel was rigged in a way that would enable it to change its appearance beyond recognition—the derricks would be folded, the upper structure and bridge would be modified, and the name of the ship would be changed.

Satellite imagery would not be able to identify the ship, or at least, so she hoped. These structural changes would begin the minute the Raptor was on board and would be completed long before it entered the ocean.

It all depended on getting away from the CIA agent before he could report the presence of the Koreans and the salvage vessel. So, she made a slight change in the getaway plans.

She would head to the salvage vessel with three of her agents—she figured that they would need a minimum of four people to carry out that part of the salvage operation—and the other two would remain at Puerto Penasco and track down the man she thought was a CIA agent.

Once they found him, they would kill him outright, without asking any questions. If they were caught by Mexican authorities, which was highly likely considering the circumstances, they would commit suicide, or if denied that option, they would have to hold their mouth closed for a minimum of three days, to allow the salvage vessel to reach the Pacific Ocean.

The two men selected for the termination job assured Chun-hee they would prefer death to interrogation and imprisonment and showed her that each of them was equipped with a 'suicide pill' sewn as a button on their suit.

***

Embassy of the DPRK, Mexico City

Kim had been closely monitoring the operation at Puerto Penasco from the basement of the North Korean embassy. He was upset when he received Chun-hee's report of the events in the sensitive area of operations.

He knew that her failure would be his death sentence, as well as hers, and probably also of Uncle Chong. He considered reporting the setback to Pyongyang and advising them to delay the delivery of the 'toy,' but thought that if there was a chance of eliminating the CIA agent and raising the plane from the seabed to the ship, the deal could go through.

He suspected that Uncle Chong had no intention of delivering a real nuke to Don Alberto, but wondered if the esteemed leader of his country wouldn't jump at the opportunity to detonate a nuke in the heart of New York or Washington, if there was a slim chance of getting away with it.

He called Chun-hee and was taken aback by her harsh tone. "Kim, I am busy. What do you want?"

"I have been following your progress. Do you need more help to take care of the CIA guy?"

"By the time your reinforcements get here, it will be too late. My people will get to him before that and carry out their mission. Successfully, I hope. I'm on board the ship and getting ready to dive, so don't call me again. I'll report as soon as we have the object on board."

Kim was disturbed by her terse response. He didn't know

her well, but she had a reputation of being the coolest, and deadliest agent the Ministry of State Security has ever recruited.

Chun-hee was under pressure and seemed to have trouble handling it. This added to Kim's uneasy feeling about the progress of the operation. He decided to share his concerns with Chong, but when he called his office at the MSS he was told the Chong was on his way to Mexico.

This unannounced visit increased his anxiety—he felt that Chong came to oversee this crucial part of the operation and wondered who was supervising the other part of the deal—the delivery of the 'toy' to the hands of Don Alberto in Bermuda.

As he had nothing better to do until hearing from Chun-hee or the arrival of Chong, Kim decided he needed some fresh air and went to have a cool beer at his favorite café, where he had met with Don Alberto.

When he arrived there, the proprietor welcomed him as one of his regular customers and told him the strange story about the beautiful woman that came looking for her husband, who was seen in the café in Kim's company.

Kim instantly grasped the significance and questioned the proprietor about the woman. When he got her description and heard how she presented the photo of her 'husband,' he was sure she wasn't a CIA agent—their style would be to come and offer money for information or threaten the café's owner.

This subtle approach was more like Mossad's *modus operandi*, and fit the information from Washington that the Israelis had joined forces with the Americans to track the Islamic terror network. He quickly drank his beer and rushed back to the embassy. He left messages for Chun-hee and Chong to call him as soon as they could, and sat by his desk in the basement, staring at the phone, willing it to ring.

***

Two hours later the phone finally rang. Kim grabbed it. Chun-hee was brisk again. "Kim, I told you I'll call you when we have the object on board. We have detached it from the seabed, but still need to tie the cables and raise it. We have come up to replace our air tanks and rest a little. What is bothering you?"

"I think the man you saw is not CIA. He is much more dangerous—probably a Mossad operative who has picked up your trail."

He told her about the conversation with the café's proprietor, and continued, "You must silence him before he gets any information to the CIA. If it's Mossad, they would have very limited resources here in Mexico. He's probably alone, and may be waiting for reinforcements, so act quickly before they complicate things any further. By the way, Chong is coming here to supervise, so don't make any mistakes."

"Kim, don't treat me like a little girl. I know what to do. Thanks for the update. I can now understand his behavior and how he managed to dupe us last night. Yes, he was too clever for CIA. I need to go back to continue with the salvage operation."

As soon as he hung up, his phone rang again. It was the sentry at the front door telling him Uncle Chong had arrived.

A minute later, the basement door opened, and a grim looking Chong marched in, accompanied by two of the embassy's security officers.

"Uncle Chong, I am glad to see you. I have information for your ears only."

Chong saw he was serious, not apprehensive, and waved the security guys away. "Kim, what is it? You look very anxious."

Kim gave him a quick update about the events at Puerto Penasco and the Mossad's involvement. Chong tried to keep a stony expression, but it was evident the news bothered him. He said, "We have to operate on three fronts. First and foremost, eliminate the Mossad agent. Second, expedite the salvage operation and get the ship out to the open sea as quickly as possible. Third, hold back the delivery of the 'toy.' Once it is in the hands of our Don Alberto, there is no way we can stop him. I don't want to lose control, and certainly don't want to lose face with our leader. I need not tell you what will happen to all of us if we deliver the 'toy' but don't get the plane."

As Chong finished speaking, the phone rang. Kim picked it up with shaking hands, fearing the worst, like a call from the leader enquiring what was going on.

It was Chun-hee. "The cargo has been loaded and we are heading south. It went without a hitch. I am waiting for the report from my two agents. The plan is for them to come to the embassy after completing their mission. See you at home in a couple weeks."

Chong smiled. "Now, it's up to the ship to get to the ocean. I'll call the leader and tell him the first phase of the project has been successfully accomplished. After the call, we can go and celebrate with the famous *chickitas* of Mexico City."

CHAPTER 18

Puerto Penasco

The jubilant mood at the Korean embassy was not shared by David in Puerto Penasco. He didn't know how many men were after him, but he was sure the Koreans would try to stop him, probably eliminate him. He was certain the Koreans, after failing to flush him out at the hotel, would be keeping an eye of his car in the parking lot.

To evade them, he pulled his baseball cap down over his face, stooped as if he was an older man and mingled with one of the tourist groups. He hopped on the bus that was taking the group to the airport and no one asked him if he belonged to the group.

His main advantage over the Koreans was that they stood out among the crowds of tourists and Mexicans, so he had a good chance of spotting them before they saw him. He considered calling his American colleague, Eugene Powers, and telling him of his suspicions concerning the salvage vessel and the involvement of the DPRK but wanted to have conclusive evidence before making a call that could possibly lead to a confrontation between the U.S. and Mexico.

Some of the tourists on the bus stared at him, wondering

what he was doing with them, but no one accosted him during the short ride to the airport. Once they all got off the bus and waited for the driver's assistant to pull their luggage out of the bus, David sauntered over to the terminal.

He checked the arrivals schedule—there were not many flights on the old-fashioned electronic board—and saw that his team would be arriving just before noon. He wandered around the small terminal, trying to remain inconspicuous, while constantly keeping an eye on the entrance to the terminal in case the Koreans figured he had gone there.

He was greatly relieved when Edna and the Fish arrived from Tijuana. Joe and Mata hired a small plane to fly across Wagner Basin from San Felipe and showed up at the terminal a few minutes later. The Mossad team rented a minivan with dark windows and drove to the beach.

On the way there, David told his team about the events of the previous evening, and how he narrowly escaped. He said now it was time to go on the offensive and turn the tables on the Korean agents—the hunters would become the hunted, in the best Mossad tradition.

They quickly devised a plan that would draw the Koreans to them, using David as bait. They would drop him off at the back entrance of the hotel and he would walk to his rental car.

The van would drive to the parking lot and take a position not far from David's car. Mata, the driver, would step out carrying the tire iron in her hand and pretend to use it to check the van's tires. Edna would also get out of the van and appear to be assisting Mata.

The two women would look guileless and not pose a

threat. As soon as the Koreans approached David, the whole team would pounce on them. Mata would use the tire iron to crush one of them, with Joe as a backup, while the Fish with David's help, would overpower the second one. They would use plastic ties to restrain them and quickly toss them into the van. They would take the van to a secluded place, David following in his car, and interrogate them.

The plan sounded simple—they had no time or means to devise something more sophisticated—and it all depended on the fact that there were only two Koreans and they were not armed with guns.

Fortunately, that was the case, and the execution of the plan was carried out flawlessly. The Koreans were overwhelmed by the sudden turn of events and didn't even have the opportunity to bite the poison-laden button sewn on their jackets.

In any case, they refused to say anything, and the language barrier didn't help. The Koreans couldn't, or wouldn't, speak English or Spanish, so the interrogation was carried out mostly in sign language.

When they were shown pictures of a ship and the F-22 plane, they were visibly startled but remained tongue tied. The older Korean agent tried to indicate he would rather be dead than speak, by dropping his head, closing his eyes, and allowing his tongue to dangle out of his mouth. The younger agent didn't budge when he saw that.

David called his team to the side and said, "I doubt we'll get anything out of them. Their reaction when they saw the plane shows our suspicions are correct—that is the reason the Koreans are here. We need to get a closer look at the salvage vessel, so I'll go to the pier and try to get a speedboat to check what they are up to. Mata and the Fish will come with me, and Joe and Edna will remain here with the Koreans. We'll have to let them go free, tomorrow, at the latest. We don't need to kill them, as they don't pose any risk to our operation, and we certainly don't want to start a blood-feud between Mossad and the DPRK."

***

They had no trouble getting a speedboat and taking it out to observe the salvage vessel. David didn't want to get too close because he worried the people on board may be armed and hostile, so they kept their distance.

They could tell some activity was taking place although the ship stayed on anchor. David assumed there were divers but couldn't see them. They didn't want to hang around for too long, so they returned to the shore and drove back to the place where the van was still parked.

Edna said that everything was in order and they decided to leave the Koreans in their custody until morning, with Joe and the Fish guarding them, while the rest of the team took rooms in the resort hotel to watch the salvage vessel from the shore.

***

When they woke up the next morning, the salvage ship was gone. Apparently, it sailed away during the night without turning on the navigation lights. David wasn't too worried because he knew the ship would need almost two days to clear the Gulf of California and travel the nearly seven hundred miles to the ocean.

He saw on the map there was a 'choke point' at Tiburon Basin, when the ship would have to pass on either side of Isla San Esteban. He planned on getting on a helicopter to do a fly-over and get a good look at the ship's cargo.

If the Raptor was on board, he would call Eugene and still have ample time to arrange an interception of the ship before it could swerve around Cabo San Lucas, the southernmost point of Baja California.

First, he took care of the two Koreans, by injecting them with a tranquilizer which would keep them heavily sedated until the late afternoon. By then, the Mossad crew would be far away from Puerto Penasco. He was disappointed there were no helicopters for charter at the airfield but found a Cessna 210N.

The plane was more than thirty years old and the pilot was at least double the plane's age, but it could seat six people, had a cruise speed of two hundred twenty miles per hour and a range of one thousand miles. It could easily cover the distance the salvage vessel travelled overnight in one hour.

The negotiation for the charter was short—the old pilot loved American dollars and was more than willing to participate in an adventure. David told him some cock and bull story about smugglers on board the ship.

The five Mossad agents boarded the plane. The pilot was cleared for take-off by the air-traffic controller, who was unaware the small Cessna was tracking the F-22 that made him a rich and happy, but frightened, man. He was also unaware that, thanks to the discovery of Chun-hee and her Korean thugs, he had been spared the interrogation David had intended to put him through.

The Cessna flew due south, following the eastern shoreline of the Gulf of California. At David's request, the pilot kept the plane at an altitude of three thousand feet that afforded a good view of the few ships heading south from Puerto Penasco.

A few minutes after take-off they could see the small airfield, really an airstrip, of Puerto Libertad that didn't even have a terminal building and seemed deserted. David wondered how many other airstrips dotted the Mexican dessert areas, and how many of those served drug traffickers and smugglers carrying out their illicit businesses.

About thirty minutes into their flight they spotted a ship about the size of the salvage vessel they were seeking, but its rigging didn't look like that of the ship they had surveyed the previous day off-shore from Puerto Penasco.

The ship was flying a Panamanian flag, but everyone knew this was often used as a 'flag of convenience' and only meant the ship was registered in Panama. David figured this must be the ship they were after, as they had passed no other vessel of similar size.

David didn't want to draw attention to the plane, so asked the pilot to continue the southwesterly course he had been following, while they took as many photos of the ship and its deck during the short period they were over it.

There was a large object on deck, but it was completely

covered with a tarpaulin. Its shape didn't look like a plane, or for that matter, like any other recognizable object. In the photos taken with a telescopic lens human figures could be seen on deck, but the features were too blurred to tell whether they were Koreans.

The pilot followed David's instructions and headed back east after the ship was out of sight. They landed at the small Guaymas airport designated as an international airport, meaning there was a Mexican passport control and customs inspection station there.

This airport was larger and better equipped than the airstrips they had passed along the way, and he reckoned they were several hours ahead of the ship. He paid the pilot and after giving him a nice tip, arranged to continue tracking the ship the following day.

The Mossad team headed to the large resort hotel of Playa de Cortes on the beach called Bahia Bacochibampo.

David didn't waste any more time and called Eugene. The line was not a secure one, so he watched his words carefully. "Eugene, you should come and join us in Baja California."

In fact, they were on the east shore of the Gulf of California that wasn't technically in Baja California. "There are very interesting things going on here, and we have seen a ship carrying a special cargo."

Eugene caught on. "Is it something that cannot be purchased outside the United States?"

"Exactly, a very rare item, that can be seen only during the daytime."

"David, can you inspect it?"

"I'd need you and your friends, many of them, and I am quite sure the people on board do not welcome visitors. They are under protection of local and international maritime laws, so they cannot be easily persuaded to stop being inhospitable. You may want to look at the ship from the sky, and then decide what you want to do about it."

"I'll make arrangements for that. What do you suggest?"

"I would advise you to wait until they are far away from the local government's jurisdiction to minimize the repercussions and avoid a conflict with your neighbor. Get ready to meet them when they head west to their home and prepare a welcome party."

"Do you propose a short visit or something more permanent?"

"Eugene, if you want to recover your property then you would have to pay a long visit. I think it would be simpler, cleaner, and without much of a fuss, if you let Archimedean laws of physics take over. Then you can shout 'not eureka, not eureka,' if you know what I mean."

The two of them were physicists and it didn't take a genius to figure out the ship would sink without displacing a significant volume of water.

***

Embassy of the DPRK, Mexico City

The Koreans on board the modified salvage vessel noticed the Cessna overhead and followed it with their eyes. There were a few other light planes they had seen since leaving Puerto Penasco, but none seemed to take a special interest in their ship.

Chun-hee was a little disturbed by the Cessna that flew lower than the other aircraft they had encountered, but as it didn't turn or circle them, she dismissed the incident. She did report it to the embassy and gave the tail number for them to check.

Kim got back to her and said the owner of the plane lived in Puerto Penasco and chartered his services to tourists who wanted to see the Gulf of California from above, or who simply needed to get from one place to the next, as an air-taxi service.

Chun-hee asked if her two agents had contacted the embassy and Kim said he hadn't heard from them. This concerned Chun-hee, but there was nothing she could do about it, except wait for them to call.

It was after noon when the senior agent finally called. "Chun-hee, we were ambushed by five Mossad agents and taken prisoner. We were interrogated but said nothing. They showed us photos of the ship and the plane, but we didn't admit we knew what those were. Eventually they set us free."

"You are to return to the embassy in Mexico City and report there. Your failure will be severely punished."

"We know and apologize. But we can confirm the man was not CIA or American, as you thought, so it may not be so bad."

"Let me consider the significance and repercussions." She terminated the call, and immediately called Kim to update him. "Kim, the two men have failed and disgraced us. Make sure they are treated accordingly."

"Don't worry about it. It's not your fault. Just continue with the goods."

***

Chong closely followed the conversation and nodded to Kim in approval. After Kim hung up, Chong said, "Do you think the ship has slipped away unnoticed? I am afraid those damn Israelis will come running to their American friends and tell them what they have uncovered. I won't feel safe until the ship docks at Nampo—not a minute before that. I would like to reinforce the crew with some of our elite troops and anti-aircraft missiles as well as torpedoes. I would also like a naval escort as soon as the salvage vessel reaches international waters. That is when the risk is greatest."

Kim said, "Perhaps we should direct the ship to the port of Wonsan, it will save at least five days of sailing, and the ship can keep its distance from the corrupt capitalists in occupied South Korea."

"You are right, but first we need to cross the vast Pacific Ocean. The Americans treat the eastern part, between Hawaii and California, as their own private pool."

Kim added, "We should have sent our navy toward the salvage vessel. If they leave our port now it will take them a couple weeks to get to Mexico."

He knew the distance between Mexico and North Korea was almost seven thousand miles by air, but the ships had to circumvent Japan, so they probably had to cover an additional seven hundred miles. He reckoned if they could sail at twenty-five knots, they could travel seven hundred miles a day.

Chong smiled. "I was pulling your leg earlier. They left port ten days ago and should be able to rendezvous with the vessel in two days' time. If the Americans dare to carry out an act of piracy on the high seas, then they will meet with our powerful naval force. In addition, our leader who is following the operation closely, will threaten the Americans with our new extended-range intercontinental missiles, that, thanks to our nuclear scientists, are now equipped with light-weight nuclear weapons. Our leader has warned the Americans that any act of aggression on their part will be answered not only by the total destruction of Seoul and its regime of collaborators, but also by taking out Los Angeles and San Francisco."

Kim laughed. "The American President would thank us for doing this—he doesn't like the people who live in those cities."

Chong ignored the humor and raised the question that really bothered him. "Do you think we should deliver the 'toy' we promised Don Alberto?"

"Not yet. We should do it only after the plane is on our soil." Then a new thought struck him. "Uncle Chong, on second thought, perhaps we should deliver the 'toy' regardless. If the plane is delivered safely, then fine, we keep our promise, but even if the ship is intercepted before it can reach our country, and the plane is taken out of our hands, then we need to retaliate. Don Alberto's plan is our best chance of doing it and getting away with it."

"Kim, you are a true asset to our country. So, we continue with the plan, and give Don Alberto as much assistance as we can."

***

Hamilton, Bermuda

Le Docteur and Lara were enjoying their vacation on the beautiful island of Bermuda, or more accurately, on the islands of Bermuda. Le Docteur had contacted the DPRK embassy in Mexico City a few times and each time was told to wait patiently for the completion of the deal.

He knew the Koreans wouldn't deliver the 'toy' until they successfully retrieved the plane from the seabed. He also realized that transporting a nuke, even a small compact one, across half the world wasn't as easy as ordering e-books from Amazon.

He hoped Uncle Chong would deliver, as promised, but wasn't entirely confident. He realized that once the plane was on board the salvage vessel the only reason the Koreans wouldn't renege on the deal was their shared interest in hurting the Americans.

He had no idea the hated Mossad was hot on the trail of the Raptor and had managed to link him to the Koreans, and Kim at the embassy didn't share this bit of information with him.

The Uyghurs he had contacted in Hamilton were

cooperative, so long as he paid them for their services. He made up some superfluous errands, just to keep them busy and strengthen their ties to him. He had them post a twenty-four-hour watch on one of the docks at Hamilton harbor, and compile a report on the shipping activities and procedures for unloading shipping containers until they were cleared to leave the port. They were very patient and didn't bother him with questions about the main task.

He had several discussions with Lara about the delivery of the 'toy' to the United States. Taking it on board a plane would be a suicide mission and she was not sure she was still that dedicated to the cause.

It was ironic that her relationship with Jacque, as she called Le Docteur, gave her a good reason to want to live and enjoy a decent life, and that changed her perspective. The 'toy' could be delivered by ship, in a standard container, with a low probability of it being found and neutralized but limited the list of potential targets and the damage the bomb could cause.

New York, and perhaps Philadelphia or Boston, were the preferred targets on the short list. Washington, DC, was the primary target for aerial delivery, in fact, detonating the 'toy' two thousand feet above the Washington Mall would decapitate the political leadership and military power of the U.S. in an instant, with one sharp blow.

Lara could do this on her own, and that would leave Le Docteur in a safe place. She wondered if he would mourn her at all, and how long it would take him to find a substitute. Whenever the subject came up, he assured her that he would be on the plane with her, but she wasn't convinced.

Then, there was another issue they had neglected until now. Le Docteur said to Lara the 'toy' would have to be armed before it could be operational. Even the cynical operators of the DPRK, with little or no regard to human-life, wouldn't send an atom bomb across half the globe without making sure that it was safe.

They didn't want an accidental atomic explosion on one of their ships or in one of their ports. Arming a nuke was not like pulling the pin out of a hand-grenade—it required an experienced scientist or engineer. When Le Docteur made the deal with Uncle Chong this was not mentioned, and he made a mental note to demand the 'toy' be accompanied by an expert who would arm the device.

Lara searched the net, looking for reports of incidents in which the pilot of a light plane managed to parachute to safety. There were numerous stories of fighter-pilots and bomber crews who had ditched their damaged planes—but those were usually from World War II.

Modern general aviation pilots didn't carry parachutes as a norm so there was no relevant information. Lara's recent experience of ejecting herself from the Raptor before it hit the water, was not a good case for comparison because the jet-fighter had been designed for such an eventuality, while light planes were not. She believed that if she would find a suitable plane, one with a door that could be opened sufficiently easily and widely enough, she could put the plane on autopilot and jump to safety, well out of the lethal radius of the bomb. Autopilot systems, she knew, were reliable enough to keep the plane on course for many miles, and the system could self-correct for the change in airflow when the door was open. She tried to find precedents on the web, but none were suitable for what she planned.

Le Docteur understood her qualms and encouraged her to devise a system that would enable the plane to deliver its deadly cargo to the target and give her a reasonable chance to survive.

Lara asked him, "Do you know the size and weight of the 'toy'?"

"I read they have managed to reduce the weight of their nukes, those intended for missiles, to four hundred and fifty pounds. This is much less than the bombs the Americans dropped on Hiroshima and Nagasaki that weighed close to five tons, but much more than the 'suitcase' bombs allegedly made by the Soviet Union or than the tactical nukes manufactured for artillery shells. Does this pose a problem?"

"Not really, I am pretty sure that all light planes that have the range to reach the U.S. from here can carry that weight."

"Lara, that reminds me of something. Did you check the distance from Bermuda to our targets?"

"The distance from here to New York is about seven hundred and seventy-five miles, and to Washington DC, about seventy miles more. This is well within the range of most light planes, certainly if they don't have to return here. I'll check which planes are available at the airport, and perhaps we'll have to ask Uncle Chong for help, if nothing here fits our needs."

While they were having this conversation Le Docteur received a coded e-mail from Kim, who was using a computer in one of the internet cafés in Mexico City, and a fictitious e-mail address. "The 'toy' you had ordered from our store will be at the port closest to you in three days' time. You'll receive notification on the details from our representative at the local office."

Le Docteur showed the message to Lara. "This means we have to finalize our plan. I think the best option is delivery by air, from a plane that will do the final part of its journey on auto-pilot. We should minimize the time the 'toy' is in our possession—so check which aircraft are available for rent. Money is no object. I'll reply to Kim's message and remind him to send a skilled technician to arm the 'toy,' as we discussed."

CHAPTER 19

Gulf of California

Chun-hee, on board the salvage vessel, that was now named Pogag (a name she made up, using every second letter of Pyongyang) was starting to relax. She looked at the flag of Panama flying in the stern of the ship and smiled.

The ship was now swerving west around Cabo San Lucas and heading out of Mexican territorial water, into the Pacific Ocean. There had been no sightings of suspect aircraft during the last twenty-four hours, and she dismissed the flight of the Cessna the previous day as a mere coincidence.

She knew the Americans had an array of other aerial observation platforms but figured if they were to stop the ship with its precious cargo they would do so in cooperation with the Mexican authorities. Once the ship passed into international waters she felt a relief, and that they would be met by an escort of naval vessels of the DPRK added to her good mood.

The only thing that kept bothering her was the presence of Mossad agents in Puerto Penasco and the failure of her two agents to eliminate the threat. She was confident the agents didn't divulge her plans but was surprised they allowed themselves to be taken alive. She didn't know that the Mossad agents who overpowered them knew about the suicide pills sewn into their jackets and removed them before they could bite on them.

She checked the tarpaulin over the F-22 and was satisfied it camouflaged the distinct shape of the jet fight. She checked the sentries on the ship and the readiness of the defensive systems. There were six heavily-armed men on duty around the clock. They carried AK-47s, pistols, and hunting knives—all kept out of sight but within easy reach.

In addition, under camouflage netting, were four surface-to-air FIM-92 Stinger missiles with infrared homing, which served as a man-portable air-defense system. These were stolen from an American army base in Afghanistan and purchased by agents of the DPRK. There were two 20mm rap-id-firing guns positioned on the bridge, under a tarpaulin, and could provide 360-degree protection, as well as be aimed at any snooping aircraft. Despite these defensive measures, she knew her mission wouldn't be accomplished until the salvage vessel was tied to a berth in Wonsan port, in North Korea.

***

Twenty miles west of Cabo San Lucas

The four Bell AH-1Z Viper attack helicopters took off from the deck of the USS Wasp, that was an amphibious assault ship, on patrol off the coast of Baja California, well into international waters.

They were directed by the ship's air traffic controller to intercept the modified salvage vessel, the Pogag. Their orders were to instruct the ship to heave to and wait to be boarded. If the ship didn't comply, they were to fire a warning shot and if the ship still disobeyed, they were to forcibly board it.

The attack helicopters were followed by two MV-22B Osprey assault tiltrotors aircraft that were carrying elite troops, trained to board ships by rappelling from the aircraft to the deck. The newly appointed Admiral Bennet, who was in command of the operation, followed every move on the plasma screens in the operations center on board the Wasp.

The Pogag, as the salvage vessel was now called, ignored the call to heave to and continued to cruise westward at the same speed. One of the Vipers fired a warning shot in front of the ship, to no effect.

The lead helicopter then launched two 70mm rockets from its Hydra rocket pods, making sure the rockets passed close to the ship's bridge, as a clear sign they meant business. A moment later, a missile streaked from the ship toward the helicopter and it exploded in a ball of fire.

The Admiral saw the whole incident on his screen, and his mouth gaped open. He had not been informed the ship may be carrying surface-to-air missiles. He ordered the remaining three Vipers to attack, but before he managed to issue the command, two more helicopters were hit by surface-to-air missiles and the remaining helicopter was peppered by 20mm canon fire, while firing flares to distract the infrared homing missile.

The admiral called the Ospreys to hold back, when he

saw on his screen that a small flotilla of unidentified ships was approaching the battle scene from the west. The camera zoomed in and the ships were clearly identified as a battle group belonging to the DPRK.

They were already spread out in a battle formation. Admiral Bennet had limited authority to board the Pogag but not to engage in a naval battle with the DPRK. He ordered Captain Ewing, the captain of the Wasp, to pursue the Pogag, that was already amid the Korean flotilla, and had maneuvered to take a defensive position around the salvage vessel.

Captain Ewing saw what was going on and gave an order to send a rescue helicopter to search for survivors from the downed Vipers, and to prepare two of the AV-8B Harrier II ground attack aircrafts for immediate take-off. These planes were the second generation of the Harrier Jump Jet family, capable of vertical take-off and landing.

He looked at Admiral Bennet for approval, but the admiral hesitated to give the go-ahead. He said, "Captain Ewing, the Harriers are to provide cover for the rescue helicopter, but not to engage the Korean vessels until I give the order."

Ewing looked at him. "Admiral, we have just lost four of our Viper attack helicopters and eight crewmen. This is an open act of war. Do we sit quietly and let this act of aggression go unpunished? My pilots can blow that ship out of the water in minutes and send the entire North Korean fleet to accompany the Pogag down to the bottom of the ocean. In fact, I can launch a barrage of missiles and sink the ships without risking any of my pilots."

Admiral Bennet said, "Captain Ewing, this is a direct

order. Stand down and do nothing until we clear this with the Pentagon and the White House." He turned to the communications officer. "Lieutenant, get me the Pentagon."

Captain Ewing was seething with rage, he gave a 'general quarters' order. Then, he stormed out of the operations center and went on deck to observe the preparations. He watched the crew manning the battle stations. Word of the fate of the four Vipers had spread and the entire crew was waiting for the order to strike back—something they had trained for and practiced, but never encountered the real deal.

Finally, word from Washington arrived. "The USS Wasp is ordered to sink the Pogag but avoid hitting any of the ships flying the DPRK flag."

The Harriers took off and within minutes were in attack position above the Korean flotilla. The pilots' earphones were ringing with the sound of warning alarms that indicated that anti-aircraft missiles were locked on them.

The lead pilot asked, "Do I have permission to engage?" But before he was answered, he saw four missiles launched at the two American planes. Without hesitation, he fired a series of flares to break the lock of heat-seeking missiles, and sent his plane into a sharp spiraling dive, that was matched by his wingman.

Flying just above the waves, he managed to evade the missiles. He brought his plane up slightly and launched two of his air-to-surface missiles toward the Pogag, but before the first missile could strike the target, one of the Korean battleships maneuvered to a position that shielded the Pogag and took the direct hit of the missile. The explosion sent the second missile off its course.

Admiral Bennet knew he was now on a collision course with the North Korean battle group, and the whole battle was being monitored in the Situation Room of the White House and waited for further orders.

There were two options: sink all the Korean ships and start a war, or stand-down and seek a political solution. This was not his call, and he could only hope the people in charge would take the first option. As a career naval officer, he was too young to serve in the Vietnam war, and the conflicts in the Middle East he had participated in as a young officer, didn't provide the opportunity to engage in a full-scale naval and aerial battle. He was anxious to test his mettle and ability to lead men into battle—he was sure he would do well.

The orders he received were unambiguous: "Sink the Pogag."

The admiral's face lit up, he turned to Captain Ewing. "Captain, I expect a clean surgical strike against the Pogag, with no collateral damage."

Captain Ewing nodded and ordered a combined strike by aircraft and surface-to-surface, radar guided anti-ship missiles. He knew there was a chance other Korean warship would be accidentally hit by missiles, but he had to take that chance.

***

On board the Pogag, the initial euphoria from shooting down the four Viper helicopters was soon replaced by comprehension of the consequences.

The Korean warship hit by the first missile had miraculously stayed afloat, although there were more than forty sailors killed or wounded by the explosion.

Chun-hee knew that in the balance of casualties, the American losses were offset by the Korean losses, so, she assumed, escalation of the skirmish to a full-fledged conflict could be avoided. However, that depended on the leadership of both sides—if cool heads prevailed that could end the battle, but anything, even a nuclear-war, could happen if one of the sides persisted for reasons on 'national pride.'

The answer to her unspoken deliberations came swiftly. Four missiles homed in on the Pogag—two surface skimming ship-launched surface-to-surface and two air-to-surface missiles launched from Harriers.

This was the last thing she saw, before the Pogag exploded and rapidly sunk to the bottom on the ocean, with its prize F-22 Raptor on board, and all her crew.

***

The commander of the North Korean flotilla saw the Pogag going down and noted the coordinates. Perhaps, he wondered, if it would be possible to retrieve the prize. In any case, he knew his small battle group was no match for the wrath of the U.S. naval forces so close to their home. He ordered his ships full steam ahead to the west.

He hoped that the knowledge of the coordinates would be his reprieve from severe punishment for failing his mission to bring the Pogag safely to Wonsan.

***

The tension was very high on board the USS Wasp. Admiral Bennet saw the four direct missile hits on the Pogag and watched with satisfaction as the ship disappeared from the surface on its way down to the ocean-bed.

He anxiously monitored the Korean flotilla and was relieved to see no missiles were launched from the battleships and that they continued their way back to the DPRK at full steam ahead. Just to be on the safe side, he called for continuous surveillance of the group, to ascertain they didn't engage in some vengeful acts on the way home.

***

Embassy of the DPRK, Mexico City

Uncle Chong was simmering with rage. "This is nothing less than an act of piracy on the high seas. How can the American devils send helicopters to attack a civilian ship, flying a flag of Panama, a neutral country not involved in any conflict? We'll get our Chinese friends to condemn the United States. The loss of the ship is something we can deal with, as is the loss of the lives of our sailors, but the loss of our Raptor," he already thought of the plane as property belonging to the DPRK, "is something we cannot tolerate. I am now convinced, Kim, that your suggestion to deliver the 'toy' to Don Alberto, has merit.

This will be the answer of the Korean people—an answer that will reverberate throughout the world."

Kim listened to this outburst with interest. "Uncle Chong, you are right. This is the only thing that may save our necks."

CHAPTER 20

Hamilton, Bermuda

Le Docteur followed the news from the Pacific. There were no details of the incident, due to the censorship imposed by the White House on the one side and the DPRK on the other side. Both sides were now trying to downplay the gravity of the incident, and the use of advanced munitions and armament.

The official version was that an accident occurred just west of Baja California, where a ship registered in Panama collided with an American helicopter carrier. As a result, the civilian ship sank and there were no survivors, and the helicopter carrier suffered severe damage that resulted in the deaths of eight crewmen and the loss of some helicopters.

He suspected that the Panamanian ship was the salvage vessel and the Raptor had been on board when it plunged to the bottom of the ocean.

He was quite sure the Koreans would now have an excuse to renege on the deal and was surprised when he was informed that the 'toy' was on its way to Hamilton and an expert 'toy-maker' would accompany it.

He was told to finalize the arrangements to 'play' with the 'toy' and share it with other children.

***

Mossad headquarters, Tel Aviv

David Avivi and his team were back in Tel Aviv when the incident of the collision between the Pogag and the USS Wasp was reported.

Although there had been several reports on accidents involving ships of the U.S. Navy, they usually occurred in narrow and crowded waterways, like the Straits of Malacca, or in the Persian Gulf. He had never heard of such an event on the open high-seas.

He knew that the Pogag was the salvage vessel he had spotted in the Gulf of California, with its precious cargo, so he treated the official reports as 'fake news.'

Haim Shimony, the Mossad chief, gathered David's team for a debriefing, and David outlined his view of the incident, and raised concerns about the Koreans' reaction. He said he felt that Le Docteur had fulfilled his part of the deal with the DPRK and they may honor their commitment to supply him with a nuke, as he had speculated.

Shimony asked if the whereabouts of Le Docteur and Lara were known and no one present had the information, so he instructed David to talk to Eugene and find out if the Americans had anything relevant.

***

Washington, DC

David called Dr. Eugene Powers but was told by his secretary that Eugene was on Capitol Hill, after being summoned by Senator McCorey, the new Chairman of the Senate Committee on Foreign Relations.

David knew of the senator's reputation and nickname as Muslim-Bashing Jimbo and expected that Eugene would not enjoy the meeting with this bully. He left a message for Eugene to call him on a secure line when he returned to his office.

***

Indeed, Eugene's meeting with MBJ didn't go well. McCorey was grandstanding for the benefit of the other committee members, and Eugene's role was to function as the punching bag.

The senator didn't mince his words. "Dr. Powers, I don't like the official version of 'the incident' off the coast of Baja California. Can you assure the Committee that the stolen F-22 sunk to the bottom of the ocean?"

Eugene was at a loss for words. His agency had nothing to do with the missing Raptor, with the renegade pilot, with the salvage vessel, or with the clash with the Korean naval battle group.

He recovered enough to reply, "Mr. Chairman, the NNSA was not involved in any of the events concerning the missing plane or the chase after it. It is only due to my personal connections with Mossad we had even heard of the whereabouts of the missing plane and thanks to that information our naval forces were able to intercept the ship. I mourn the loss of lives, but I think your queries should be addressed to other government agencies and the air force."

Senator McCorey didn't like getting advice from anyone, let alone civil servants who he regarded as losers and failures. "Dr. Powers, let me remind you that your testimony here is in the line of your duties as a government employee. I didn't ask for your opinion or advice—only if you were certain the plane could not be retrieved later. Can you tell us how come you have a direct connection with a foreign intelligence organization, that bypasses official channels? You know it is against the rules and punishable by law."

"Senator McCorey, the NNSA is responsible to provide nuclear security to our nation. It does this by guarding our nuclear facilities, our nuclear materials, and personnel at the National Laboratories. We also work with friendly organizations to prevent hostile regimes and terrorists obtaining nuclear devices that may be used against the United States and its allies. That is the context of my connection with Mossad. You may be aware that Israel's dire enemies are the terrorist organizations headed by Muslims bent on the annihilation of the country that is our most friendly and staunchest ally."

This further infuriated McCorey. "Dr. Powers, you just said the NNSA is responsible for nuclear matters. I don't need a lesson in global politics and don't need your opinion on who is, and who isn't, our enemy or our ally. I repeat, can you guarantee that our plane will not be retrieved, and our coveted secrets revealed?"

"Mr. Chairman, I cannot give such a guarantee. It is not in the charter of the NNSA to do that." This time, he refrained from pointing to the agencies involved.

Apparently, this satisfied the senator, who saw that his bullying and intimidation were working. He dismissed the scientist. "Dr. Powers, thank you for not wasting more of the Committee's time."

***

Eugene returned to his office feeling like the sacrificial lamb about to be publicly sacrificed, not for the common good, but solely for the promotion of the ambitions of Senator McCorey.

The NNSA was an easy target—few people understood what those brainy scientists and strange engineers did—while other intelligence agencies like the CIA, FBI, and DHS were portrayed in countless movies and TV-series as the heroes who saved the nation.

The scientist was no fool—he recognized a dupe when he saw one, and when a true bully was tearing into him. Eugene wondered if McCorey would call for his dismissal, preferably with a public trial in which he would place the blame for the debacle on the NNSA and him, personally.

When his secretary said that David had asked him to call back, he was in foul mood. "David, I have had the most abusive treatment of my life." He went on to tell David about the committee and its chairman, and concluded, "I think I'll be the scapegoat for all the security fiascos regarding the stolen plane. Although, thanks to you, I am the one who notified the intelligence community of the plane's whereabouts, and that's how it was intercepted before falling into the hands of the Koreans."

David interjected, "Eugene, this is exactly why I have called. We know the official report of 'a collision' between the Pogag and a USS Wasp is nothing but a big pile of 'fake news' mixed with 'alternative facts.' I wish to confirm that the missing plane is once again at the bottom of the ocean."

"Yes, it is, and much deeper this time."

"Have you managed to locate Lara and Le Docteur? We fear they are up to something really bad, with the help of the Koreans."

"David, the United States main interest was to prevent the Raptor falling into the wrong hands—and this has been done. Our intelligence community is no longer concerned about the perpetrators. Sure, they would like to bring them to justice, even if it takes years, but they don't feel threatened by them. It also looks as if the DPRK has accepted the loss of their prize and damage to their ships and national pride."

"Eugene, I think you don't understand the mentality of the people in Asia. They hate nothing more than 'losing face.' They must redeem their national pride and self-esteem as this is the most valued currency in that part of the world. Believe me, most Israelis have the same blind spot—they regard our Arab neighbors as rational people who think with their brain and mind, which is true until matters of pride enter the picture. Then gut-feelings of disrespect come into play and dictate the reaction, that is often irrational and emotional. If

I were responsible for U.S. security, I would do my utmost to find these two people and neutralize them."

"David, all I can do is convey your thoughts to those responsible. I already feel better after talking to you. Let's stay in touch, that is if Senator McCorey doesn't have my head delivered on a platter."

***

Hamilton, Bermuda

Le Docteur and Lara were enjoying cocktails at the Pickled Onion, when his phone rang. The only people who knew the number were the North Koreans at the embassy in Mexico City, so he answered, expecting Kim or Chong.

An unfamiliar voice said, "Don Alberto, this is the 'toy-maker'. Look behind you and you'll see me in a floral shirt and striped Bermuda shorts."

Le Docteur turned his head and saw a couple of Korean tourists grinning at him. The man was small and wore rimless glasses and the woman was quite large and similarly attired.

Le Docteur didn't want to be seen in public with the Koreans, so answered, "Please, meet us at Point Pleasant Park at nine this evening. We'll be sitting on the bench at the edge of the park." He hung up and continued his conversation with Lara, as if nothing had happened. "Lara, we have been contacted by the 'toy-maker' and his colleague. From the looks of it, I believe he is the brain and she provides the security. Their presence here probably means the 'toy' has also arrived at Hamilton port, and means we need to prepare the Uyghurs for their real mission. I suggest we go to the airport to take another look at the plane, and then tell Ding and his men to get ready."

Lara turned pale. "Is this the end?" She looked anxiously at her man. "Jacque, will you accompany me on the plane? I wouldn't feel good if you didn't."

"We'll stay together, no matter what happens." He held her hand in his. "I think we have another couple days before we leave. Let's go to the hotel and make them unforgettable."

***

Later that evening, they sat on the bench overlooking the bay and waited for the Koreans.

The jovial little man approached with the woman in tow. "Don Alberto, it is an honor to meet you. Please allow me to introduce myself and my colleague. I am Professor Mal-Chin Park from the research facility at Yongbyon and this is Soo-Jin Ree from our security service. I have heard so much about you from Uncle Chong and he told me you are on a sacred mission. I am here to help. Soo-Jin speaks very little English but, I can assure you, she is an expert in handling conventional explosives and weapons of all kinds. She wishes to tell you the 'toy' has arrived and is in a container packed with musical instruments about to be unloaded tomorrow night. I was instructed by Uncle Chong to make sure that piano in which the 'toy' is concealed is delivered intact to the office of *NK Import and Export Services*. Once it is there,

I'll assemble it and arm it. You are welcome to watch, but do not interfere because it is a delicate job, and we don't want an accident on our hands that could flatten Bermuda and submerge the islands."

This seemed to amuse him, and he laughed when he said that, and Lara who had been following every word started to worry about his sanity.

Le Docteur said, "I am pleased to meet you both and appreciate what you are doing to help us. Just let me clarify that the address of *NK Import and Export Services* is a small apartment belonging to our Uyghur collaborators. The delivery of a piano would be frowned upon by the residents and their curious neighbors. We'll have to find a different place for assembling the 'toy.' I'll rent a more suitable place tomorrow morning, so the piano can be delivered there in the evening. I assume you two are staying at one of the resort hotels as a married couple."

He waited for Professor Park to translate this to his colleague and saw that she blushed.

"Of course, we are posing as couple from South Korea, not to arouse suspicion."

"So, it is best if we are not seen together more than necessary. I have your cell phone number from your call earlier today, and I'll text you the new address as soon as the arrangements are completed."

The Koreans bowed politely and left the park. As soon as they were out of earshot, Lara said, "I don't like this. It is so unprofessional and that worries me. The woman scares me. She didn't utter a word and kept observing us like specimen under a microscope. I kept wondering if she would pull out a gun or a knife and eliminate us in this isolated spot. Even Professor Park seems to fear her. She is the opposite of Chun-hee, although they could well be graduates of the same training course."

Le Docteur nodded. "I cannot imagine a *menage a trois* with Soo-Jin, can you?" This helped break the tension.

***

The next morning Le Docteur found a small cottage on Grape Bay in a relatively isolated spot. It was fully furnished, but Lara told the real estate agent she was a pianist and expected her piano to be delivered.

The real estate agent said that it was not a problem—they had already signed a contract for a month's rental at an exorbitant price—so she didn't care if a dozen grand pianos were delivered.

Le Docteur texted the address to Professor Park and contacted his Uyghurs to ensure they handled the delivery of the extra-heavy piano.

The container with the musical instruments was unloaded and passed through the Bermudan customs without a hitch. It was sent to the warehouse, where the special piano was separated from the rest of the merchandise and, with the help of the Uyghurs, was loaded on a van that transported it to the cottage.

Le Docteur paid the Uyghurs for their labor and asked them to report back to the cottage at noon, the next day.

After the Chinese left, Park and Soo-Jin arrived with a small suitcase that contained a set of specialized tools, and the professor got to work.

Le Docteur and Lara watched closely as he removed the panels from the piano and saw that instead of the usual mechanism of hammers and strings, there were metal and wooden boxes of different sizes.

Park donned overalls, a face mask, a pair of nitrile gloves, and started opening the boxes. He first opened the smallest metal box, that was filled with polyurethane foam. He separated the two sheets of foam and a small metallic sphere, the size of a grapefruit, could be seen.

He left it in its protective foam packaging and pulled a small device out of his suitcase and explained that it was a radiation detector. He switched it on, and it clicked slowly, but when he brought it closer to the sphere it started chirping like crazy.

He smiled. "This is the heart of the 'toy.' It is a special composite of fissile materials, developed by our laboratory, and I can assure you that no forensic lab in the world would be able to trace its origin."

Next, he opened a slightly larger wooden crate, removed the two metallic hemispheres packed inside it, and explained, "These will help the 'toy' increase the yield, by holding it together for a longer time and reflecting neutron back to the core."

He gingerly removed the sphere from its protective foam and placed it in one of the hemispheres and then covered it with the other hemisphere—forming a slightly larger sphere.

Lara watched fascinated and fearful.

Next, Park opened the wooden boxes and removed a batch of strangely shaped objects and arranged them around the metallic sphere, so that a larger sphere was formed.

This pattern was like a football. Then he opened another metal box and cautiously took out a bunch of objects that looked like small pens, each of which connected to a pair of electric leads. He inserted each of those into a readymade hole in the strange objects. "These are the detonators inserted into the plastic charges of high-explosives. When they receive an electric pulse, they will detonate the explosives and this will create a shockwave that will compress the core of fissile materials, producing an atomic explosion. It is important that this is done simultaneously, or this wonderful little device will produce a fizzle, with a small yield."

Then he took the electrical leads from all the detonators and arranged them in two bunches, that he connected to a couple of plugs. "Now we come to the most interesting part—setting the trigger. I understand you want the 'toy' to detonate at an altitude of two thousand feet over the target. So, I am setting this barometric trigger to that height. It will arm itself when your plane soars above this altitude and will remain armed as long as you remain above two thousand feet. It will automatically detonate when the plane descends below this altitude. The only way to disarm the device, after it is armed, is to disconnect the power supply that I'll hook up once the 'toy' is in the plane. It is perfectly safe now, just make sure not to take it above two thousand feet."

He laughed, because he knew the highest spot in Bermuda,

Town Hill, was two hundred sixty feet above sea level. He added, "Normally, the whole device would be contained in a stainless-steel shell, but to save weight this 'toy' will only be wrapped in a tarpaulin to hide it. After all, we don't want anyone to start asking what this bunch of wires is for, do we?"

He laughed again with the strange tone that had made Lara and Le Docteur nervous the previous evening.

By the time the assembly job was complete it was almost dawn. The Koreans returned to their hotel after explaining again that the device would be armed once it reached an altitude of two thousand feet. He repeated the warning it would detonate automatically once the armed device descended below this altitude.

Le Docteur said that he and Lara would remain at the cottage to guard the 'toy,' and wait for their Uyghurs to load it on to the plane.

***

The four Uyghurs arrived at the cottage, close to noon the next day. They viewed the tarpaulin with obvious suspicion. They could discern that it was wrapped around some heavy spherical object placed on a standard four by four wooden pallet, used to transport merchandise.

The object was secured to the pallet with four ropes. The four men couldn't lift it, so Le Docteur and Lara came to their aid, and together the six of them managed to hoist it aboard the truck.

Le Docteur said he would drive the truck with the wrapped

object, with Lara at his side. He gave Ding the keys of his rental car and the other men got in the car.

The car followed the truck to the airport, where the twin-engine turbo-prop plane was already fueled and waiting.

Lara had taken care of getting the plane from a firm about to go bankrupt. In fact, she bought the plane outright, so no questions were asked.

Transferring the 'toy' from the truck to the side-door of the plane required a lot of maneuvering because it barely passed through the door.

Le Docteur paid off the Uyghurs and they wished him luck and success.

Before parting, he called Ding over and placed a thumb drive wrapped up in a note in his hand. He told the Uyghur to take it to the police in the evening—not a minute before nine. He instructed Ding to enter the station, say he found the thumb drive with the note, and leave the station immediately.

***

Lara had filed a flight plan to Washington, DC, and they were cleared for take-off. However, before climbing into the left seat, she checked the parachute she had purchased from a sky-diving shop and strapped it on.

Le Docteur climbed into the right seat and did the same with his parachute. He didn't notice the package hidden under his seat—Lara had placed it there when he was busy supervising the loading of the wrapped 'toy' by the Uyghurs.

She knew that if she wouldn't manage to persuade Le

Docteur to accept her newly hatched plan, the folded dinghy contained in the package wouldn't be used. She also surreptitiously checked the door on her side to make sure it would open easily.

She asked, "Do you trust Ding to deliver the thumb drive?"

Le Docteur replied, "I do, but just to be on the safe side I have also posted its content on the web, with a delay of eight hours before it will be mailed to all major networks."

***

Le Docteur removed part of the tarpaulin that covered the 'toy,' found the two main electrical plugs and connected them to the heavy-duty car battery he had acquired, according to the specifications of Professor Park. A green light flickered for twenty seconds, and then remained on.

Park had told him that once the device was armed the green light would become red, indicating the device was ready.

***

The plane taxied on to runway thirty and took off in a northwesterly direction, which corresponded to the route they were taking. Lara figured that the flight time would be a little over three hours, so after reaching her cruising altitude, she relaxed a little.

Not an easy task when you know that there is an armed nuke on the seat behind you. Le Docteur turned his neck and saw that the light on the device had turned red and told her so.

She put the plane on autopilot and took Le Docteur's hand and said, "Jacque, I have studied the aircraft's flight manual and I have a plan that will ensure that the 'toy' is detonated over Washington, DC, and will allow us to survive."

When he looked at her inquisitively, she continued, "The autopilot has a feature that can make it glide at a fixed angle, while maintaining its compass heading. For example, I can set it at a glide-ratio of zero point five percent, so that for each altitude loss of one mile it will travel two hundred miles in the direction I set it. If we climb to two and a quarter miles and I set it at zero point five percent glide-ratio, it will travel about four hundred miles before it reaches two thousand feet and the 'toy' goes off. We can parachute to safety, long before that, far away from the target."

Le Docteur interrupted, "This will be in the ocean. We'll drown or be eaten by sharks."

"Jacque, look under your seat. The package is an inflatable dinghy, equipped for survival in mid-ocean for a few days. We have flares and can attract the attention of a ship or plane that will come to our rescue. We'll say that our plane developed engine trouble and plunged into the ocean. If they check the flight record, they'll see that we took off from Bermuda and filed a flight plan to Washington—"

"Lara, I thought we agreed this will be a one-way ticket to paradise."

"I know. But we have found paradise and happiness here, in this life. Let's enjoy it. We can continue our fight and, I repeat and, see the fruits of our enterprise. Don't you want to know what will happen after we destroy Washington?"

She knew this could be the decisive argument that would change his mind. The combination of enjoyment of their blissful life together, with the opportunity to satisfy his curiosity about the results of his life's most ambitious act against his hated enemies, could be irresistible.

"Lara, are you sure it will work?"

She smiled at him and nodded.

***

Lara replayed in her mind the video message he had recorded at the hotel, before leaving it two days earlier. In the message, he reiterated the story of his connection with Senator Jim McCorey. *I am the most wanted man on the face of the earth, because I stood up for the rights of my Muslim brothers. My crime is that I attempted to avenge some of the injustices my brethren suffered throughout history in the hands of the crusaders, colonialists, communists, capitalists and Jews. I have created NEMESIS and worked for the cause in Europe, but due to a misfortune there I had to seek refuge in Canada.*

I adopted the motto attributed to Lenin 'the worse, the better,' meaning that the worse things got the better it was for the Marxist revolution. I modified it to suit the situation of the Muslims—the worse it got for them in the United States, the better it would be for them in the world. Persecution of Muslims in America would surely raise an outcry not only among the Ummah of Islam worldwide, but also in non-Muslim democratic societies everywhere.

I moved down to the United States and found a person who was the most vocal speaker for persecuting Muslims. We agreed to cooperate—I would carry out blatant terrorist attacks in the name of Islam and he would intensify his attacks on Muslims, blaming them for these attacks. With his support, I orchestrated the attack on the Capitol with radioactive substances, I arranged the incident at Yankee Stadium, I, personally, destroyed the unique exhibit at the National Museum of Nuclear Science and History in Albuquerque, and planted the bomb at the powwow in Gallup, New Mexico. After each of these attacks, the distinguished senator gained more popularity, more power, and more influence. He announced that he would run for the office of the President of the United States in the coming election. Imagine this man holding the highest office in the land, and becoming the leader of what you unashamedly call, 'The Free World.'

All these acts of terror were miniscule compared to what we did afterward. You may have heard the true story about the pilot who stole a F-22A, Raptor, the most advanced, most expensive, and most secret fighter-jet made by the U.S. The brave woman who flew this plane, shot down her commanding officer, and single-handedly, audaciously attacked a U.S. naval base in San Diego. She then ditched the plane in shallow waters, and it remained almost intact—a feat few pilots would dare to attempt. This brave woman walked away, or more precisely, swam away unharmed, from the crash landing.

When you see this video clip you will know that Washington is again a swamp, as it was three hundred years ago. In case anyone doesn't know to whom I was referring—Senator Jim McCorey, MBJ, Muslim-Bashing Jimbo, is the man who was willing and ready to sacrifice his fellow Americans to gain publicity and power.

This is the final act of NEMESIS. It may take a century or two, but Islam will prevail once again, as it did for centuries less than fifteen hundred years ago. Bismillah—in the name of Allah—I bid you all good-bye.

***

They were about one hour from Bermuda when Lara said, "Jacque, this is the correct place and time. We are four hundred miles from Washington. I'll climb to an altitude two and a quarter miles and we'll parachute out of the plane after I set the autopilot on course and adjust the glide-ratio to zero point five percent."

She unbuckled her seatbelt, leaned over and kissed him full on the mouth. He responded and unbuckled his own seatbelt and hugged her for a short moment. She fiddled with the setting of the autopilot for a couple minutes, checked the exact position on the GPS system, and opened the door on her side.

"Jacque, pull the dinghy from under your seat, open the door, and get ready to bail out with it, on my count down from ten."

She looked at him as he struggled to retrieve the package in the confined space of the cabin. When she saw he was ready she said, "Okay. Hold on to the package. You'll freefall for about eighty seconds, and then the parachute will open automatically, and you'll glide down to the ocean. The package will probably slip out of your hands when the parachute opens. Don't worry, it will inflate when it touches the water. I'll meet you on the dinghy. Ten, nine, eight, seven, six, five, four, three, two, one, go. I love you."

The freefall skydive was thrilling. Lara heard Le Docteur yelling as he fell, and knew it was cathartic. A combination of primal fear of falling and of exhilaration. She had felt the exact emotions when ejecting from the fighter-jet.

She was very glad their two parachutes opened almost at the exact same time. She guided her parachute away from his, using the guide-strings, and they both hit the water seconds apart. The inflated dinghy was close by, and they swam to it and boarded it at the same time.

They lay exhausted on the rubberized bottom and looked up to the sky. They could barely see their plane continuing its flight toward Washington. They were still catching their breath when they saw an immensely bright flash in the direction the plane was travelling.

Moments later they felt a rush of air that overturned their dinghy and threw them overboard. They swam frantically and managed to climb back into the dinghy and looked at each other in confusion.

Le Docteur was the first to speak, "Something must have gone wrong with the trigger."

She answered, "It couldn't have dropped this fast to two thousand feet. It's either a malfunction of the mechanism or the Koreans fooled us."

She stared at Jacque. "It's good we escaped a useless, futile, death."

"Maybe it's just the infamous Bermuda Triangle. Let's hope we get picked up soon."

***

One day later they saw a small ship heading south a couple miles from their position. Lara fired three flares and they were glad to see the ship change course and approach them.

A rope ladder was thrown to them and they gingerly climbed it. They were met by a couple men, obviously merchant marine sailors. One of them must have been the captain of the ship. Before they could thank them for saving their lives, Le Docteur and Lara noticed the pallor and ugly, fresh lesions and blisters on the exposed faces of their rescuers.

The older man said, "I am John Stone, the captain of the ship. We were on our way from Canada to Cuba when we saw a flash of light, brighter than the sun, and then heard what sounded like thunder. Minutes later a heavy rain started falling. I suspect the light and thunder were from a nuke, and the rain was contaminated by radioactivity. During my engineering studies, I had read about this. I quickly ordered the crew below deck to take shelter, but I guess it was too late. Several started vomiting and burning with fever. Hours later ugly lesions developed," he pointed to his face, "now only Diego and I can function. All the others are either dead or hopelessly sick. All my electronic equipment is not functioning. I guess it was fried by the electromagnetic pulse that accompanied the nuke blast."

Le Docteur said, "I am sorry to hear that. Can we help

bring the ship to a port?"

He looked at Lara and saw that she was probably thinking the same thing he was: *we have killed the people who saved us.*

He asked, although he knew the answer, "Captain Stone, have there been any reports on an accidental nuclear explosion?"

The captain shook his head. "I said all our electronic equipment is out of order."

The ship arrived at Havana and was quarantined. The dead crew members were carried away in lead-coated caskets, the two survivors were treated at the local hospital, but only the captain lived.

Le Docteur and Lara were examined and after their story was accepted, were free to leave.

***

Pyongyang, Residence of the Leader

The eccentric young leader of the Democratic People's Republic of Korea was enraged by the news of the loss of his salvage ship with its prize, the F-22 Raptor, off the Mexican coast. When he was informed his precious nuke detonated in the middle of nowhere, hundreds of miles from American soil, he immediately had the bearer of the news, his Military Adjutant, executed.

He badly needed something to distract him, and called for his favorite concubine, Chun-hwa, who was Chun-hee's twin sister. She, too, was a graduate of the country's top course for spies, and her sexual skills surpassed those of her sister.

Few people knew that the leader was married and had sired a boy and a girl, because his formal wife was never seen in public, and there were no photographs of her on record. In times of stress, the leader preferred Chun-hwa.

They had this new game they played: She called him Little Rocket Man and faked running away from him. He pretended to be infuriated by this and chased her around the bed. When he caught her, he tore off her clothes, shouting at the top of his voice, "Look at the rocket—isn't it the largest rocket you have ever seen."

She donned a straw-colored wig, that was stylized to look like the hair of his famous arch-rival, as he grabbed her from behind and continued shouting, "I'll show you who is boss—you mentally deranged dotard."

A moment later he collapsed on Chun-hwa's back, wasted and satiated.

EPILOGUE

A small number of people on board cruise ships or merchant mariners saw the strange mushroom shaped cloud. Those that were wise, or warned by knowledgeable people, quickly sought shelter and didn't stand outside and wait for the rain that was sure to follow with its radioactive material.

A couple of commercial passenger planes couldn't avoid flying through the rapidly rising cloud and had to be thoroughly decontaminated before anyone was allowed off. Other than those unfortunate people, no one was hurt by the detonation of the atomic bomb.

Samples of air and water were collected and sent to military forensic laboratories, but other than showing that the bomb had contained fissile material, there was no conclusive evidence pointing to the origin of the bomb.

Mossad and the NNSA had no doubt it was manufactured by the DPRK, but without irrefutable proof no politician was willing to act against this strange country and its eccentric leader.

Senator McCorey committed suicide rather than face charges of high treason and murder by proxy, as well as a myriad of other charges.

Blossom's body was found in a deep ravine on the east side

of the Sandia mountains. No foul play was suspected by the police, but her parents were sure she was murdered by her former lover, who had mysteriously disappeared.

Uncle Chong returned to Pyongyang and was never heard from again. There were rumors the eccentric ruler of the country had fed him to the dogs, literally.

Kim died in Mexico City, in what appeared to be a fluke accident, when a heavy bookcase collapsed in the public library and crushed him.

At the small celebration that was held at Mossad headquarters in Tel Aviv, the chief said the world was a better place without NEMESIS and Le Docteur, thanks to David and his team. David modestly said the battle was won but the war wasn't over.

Le Docteur and Lara stayed in Cuba for a few weeks, recuperating, and trying to get over the failure of their mission. He told her the video he had left was their passport to safety and freedom. Everyone would be convinced they died aboard the plane with the nuke's premature explosion. He suggested they go back to Europe and start afresh there. Lara smiled and nodded.

ACKNOWLEDGEMENTS AND NOTES

One of the main points of the plot involves the use, or more accurately, the abuse, of a military plane in an act of terror against its own people and country. In theory, any pilot in a single-seat jet-fighter, or the flight crew colluding in a twin-seat plane, can use the plane's armament for an unauthorized attack. The selected target may be in the country, or as a blatant provocation in a neighboring country. For example, imagine an overly-patriotic radicalized pilot of the Israeli air-force, diverting from a routine mission and bombing the mosques on Temple Mount in Jerusalem. This would undoubtedly ignite a religious war between Muslims and Israel (or the war of civilizations between Islam and the West). Is this farfetched? Yes. But is it impossible? Certainly, no.

Some notorious cases that demonstrate what lone pilots can do: During the failed coup in Turkey, on July 15, 2016, pilots from the Turkish air-force bombed and strafed facilities of their own government. Or, the Iraqi pilot who in 1966 deserted his country and flew with his Mig-21 jet-fighter across Iraq and Jordan to land in an Israeli military airfield, as part of a Mossad brilliant operation. Not to mention the Catch-22 fictitious incident in which U.S. bombers stationed in Italy during WWII bombed their own airfield. I don't think there is any other example of a single person having so much power at the tips of their fingers, and the ability to carry out an attack of this sort with impunity.

I know F-22A planes are no longer operated out of Holloman Air Force Base (since 2014, I read), but I decided to place them there for the development of the plot. In this story, Lara didn't have to shoot down Major Buchanan, she could have probably evaded him, with the element of surprise on her side. However, I used this to intensify the feeling that she was performing the ultimate act of treason—shooting down, killing, a comrade in arms.

There are not many precedents of planes landing on water without disintegrating. I did mention the 'Miracle on the Hudson' incident, as a unique example. During the Battle of the Pacific in WWII, numerous American and Japanese pilots, operating from aircraft carriers, had to ditch their planes in the ocean, either because the plane was damaged or because they were unable to land on a carrier. Some of them survived the impact with the ocean and were rescued, others didn't.

I am not aware of any cases of salvaging a jet-fighter from the seabed, although there are reports, and videos, of salvaging a German WWII bomber from the English Channel and a Japanese fighter (N1K2 Shiden-Kai) from the bay of Jouhen Town in Shikoku, and light planes from the bottom of the sea or a lake. Nowadays, there is a plan to recover sunken Avro Arrow models from Lake Ontario in Canada. On the other hand, ships and submarines have been salvaged from great depths. So, Lara's successful crash-landing on water is a daring and audacious feat—do not try this at home—and the salvage operation of the F-22 at a depth of 25 meters may be difficult, but not impossible.

While writing this thriller, I came across an article by Graham Allison published in the Bulletin of the Atomic Scientists, in 2006. The article's title, *The ongoing failure of imagination* highlights its main point: the principle failure to prevent 9/11 was a failure of imagination. The article then reviews, in brief, the 'who, what, where, when, and how,' nuclear weapons may be obtained by terrorists and used against the United States (*Bull. Atom. Sci. Vol. 62, pp. 36-41, 2006*).

In my previous thrillers (see the list below), I tried to imagine the unimaginable—a nuclear device in the hands of a terrorist organization. Hopefully, my nightmares will remain in the realm of fiction, but foreknowledge of these (and other) scenarios may be helpful in thwarting them. The literature (fiction and non-fiction) and the web, mention numerous ways of producing or obtaining fissile materials, and I have invented a few new ones (without real scientific basis, of course). Thus, I have avoided giving useful or practical ideas to 'the bad guys' by providing 'fake physics.' So, my readers who have expressed concerns that I may giving the terrorists blueprints for acquiring atomic weapons, can rest assured that I have not done so.

In an address on, *National Security and Strategy for a New Century,*' made by the Clinton administration in the year 2000 (before 9/11), it was noted that, *Proliferation of advanced weapons and technologies threatens to provide rogue states, terrorists, and international crime organizations with the means to inflict terrible damage on the United States, our allies, U.S. citizens, and troops abroad*." Words to that effect were repeated time and again, in official documents and unofficial conversations. My books take these concerns from the general statements to specific, imaginary so far, situations. Today's grim fantasy might be tomorrow's horrible news.

I wish to thank Rob Carnell for his critical reading of the manuscript and helpful comments. If you like stories about international conspiracies and nuclear terror, you should look-up his two books: *Smuggler's surprise*, and *Nuclear surprise*, available on Amazon.

Finally, I wish to thank my wife, Hana, and my sons, for their useful suggestions.

Other books by Charlie Wolfe, published on Amazon:

Mission Alchemist,

Mission Renegade,

Mission Patriot,

Mission Rocket Man,

Mission Tango

Mission Senator.

Each of these books can be read independently. Mossad agent David Avivi plays a crucial part in all these books.

Printed in Great Britain
by Amazon

43394246R00194